D1799652

AGAINST ALL ODDS

A BROOK BROTHERS NOVEL

TRACIE DELANEY

ﾞ ﾞ eﾞs and Puzzles

ﾞ Victoria Road West Cleveleys
FY5 1BU (01253) 855111

firefly publishing limited

Copyright © 2018 Tracie Delaney

Edited by *Sarah Carleton - Red Adept Editing*
Edited by Emmy Ellis - Studioenp
Cover art by *Tiffany @TEBlack Designs*
Cover Photographer - *Wander Aguiar*
(Facebook) Wander Book Club
Cover Model - Forest Harrison
(Facebook) Model-Forest

All rights reserved. No part of this publication may be reproduced, stored in any retrieval system, or transmitted, in uniform or by any means, electronic, mechanical, photocopying, recording or otherwise without prior written permission of the author.

This is a work of fiction. Names, characters, places, and incidents are either the products of the author's imagination or are used fictitiously, and any resemblance to actual persons, living or dead, business establishments, events, or locales is entirely coincidental.

BOOKS BY TRACIE DELANEY

The Winning Ace Series

Cash - A Winning Ace Short Story

Winning Ace

Losing Game

Grand Slam

Winning Ace Boxset

Mismatch

Break Point - A Winning Ace Novella

Stand-alone

My Gift To You

The Brook Brothers Series

The Blame Game

Against All Odds

His To Protect

Web of Lies

To Louise - my rock

CHAPTER 1

Calum Brook strode into the boardroom and scanned around the large oval mahogany table where the board members of Necron Drinks Inc. were seated. And then his gaze fell on *her*. Laurella Ricci. Instinctively, he knew he'd been right.

She was trouble—with a capital T.

The moment her dark, almost black gaze settled on him irritation crept over his skin, and the hairs on the back of his neck stood on end. Calum always sat to Zane's right, but this newcomer had planted her perfect ass into *his* chair. Not that he knew what her ass looked like, considering she was sitting on it, but if it matched up to the rest of her, *perfect* would undoubtedly be a good adjective to use.

"Calum." Zane got to his feet and strode across the room. The two men shook hands warmly. "It's great to have you back. How's Jax?"

"Almost fully recovered, thanks," Calum replied. His older brother, Jax, had been recuperating after his girlfriend's crazy-as-fuck, now-dead brother had tried to kill him.

Girlfriend. Calum almost laughed. Jax might have forgiven India for nearly getting him killed, lying to him, and setting him up then professing to love him, but she'd have to work a hell of a lot harder to win Calum over.

"I'm so glad." Zane gestured to the chair on his left.

The wrong fucking chair.

"Take a seat. I'm sorry I haven't stopped by for a couple weeks, but it's been a bit busy without my right-hand man," Zane said.

Calum stared pointedly at Laurella. "Well, I'm back now."

She settled her unflinching cool gaze on him as she half stood and extended her hand. "Laurella Ricci," she said, a faint trace of a Mediterranean accent giving her voice a soft lilt that belied her hard-nosed, all-business expression. "The new marketing director."

Calum reluctantly took her hand and shook it. Her skin was cool and smooth to the touch, her handshake firm and brief. "Calum Brook. The definitely not-new sales director."

Zane touched his forehead. "Damn, I'm sorry. I forgot you two hadn't met yet. Laurella, Calum. Calum, Laurella." He let out a low chuckle. "Laurella's been here… what, six weeks now?"

Laurella nodded demurely. "This is my seventh week."

Calum still didn't understand why Zane had been so adamant that they bring in a marketing director. Necron, the niche liquor company Zane had started when they'd graduated from college five years before, had done very well without a marketing head so far. And to poach someone from Spirito, one of the largest alcoholic-beverages companies in the world? Completely unnecessary. Yet every time Calum had broached the subject when he'd seen Zane socially over the last few weeks, his friend had waved his concerns away with a flick of his wrist and told him not to worry. Now that Calum was back, however, he wasn't going to allow Zane to dodge the conversation. They were supposed to be business partners, not to mention best buddies.

"Hope you're settling in well," he said without feeling.

"Very well, thank you," she replied, equally without feeling.

Laurella retook her seat and opened a leather-bound book. She flicked on a few pages until she found a blank one. With her pen poised, she focused on Zane, who'd resumed his seat at the head of the table, then bent her dark head to make a couple of notes. Her handwriting was small, neat, flawless. Calum strained to see what she'd written but couldn't make it out.

He shook hands with the remaining board members then sat in the spare chair to Zane's left—the one and only fucking time he'd be sitting on this side of the room. It pissed him off that Zane hadn't seen fit to tell Laurella to move her butt.

Yeah, Calum knew he was an egotistical dick. He'd learned to live with it.

"Okay, down to business," Zane said, pulling up a Power-Point presentation and projecting it onto the large screen at the far side of the boardroom. "Laurella, why don't you take us through the plan."

"Of course." She eased to her feet, and with a precision that was already getting on Calum's nerves, she placed her pen next to her now-closed notebook, correcting it when it dared to roll to the side.

She walked to the front of the boardroom. He'd been right about her ass, which was round, pert, and superbly accentuated by a tight-fitting pencil skirt that skimmed her knees and clung to her hips. Four-inch black patent-leather designer shoes completed the lower half of the ensemble.

Hmm. Wonder if she's wearing nylons or hold-ups?

Laurella coughed, attracting his attention. Only then did Calum realize he'd been caught checking her out. He slowly inched his gaze up to her face, schooling his expression into a flat stare. Laurella returned his impassive glare with one of her own.

"Gentlemen," she said, "over the past six weeks, I have been gradually getting to know you all and familiarizing myself with the company—where its strengths lie and what its growth potential is. I've come to a very swift conclusion. While you're doing well, there is room for significant improvement. You're thinking too small. You're too focused on the domestic market. In order to take the business to the next level, you need to think globally. You've also been too driven by short-term incentives to sell rather than developing and building your brand." Her attention turned to Calum. "I'm here to change all that."

Calum ground his teeth as she flat-out taunted him. Six weeks into her tenure at a company he'd spent five fucking years pouring blood, sweat, and tears into, she'd already made her conclusions. During those five years, he'd been Zane's right-hand man, transforming a completely unknown liquor company into a preferred supplier to half the eastern seaboard's restaurants and bars. Yet in had waltzed a virtual stranger who had the gall to tell them all how they'd been doing it wrong.

Fuck. Her.

He flashed a look at Zane, expecting to see irritation or at the very least agitation on his face. Instead, Zane was gazing at Laurella with something akin to reverence or, at the very least, respect.

Shit. He was going to have a tough fight on his hands, persuading Zane that the company had been doing just fine without Laurella Ricci and would continue to do just fine after he fired her ass.

She continued, but Calum had stopped listening. Instead, he began mentally drafting his pitch to Zane while doodling on his notepad. The second this board meeting was over, he was going to take his friend to one side and share how he'd come up with a great cost-saving initiative—the termination of Laurella Ricci's contract.

After she'd held the floor for at least thirty minutes, Laurella strolled back to her seat with a confident air that said she'd nailed it. As she sat, her gaze fell on him, and a small, triumphant smile played around her lips.

"Great presentation, Laurella," Zane gushed.

Calum clamped his jaw shut before he said something he wouldn't be able to retract.

"Calum, did you have any questions?" Zane asked.

Calum stared down Laurella. "Not right now, but I'm sure once I've had a chance to absorb the copious amounts of material Laurella has collated, I'll have plenty."

The gibe was direct and purposeful. He expected her to show at least a modicum of annoyance. Instead, she flashed him a brilliant white-toothed smile that appeared even brighter against her olive skin. *Bravo.* She was playing the game beautifully.

"I'll be happy to answer any questions you have, Calum. After all, we'll be working very closely together, so it's important we're on the same page."

The same page? Sweetheart, we're not even reading from the same fucking book.

"Wonderful," he said, his tone dripping with sarcasm. "I look forward to it."

～

"I still don't get it, Zane," Calum said, pacing around Zane's office, hands stuffed deep into the pocket of his suit pants. "We were doing just fine. The company has gone from strength to strength. We don't need anyone to head up marketing. And even if we did, you could have found a cheaper option here in the US, without the expense of the goddamn green card."

"I disagree on both counts." Zane rose from his chair, his calm standing in contrast to Calum's agitation, and walked over to the coffee machine in the corner of his office. He made them both a cup.

"I might need something stronger," Calum muttered.

Zane ignored him. Apart from his brothers, no one knew Calum better than Zane. They'd met in college, quickly becoming close friends, and when Zane had the idea for a niche liquor company, he'd asked Calum to come on board and head up the sales department. Back then, the department had consisted of one—Calum himself. But over the past five years, Calum had gradually increased the team to seventeen, and the sales were off the charts for such a relative newbie in a competitive market. The fact that his best friend thought they needed suggestions for something different, and from an outsider no less, really pissed him off.

"At the risk of repeating myself, she comes with a top-class résumé. Yes, we've seen outstanding performance over the past five years, and you've been a massive part of that, but our growth is stalling, Calum. If we want to break into the big leagues, we need the big guns. Laurella knows how to grow a brand. Hell, she catapulted her last company into the top one hundred businesses in Italy. And *that's* why I hired her. That's why she's worth the additional expense."

"This isn't Italy," Calum said, his tone leaning toward cynical.

Zane grinned. "No shit." He slurped his coffee and wandered over to the window. Glancing over his shoulder, he beckoned to Calum. "See that?" he said, pointing upward when Calum joined him.

Calum craned his neck. The head office of one of the biggest liquor companies in the US loomed over them, the large smoked-glass building dominating the neighborhood. "Can't miss it. Fucking monstrosity."

Zane chuckled. "It's modern. It's happening. It's now. *That's* what I want for Necron—the kind of success that will reward us all. And to do that, we need to grow the brand. Laurella has contacts all over the globe. She can enable us to make the step change needed to launch this business into the stratosphere."

"She sat in my fucking chair," Calum grumbled with a sullen glance at Zane who, obviously hearing the petulance in Calum's tone, threw back his head and laughed.

"Fine. I'll tell her to sit on the other side at the next board meeting." He clinked his mug against Calum's. "I've missed you, dickhead."

Calum grinned, the tension that had been riding him since he walked into his office building two hours earlier dissipating under Zane's teasing. "Okay. I'll try to make it work, but she'd better take that snooty attitude she threw down back there and shove it up her ass."

Zane laughed once more, his loud guffaw echoing around the room. He set his coffee on the desk and then rubbed his hands together. "Man, I'm going to enjoy this. Might even get a popcorn machine installed—this is going to be one hell of a show."

"Screw you." Calum left the room, his best friend's chuckles following him down the hall as he retreated to his own office. He kicked the door closed and flopped into his chair. After firing up his computer, he spent the next couple of hours clearing out junk mail and catching up on what had been happening around the place during his relatively short absence.

A light tapping at the door had him lifting his head. Jules, his number two, poked her head inside. With a broad smile, he beckoned to her.

"I'm so glad you're back." She placed her notebook on Calum's desk as he stood to embrace her. "You look well. Is everything okay with your brother?"

Calum nodded. "He's getting there. Thanks for asking." He pointed at the chair opposite his. "How've things been?"

Jules let out a heavy sigh. "Crazy. I've been pulling sixteen-hour days. Hence my relief that you're back."

Calum waggled his eyebrows. "And you've missed my charm and repartee, of course."

Her lips twitched. "That goes without saying," she said, her sarcasm obvious.

He laughed. Jules was an absolute godsend, and Calum adored her. They acted more like brother and sister than boss and employee, and she was one of only a few people unafraid to call him out on his shit. And he'd take it from her—and dish out plenty in return.

She picked up her notebook. "So, want the debrief?"

He nodded, and for the next thirty minutes, Jules gave him the rundown on sales, forecasts, and the latest client who was trying to pull a fast one and renege on a pricing deal.

"I think I've resolved it," she said, "but it'd be good if you could swing by their offices sometime this week."

Calum made a note in his calendar. "Consider it done." He leaned back in his chair and rolled a pen between his fingers. "What do you think of the new marketing director?" He kept his voice calm and steady, even though his annoyance meter spiked at the mere mention of her title.

"Laurella? She's settling in well. Seems to know her stuff, although I can't profess to be a marketing expert. She has... an interesting perspective on sales."

Calum narrowed his eyes. "What do you mean?"

"Well, when she started, she met with each of us in your department. She laid out her strategy and said that from what she'd observed, we took a short-term view. Said she'd reviewed our recent sales and that we'd been too focused on closing the deal at any price rather than working to connect with the client and build a long-term relationship."

"She fucking what?" Calum shot to his feet. Laurella had said as much in her presentation, but Jules's confirmation, and the fact his team had been spoken to without his express permission, annoyed the shit out of him.

Jules made a calming motion with her hands. "Take it easy. She's entitled to her opinion, and who knows—we might be able to learn a thing or two."

"She'll learn a thing or two all right. Starting with keeping her nose out of my goddamn department."

Jules chuckled. "I see the break hasn't done anything for your temper." Jules had known Calum too long to be bothered by his outbursts.

"What else did she say?" he asked through gritted teeth.

Jules shrugged. "Not much."

When Calum continued to scowl, Jules reached across the desk and patted his arm. "Go easy, Calum. Zane thinks she's fucking amazing. I know he's your friend, but at the end of the day, this is his business. You're a minority shareholder, so you'd do well to remember that. Don't say anything you might later regret."

Calum's answering smile was tight. "What, me?"

"Yes, you." Jules got to her feet. She made her way across his office but paused with one hand on the door handle. She glanced over her shoulder. "She's smart, Calum. Don't toss her ideas in the trash before listening to them."

After Jules had left him alone, Calum mused over what she'd said. He was annoyed by Zane's decision, but it had been made. Laurella Ricci was right there, on his turf, which meant he should try to make it work.

Or not.

CHAPTER 2

Laurella headed back to her office after the board meeting. It hadn't gone too badly, although it could have been better. She'd been anxious about meeting Calum, and from his initial response in there, her anxiety had been well-founded. From what she'd gleaned during the last few weeks, he commanded an enormous amount of respect, as well as a healthy dose of fear.

Zane hadn't told her why Calum had been out of the business. Not that it mattered. She was there to do a job—and do it she would, regardless of his clearly intended resistance.

She'd come across salesmen like Calum before. The way he'd sneered throughout her presentation had been textbook. And then he'd baited her regarding the level of detail in the material she'd presented. Well, screw him. He'd have to work a hell of a lot harder than that to get a rise out of her.

She spotted an email from her dear friend at Spirito and grinned at the subject line: *Crushed any balls yet?* She reached for her cell phone and Facetimed him. While she waited for him to answer, a sense of nostalgia washed over her. It had been the right time to leave Spirito. She needed to prove herself in a smaller company, one that didn't have its entire strategy already in place that limited her ability to influence. However, that didn't stop her missing her previous employer or the fabulous team she'd been a key part of.

"Laurie, *mia cara*. How are you doing?"

She grinned at Andrew's nickname for her as well as his attempt at an Italian endearment. Even after spending five years living and working in Italy, his English accent still shined through. "I'm well, Andrew. How are things in Milan? Missing me yet?"

"Every day, my sweet girl. I hope Zane Quinlan knows how lucky he is to have snagged you. Are you settling in okay? Enjoying the Big Apple?"

"It's wonderful. As vibrant as you described."

"So you don't think you've made a huge mistake and are calling to beg for your job back?" His voice held a tinge of hope mixed with anticipated disappointment.

Laurella laughed. "You're persistent, I'll give you that."

"One can hope, my dear."

She expelled a soft sigh. "I do miss you all."

"You'll miss us for a while. And then you'll forget us like that." Andrew snapped his fingers.

She laughed. "Never. I have to admit, I hadn't appreciated the challenge of moving companies and countries at the same time."

"Well, at least it's not your first trip across the pond, although I'd imagine New York is a little different from Harvard."

"You're not kidding," she said. "Although, thank goodness, those four years taught me some of the lingo."

Andrew laughed. "You've remembered some slang at least. You'll do fine, Laurie. I'm always here if you need anything."

"Thank you, Andrew. I'm so lucky to know you."

"I think you have that the wrong way around, Laurie."

She chuckled, said goodbye, and hung up. She caught her breath as a slug of homesickness rushed through her. She sucked in some air, taking it through her nose then let it out slowly. "*Calmati*, Laurella," she said. "Calm down."

She fired up the design app and opened the file that held a logo she'd been working on for Necron. She hadn't shared this with Zane yet. She still had a few hours of work to do before it would be good enough to show him, but already, the buzz of knowing she was working on something with real promise zipped through her. Her first essential task was to give Necron a recognizable brand. From what she'd observed so far, the company's brand awareness wasn't consistent, and its success had far too much reliance on people. All it took was for one of those people—say, someone like Calum Brook—to decide to leave, and bam! The company would take a hit that it might never recover from. She was there to provide *sustainability* as well as expand growth into new markets.

After she'd worked for another hour or so, her stomach rumbled with hunger. Laurella stood and stretched out her back then grabbed her purse, ready to head out to the deli across the street. She'd only made it halfway to her office door when Calum Brook entered—without knocking.

"Going somewhere?" he drawled, his easy manner, after his earlier rudeness, grating on her.

Laurella lifted an eyebrow. "To lunch, actually." Her tone might have been the epitome of politeness, but her message was clear. Her stomach rumbled again, and Laurella clutched it. Calum's lips twitched. *What a child.*

Calum moved the sleeve of his crisp white shirt and glanced at his watch. "I'll join you."

Going to lunch with Calum, even if that meant simply standing in line at the deli, was the very last thing she wanted to do. The air of arrogance he wore, as if he owned the place, set her teeth on edge. Her relationship with the sales director at her previous company had been based on mutual respect, even if their often-opposing goals created conflict. They'd always found a way through. She had a feeling her relationship with Calum was going to be very different. Unfortunately for him, Laurella had never run away from a fight in her life. Between her three brothers, two sisters, and herself, arguments in the Ricci household had been frequent and brutal. She'd rarely lost.

Laurella swept past him and reached for the door handle, but he got there first.

"After you," he said, gesturing, a hint of challenge to his tone.

She clamped her teeth together at the insincerity in his voice but somehow managed to suppress a sarcastic retort. She stepped around him and headed for the elevators.

They traveled down to street level in silence, Calum lounging against the back wall of the elevator, one foot crossed over the opposing ankle, while he tapped on his cell phone. *Good.* She didn't want to converse with him anyway.

When they arrived at the deli, the line curved around the block. Laurella figured it would take them at least ten minutes to reach the front, and she inwardly cursed her bad luck. Calum stood beside her, his body closer than she felt comfortable with, almost as though he was surreptitiously invading her personal space. Something about the man made her nervous, but she couldn't put her finger on precisely what. Regardless of the reason, she needed to shake it off—fast. She would bet he had a nose like a bloodhound and was able to smell fear—or victory—from twenty paces away. Even though they'd barely spoken, she'd already figured out his agenda, and Laurella believed attack was the best form of defense.

"I know you're not happy that Zane has brought me in to drive the company forward, but it's too bad, because I'm going nowhere."

Calum gazed down at her, his height providing a significant advantage despite the fact she was wearing four-inch heels. His intense green eyes and designer stubble gave him a dangerous air. Laurella refused to look away, even with every instinct she possessed screaming at her to do so.

"Is that right?" he murmured. He leaned toward her, his warm breath blowing her hair. "We'll see."

He moved forward with the line, standing slightly in front of her. Laurella itched to smack the smug curve to his lips right off his face. If her sister Caterina were present, she already would have, but Laurella had always been calmer than both her sisters, who had stereotypical fiery Italian temperaments. Make no mistake—Laurella's fierce spirit could rival anyone's, but she recognized the necessity to keep it tightly contained, especially when outside of Italy. During the years she'd spent at Harvard Business School, she'd learned the American way—to be much more restrained. She'd mastered the ability to hold her tongue and win arguments using intellect rather than bluster, and it had served her well.

Laurella remained silent until it was their turn to be served. As Calum opened his mouth to order—he was certainly no gentleman—she cut across him.

"Pastrami on rye, please," she said, giving the server a sweet smile.

"Are you together?" the man behind the counter asked.

"No."

"Yes."

The man stared at them both, confused, while Laurella flashed a fierce glare in Calum's direction and scowled.

"No, we're not together." She handed over a twenty-dollar bill and took her sandwich. "And a bottle of water, please."

Instead of looking peeved, Calum seemed much more amused. His lips twitched again, and his eyes twinkled with a mischievous spirit Laurella wouldn't have expected from him. She took her change and spun around. As she began to walk away, a firm hand gripped her upper arm.

"Wait," he commanded in a tone that brooked no argument.

Laurella launched her shoulder upward, dislodging his hand. "What for? So I can be treated to more of your scintillating conversation? It's chilly, and I'm hungry."

She stalked off, resisting the growing urge to glance over her shoulder to see if Calum was watching. She arrived back at the office building and stepped into the elevator. She pressed the button for the tenth floor. A hand shot through the gap, and the doors sprang back open. In walked Calum, a cocky smirk on his runway-model-handsome face. Laurella preferred a more rugged man, one who looked as if he'd lived and maybe even been in the odd brawl or two, but apart from a tiny scar under his left eye—which Laurella pretended was the remnant of cosmetic surgery, to amuse herself—Calum Brook was too goddamn perfect.

"That was a little rude," he said as the elevator doors closed once more.

Laurella bit her lip, because if she didn't, she'd likely take a bite out of him—and not one he'd enjoy. "I told you. I was cold and hungry, and as you invited yourself along without my permission, I didn't feel I owed you anything."

"Your *permission?*" Calum hit the stop button. The elevator juddered to a halt. He turned around slowly, his tall frame dwarfing the space inside the square box. It might have been stamped on the wall that eight people could easily fit inside, but with Calum making his presence felt, they'd have been lucky to fit in another two or three.

He stared directly at her. "Let's get something straight, shall we, Laurella? I don't need your *permission* for anything. Right now, Zane might be dribbling all over you like a virgin at a strip club, but trust me when I say I've known him a hell of a lot longer than you. He already knows what I can do. You, on the other hand, are an unknown commodity. If you don't perform, and damned quick, make no mistake: I'll be whispering in his ear over drinks that you're a cash-flow problem we can solve with a simple 'Sorry, sweetheart, you're fired.' It would be such a terrible shame if your green card got cancelled."

Laurella sucked in a breath so quickly it hissed through her teeth. She narrowed her eyes. "This is the twenty-first century,

Calum. In case you hadn't noticed, the old-boys' network is long dead."

He leaned forward until they were so close she smelled mints on his breath. "That's what you think, sweetheart."

With his gaze burning through her, he reached behind him. The elevator jerked into action. After a couple of seconds, a ping sounded, and the doors groaned open as if in agony. They definitely mirrored her feelings at that moment.

She refused to back down from Calum's fiery glare, but when he didn't break eye contact either, she pursed her lips and brushed past him. "Excuse me, but I have work to do. I don't have time to play your childish games."

She strode down the corridor, her heels clicking on the marble tile. The second she escaped into her office, she sagged against the closed door. Calum Brook was going to test every single nerve in her body, and the way things were going, she expected him to snap each one.

CHAPTER 3

Calum stepped through the front entrance of the hotel. Jax ran it, although the whole family had an equal stake in the business. Past the lobby, off to the right of the long hallway, the communal lounge room and bar was full of guests.

He spotted Jax behind the bar and hovered until he caught his eye. "You okay?" he mouthed.

Jax nodded and grinned then turned away to serve the next customer. Jax was born to work in the hospitality trade—and he was damn good at it. Calum considered grabbing a quick drink and mingling with the hotel guests, but after the day he'd had, making small talk was too much effort.

Taking a left turn at the end of the hallway, he descended the steps into the basement that doubled as their private quarters. When Jax had come up with this harebrained idea to open a hotel and have them all move in, Calum had thought his older brother had gone nuts. But now, a few months later, he had to admit it worked—and they all saved a shitload on rent.

At the bottom of the stairs, he entered the family room. His twin, Cole, was dressed in his cop uniform, apart from his duty belt, which lay across the breakfast bar. He was leaning against the kitchen countertop, his hand cupped underneath a bowl, shoveling cereal into his mouth.

"You on tonight?" Calum asked, dropping his gym bag on the floor.

Cole nodded. "Twelve-hour shift coming up."

Calum's disappointment must have shown on his face, because Cole frowned. "Something up?"

"Nah. It's fine." Calum opened the fridge and grabbed a beer. He twisted off the cap and took a long drink. He wiped the back of his hand across his mouth and flicked the bottle top into the trash. "I needed that."

"Gym session followed by a beer?" Cole laughed. "Something wrong with that picture, bro."

Calum grimaced. "After the day I've had, it ought to be gin."

Cole placed his bowl in the dishwasher. "I've got a few minutes, and they're all yours. Tell me how your first day back went."

Calum eased onto a stool at the breakfast bar and picked at the label on his beer bottle. "Met the new marketing woman today."

"Ah." Cole pulled up a seat next to him. "And?"

Calum shrugged. "As I expected—a complete know-it-all. Told me I'm shit at my job, without saying the actual words. She's only been at Necron five minutes, yet she thinks she's top fucking dog. If I get my way, she'll be looking for a new job this time next month."

Cole twisted the cap on a bottle of water and took a sip. "That's a passionate outburst for a woman you barely know."

Calum scowled. "If all you're going to bring to the party is unhelpful comments, you can just go to work."

Cole chuckled. "Bro, give the woman a chance. Who knows? You might learn something."

"The only thing I'm likely to learn is how to refrain from

sharpening my tongue on her shitty attitude. Something tells me I'm going to fail."

Cole let out a low whistle. "She's really gotten to you, huh? Better start examining those strong feelings, brother. Sounds to me like you've got the hots for this woman."

"Bullshit," Calum scoffed. "When someone who doesn't even know me or the company I work for stands up at a board meeting and basically tells us all how wrong we've been running things for the past five years, forgive me if I don't just bend over and take it up the ass."

Cole grabbed his belt and slung it around his waist. He removed his Glock, checked it, then put it back into the holster. "Gotta go." He walked past Calum and laid a hand on his arm. "As much as I love you, you can be a total dick at times. And who knows, in time, you might even end up liking her."

"Fat fucking chance," Calum muttered.

Alone, he paced, his irritation growing with every passing second. He played over the events of the day, from the meeting in the morning to what Jules had debriefed him on and then the trip to the deli. When Laurella had left him basically holding his dick in the elevator, he'd almost stormed into her office and given her a piece of his mind. But instinct had told him he had to be clever with this one. She had her high-heel-clad feet well and truly under the table, despite only starting with the company a few weeks earlier. Instead of his usual style of firing with both barrels, he'd need to be cautious—watch and listen, and when the time was right, strike. There was only space for one of them at Necron, and *he* would be taking that spot.

The earlier solitude he'd craved became an urge to be surrounded by people. He jogged upstairs and entered the bar. Jax was still running around and doing far too much, considering he wasn't fully recovered yet. Calum shared a few words with a couple of the regulars then eased onto a chair at the bar.

"You want some help?" he said to Jax, who was mixing a martini with one hand and pouring a beer with the other.

"I'm good," Jax replied. "Besides, you've done a full day already."

"No more than you, and you're still going."

"It's all good. I'm actually thrilled to be back at the helm. I'm only covering the bar tonight and tomorrow. Isa will be back from vacation then, so she'll be able to take over the evening shift." He finished serving a customer then set a glass of Barolo in front of Calum. "How was your first day back?"

For some reason, Calum didn't want to share his thoughts about Laurella with Jax. Cole was a different matter. His twin knew the right things to say to keep him calm. Jax would ask too many questions and get his back up.

"Good. It was great to see everyone."

Jax nodded. "It's where you belong. I don't think hotel management quite suits you."

Calum painted on a faux-aggrieved expression. "How could you say that? The guests love me."

Jax laughed and stepped to one side to serve another customer. Calum glanced around. Every table was taken up with guests of the hotel and some nonresidents. Early indications were that Jax was going to make a real success of this business. Calum had been the first to share his skepticism about this venture in the beginning, before the renovation had been completed. However, if bookings continued at their current rate and the buzz about the place didn't let up, his brother would have a winner on his hands. That kind of success was no more than he deserved.

As the clock edged toward nine, more customers arrived, and Jax barely had a minute to breathe.

"Let me help." Calum got down from his chair.

"No need." Jax pointed his chin toward the entranceway. "My cavalry is here."

Calum glanced over his shoulder. His gaze sliced to Jax's girlfriend as she walked toward them, and he clenched his jaw. *Fucking India.* Jax may have forgiven her for almost getting him killed and nearly succeeding in ruining them financially, but Calum was a long way from that. Jax was blind when it came to her, but as sucking Calum's cock to secure his forgiveness wasn't exactly on the table, India would have to use different tactics to get him to look at her with anything other than barely veiled hatred.

"I'm so sorry," she gushed, tossing her purse and coat behind the bar. "I tried to get here earlier, but work has been crazy."

"You're here now." Jax's eyes filled with adoration, and he bent down for a kiss. "That's all that matters."

"Yeah, that's *all* that matters," Calum repeated, his tone laden with sarcasm. "Well, seeing as you don't need me, I'll be off."

He stomped out, but before he reached the door that led to their private quarters, India appeared behind him.

"Calum, wait," she called out.

Yanking open the door, he jogged downstairs. The damn woman followed him. He stalked into the living room and turned around, hands planted on his hips, eyes narrowed. He glared at her. "I thought you were helping Jax. So fuck off back upstairs and do what you came to do."

She met his venomous gaze with one of her own. "This can't go on, Calum. You need to face facts. I'm going nowhere, and as you aren't either"—she gestured between them—"we *have* to figure this out."

He stepped toward her. To her credit, India stood her ground when Calum got right up in her face. "I don't *have* to do anything—not where you're concerned." He laughed, the sound short and bitter. "You might have Jax conned, but you don't fool me. After what you did, how he can bear to look at you—let alone stick his cock inside you—is beyond me."

The slap to his face sent a ringing sound ricocheting off the walls. Despite the sting, Calum didn't touch his cheek. Anger and adrenaline rushed through his body, and the muscles in his legs quivered.

"That's a freebie." He moved in closer, which brought them nose to nose. "Next time, I'll return the favor."

"I'll bet you will," she sneered. "Hitting women is something you're sadistic enough to get off on, right? Calum Brook— thinks he's a big shot. In reality, you're just a bully. Well, go and find someone else to pick on, Calum, because you don't scare me."

"No?" he said, his voice menacingly low. "You should be scared, sweetheart."

Despite her bravado, India's bottom lip quivered. She bit down, but too late. She'd shown her hand. "If you bothered to listen—and I mean really listen—to the full story, you might be more understanding."

Calum snorted, turned his back, and strode across the living room. He grabbed another beer from the fridge—without offering *her* one. He twisted off the cap and flicked it in her direction. It bounced harmlessly off the wall behind her head, but she flinched regardless.

"Go on, then." Derision laced his tone. "I'll give you airtime. Five minutes to prove to me you're not a manipulative bitch who set my brother up and almost got him killed."

Her chin fell to her chest. "I never meant for Jax to get hurt. Not like that. But Phil—"

"Oh, here we go again. I guess it's easy to blame a dead guy. Your brother might have been crazy as fuck, but at least he owned his part in your little scheme. Yet you stand there, pretending like you didn't have a mind of your own. I don't buy it, India, but go on. Do your best to convince me you're the innocent party."

A flush crept up her neck, inching over her jaw, bleeding into her cheeks. "What's the point?" she said with a slow shake of her head. "You'll believe what you want to believe."

She went to leave then paused on the threshold and glanced

over her shoulder. "Like I said, Calum, I'm going nowhere. Jax has forgiven me, and we're together. The sooner you accept that, the easier this situation will be for all of us."

Before he could think up a suitable retort that didn't involve the words *fuck* and *off*, India spun on her heel and left. Her footsteps sounded on the carpeting as she jogged upstairs, then came the slam of a door, and silence.

Calum stared at the empty space she'd occupied until five seconds before. She sure knew how to press his buttons, but she was right about one thing—Jax was completely smitten. Sooner or later, Calum would have to call time on his antipathy toward her, for the sake of his relationship with his brother. When Calum had made to leave a few minutes earlier, he hadn't missed the pleading in Jax's eyes, and no doubt, they'd have an argument about his treatment of India as soon as Jax closed up for the night.

With a heavy sigh, Calum flopped onto the couch. The beginnings of a headache pounded behind his eyes, and he closed them for a moment, pinching the bridge of his nose with a thumb and forefinger.

He reached for his iPad. He'd meant to do more digging on Laurella Ricci before going back to work, but apart from a brief review when Zane had told him he'd hired her, Calum had been too busy. As Jax could no doubt testify, running a hotel didn't leave much spare time.

He started his search in Google. After thirty minutes, he'd managed to glean that she was one of six siblings—three brothers, two sisters. Laurella had been born and raised in Milan, but her British mother had made sure she'd received English lessons from a very early age, which no doubt accounted for her near-flawless command of the language. Well, that and the fact she'd attended Harvard Business School, gaining a double major in business administration and marketing after four years. This pissed him off even more because such an achievement reaffirmed her brilliance.

From there, she'd returned to Italy where, for the past seven years, she'd gradually worked her way up at Spirito, ending her career there as second-in-command to the marketing director. And now, at the age of thirty, two years older than him, she'd turned up on his doorstep to make his life a goddamn misery.

He cast his iPad to one side. Something told him that getting rid of Laurella Ricci wasn't going to be as easy as he'd first imagined. Still, understanding the enemy was the first step. Next step? Get creative.

CHAPTER 4

After a night of tossing and turning, Calum arrived at the office in a foul mood—which got a hell of a lot worse when he found Laurella Ricci sitting behind his desk. *For fuck's sake.* First she'd stolen his chair in the boardroom, and now the damn woman was pissing all over his office, metaphorically speaking.

"What do you want?" He slammed his briefcase on top of his desk and walked around to where she was sitting. He glared down at her, hands on his hips.

Laurella uncrossed her legs, the movement drawing his attention. With considerable effort, he forced his gaze upward. It didn't matter how shapely her legs were or how good they looked in heels. She wasn't going to be in her position long enough for him to care one way or the other.

Laurella eased to her feet and stepped aside. "To talk to you."

Calum sat in the recently vacated chair, and the heat from Laurella's body warmed his ass—almost as if they were touching. A slight tremor ran through him. Disgust... or desire? Cole's words from the previous night came back to haunt him. He was *not* attracted to Laurella Ricci. Sure, she had a smoking figure. Even a monk would give a second glance at a woman with a body like hers, but what use was physical attractiveness when he couldn't stand the woman?

He painted on a bored expression. "About what?"

She sat in his guest chair and refolded those slender legs finished off with expensive-looking shoes. He had to hand it to her—she oozed class and style.

"I feel like we got off on the wrong foot yesterday. I'm here to suggest a fresh start."

Calum narrowed his gaze. "What makes you think we got off on the wrong foot?"

She smiled. "You honestly want me to answer that?"

When he remained silent, his eyes hooded while he waited for her to make her next move, she quietly sighed. "I know that marketing and sales often have a… tempestuous relationship. But it doesn't have to be that way. At my last company, the sales team and I found a way to work together toward a common goal. Can't we agree to that for Zane's sake? For the sake of Necron?"

"Why did you leave?" he asked, ignoring her plea for peace. If she thought he was going to make it easy for her, she was living in la-la land. "How can Necron possibly hope to compete with a company with the size and history of Spirito?"

She brushed at an imaginary piece of fluff on her stylish suit before raising her head. Her eyes held an emotion he couldn't read, but when he peered closer, her gaze became shuttered. "I needed a new challenge."

He snorted. "That's it?"

She jutted her chin, clearly annoyed by his dismissal of her reasoning. "Yes. That's it. I'd been at Spirito since I left Harvard seven years ago. I could have stayed, waited for the current marketing director to leave, but that might take years." She leaned toward him. "I'm good at what I do, Calum. Actually, I'm better than good. If we work together, rather than in direct competition, we can really take this company places."

He raised his eyebrows at her confident play. He, too, leaned forward, mirroring her posture, except that he also placed his hands flat on the desk in an assertive manner. "This company was going places before you. It will *still* be going places after you've gone."

Realization of his underlying threat swept across her face, and then her features hardened. She pressed her lips together. "If that's how it's to be." She flicked her midnight-black hair over her shoulder, rose from her chair, and smoothed a hand down her shirt. "You want a fight, Calum?" She rested the tips of her fingers on his desk. "You've got one."

Calum's lips curved upward. He picked up his empty mug and raised it to her. "I look forward to it, sweetheart."

She straightened. A ripple of excitement surged through him as he met her furious gaze. Sparring was in his blood. He lived for it. And although Laurella Ricci was clearly going to be a worthy opponent, there would only be one winner.

"*Stronzo*," she muttered before spinning on her heel. She left his office, slamming the door behind her. The glass on either side rattled.

He tried for a triumphant grin, but for some reason, his lips wouldn't move. What the fuck did *stronzo* mean? He'd bet it wasn't complimentary, especially considering the way she'd almost spat the word. He typed it into Google and waited for the search engine to return the results. When it did, he ground his teeth.

She'd called him an asshole. Still, he'd been called worse.

A tightening sensation gripped his chest. *Must be heartburn.* He reached into the drawer to his right and took out a bottle of Pepto-Bismol, drinking a dose straight from the bottle.

Zane's head poked around Calum's door. "Got a minute?"

"Sure," Calum said, replacing the bottle of pink liquid and shutting the drawer.

"Everything okay?" Zane asked with a concerned head tilt.

"Yeah, fine. I must have eaten something that disagreed with me."

Or you want *to eat something that disagrees with you.*

Zane took a seat as Calum forced the unsolicited thought from his mind.

"I just saw Laurella stomping down the corridor. What gives?"

Calum ruffled the top of his head. "She is one frustrating woman." *But oh so hot when she's angry.* He shifted uncomfortably. *For fuck's sake.* His dick needed to take a goddamn vacation.

Zane laughed. "She's Italian. You'll get used to her."

"Don't bank on it."

The laughter drained from Zane's eyes. "Is there something I should know?"

Calum hesitated. Zane might be his best friend, but he still owned the company. Best to go for a half-baked response.

"She's a marketer. You must have known when you brought her in that she and I were going to clash."

Zane expelled a frustrated breath. "Give her a chance, Calum. You've been a fantastic support to me and helped grow this company these past five years, but you and I both know we've taken Necron as far as we can without bringing in new talent."

"If you want to bring in new talent, then why don't we hire some young, hungry interns? They'll work for a pittance and slave away like dogs."

"Because I need *experience.* Laurella was responsible for some phenomenal achievements at Spirito throughout the last seven years. If she replicates even a fraction of that success here, this company will grow exponentially." Zane rubbed his thumb over his fingertips. "You're a shareholder. Think of the money."

Calum grinned. "You always did know how to motivate me."

Zane stood. "Try to get along with her, for the well-being of Necron if not for my sanity. Undoubtedly, there will be times when you'll disagree, but you're a professional, as is she. Work it out."

"I'll do my best not to kill her," Calum said, softening his tone for Zane's benefit.

Zane laughed then crossed to the door. "I'm more worried that she'll kill you."

Calum stared at the closed door for a few moments then leaned back in his chair and glanced out the window. He was going to murder Cole for putting stupid thoughts in his head, because now he couldn't shut them off. He needed to think about Laurella differently. Perhaps he could think of her as an attractive sculpture that he could look at and admire for its external beauty—even if it was the last thing he'd want next to him in bed.

He tongued his top teeth. Working with her was going to be the equivalent of having pins pushed underneath his fingernails. Fucking torturous.

CHAPTER 5

Calum counted four separate huge arguments with Laurella during the following month. They bickered over everything. Strategy, direction, pricing, deals, offers. In fact, the only thing they could agree on was that they hated each other. Despite promising Zane he'd try, she had a special skill for doing the complete opposite of what Calum thought was the right thing, and he couldn't keep his mouth shut—or turn a blind eye.

Finally, when Zane had asked if he wouldn't mind preparing a financial review on a project Laurella had presented to Zane earlier that week, Calum jumped at the chance. Zane wasn't sure her idea would work, and if Calum had his way, he'd make sure it failed spectacularly.

He spent the entire weekend working on the report. He couldn't keep the smile off of his face when he hit Send late on Sunday evening. The report concluded that her project wouldn't make money.

He arrived at the office early the following morning, keen to go over his findings with Zane. He grabbed two coffees from the deli across the street, hung up his coat, then headed to Zane's office. He nudged it open with his hip.

"Morning." He placed a coffee and a bunch of sugar packets on Zane's side of the desk.

Zane removed the plastic lid and added three sugars. "Lifesaver."

"When you hit thirty, you're going to regret pumping all that sugar into your body." Calum made a motion with his hands as if rubbing a fat belly.

Zane laughed. "We can't all have bodies like temples."

"Doesn't come for free," Calum said, smoothing a hand over his abdomen. "But the benefits make the hours in the gym worthwhile."

"Some of us are happy with just one woman," Zane said, referring to his girlfriend, Brienne.

Calum snorted. "Not for me, my friend. I've always preferred the variety of a buffet."

Zane laughed again. "One of these days, you'll get sucker-punched, and bam!" He clapped his hands together. "A woman you never saw coming will have you down the aisle before you can blink."

"You're clearly mistaking me for someone else," Calum said.

Zane wagged his finger. "We all fall in the end. You won't be any different."

"Maybe… when I'm like, fifty. Until then, it's all-you-can-eat for me."

"I give up," Zane said, turning his attention to his laptop. "Now, about this report you sent last night."

Calum grinned, pulled out a chair, and sat. "It's a good idea, but in its current format, it won't work."

Zane steepled his hands beneath his chin. "Tell me more."

Calum explained what his research had thrown up and how he'd come to his final conclusion. Zane interrupted with the odd question a couple of times, but on the whole, he listened quietly.

"I see," he said when Calum had finished. "She should be in by now. I'll give her a call so we can talk it through."

Calum withheld a grin. *This should be good.*

31

While Zane contacted Laurella, Calum wandered over to the window and drank his coffee, staring at people on the street below, all dashing around in their urgency to be somewhere. Thirty seconds later, the door creaked open behind him. He turned around in time to catch Laurella quickly frowning, then she smoothed her expression.

"Morning, Calum," she said in a tight voice. "Nice weekend?"

"Excellent, thanks."

"Good." Her tone told him she didn't care about his weekend. That was fine by him. He couldn't give a shit about hers either.

She sat and crossed her legs. "What's this about?"

That was the thing with Laurella. Small talk was something to be gotten out of the way, almost as if she'd read a *How to Engage with Coworkers* manual and was ticking off a list. Give a greeting: check. Ask about weekend or previous night: check. Acknowledge answer: check. Move on quickly, hoping no one will notice blatant lack of interest: double check.

Zane took a seat behind his desk. Calum remained standing to Zane's right. Laurella's mouth was pinched around the edges. *Good.* She'd read the situation correctly.

"I asked Calum to take a look at your proposal," Zane said.

Her eyes widened, and she gave a slow, disbelieving headshake. And then her chin actually trembled before she clamped her jaw tight.

Fuck! The ice queen was actually hurt that Zane had gone behind her back. A tight feeling spread across Calum's chest. Maybe he should have at least tipped her off or given her a heads-up that their conclusions differed. His guilt lasted a microsecond, ending when she met his gaze with an icy stare intended to give his balls frostbite.

"Why?" The question came out short and sharp as she quickly recovered her composure.

"I wanted a fresh pair of eyes from someone who's been in

the company longer than you. It doesn't mean I don't trust you."

Her eyes cut to Zane's. "That's exactly what it means." When his eyebrows shot upward, she backtracked. "Sorry if you think that was blunt, but I can't pretend I'm not disappointed. I thought we operated as a team here."

Zane winced while Calum remained stoic. She wouldn't get a reaction out of him.

"We do," Zane said. "I wanted a second opinion—that's all —and Calum is my number two. Please don't worry about being blunt." He cocked his head toward Calum. "There's the master."

Laurella's eyes didn't even flicker in Calum's direction. They remained fixed on Zane. "And what is Calum's conclusion?"

"It's a good idea," Calum said. "But it won't make money in its current form."

She took a deep breath through her nose, her gaze still averted. "Yes, it will."

"I disagree. And that's what I put in my report."

She finally looked at him, her irises tinged with an emotion he couldn't place. Sadness maybe? No, it couldn't be that. He was reading the signs wrong. Before he could take a closer look, her face became shuttered.

She turned her attention back to Zane. "It will make money. I will prove it."

Easing to her feet, her posture stiff and unyielding, she smoothed her skirt—a regular habit, Calum noticed—and set her mouth in a firm line. "Would you do me the courtesy of sending Calum's findings to my email please, Zane? It seems I was left off the distribution list."

Ouch.

"Of course. Although that's not Calum's fault. I asked him to report back to me. I am sorry. I should have suggested he discuss his findings with you."

"Or he could have come to that conclusion on his own," she

said. "But then, that would mean he had to think like a team player, and it's becoming more and more obvious that Calum believes in the old adage of, 'There is no *I* in team, but there is most definitely a *me*.'"

Double ouch.

Her final jibe having been delivered with scalpel-like precision, she swept out of the room, closing the door with a quiet click. *Hmm.* Calum had expected a slam. Another twinge of guilt crept in. Irritated with himself, he shoved the feeling to one side. Laurella Ricci wasn't some helpless female being pushed around by the big boys. She was a tough competitor who gave as good as she got.

Zane looked positively distraught. His eyebrows were drawn low, and he repetitively drew his teeth across his bottom lip. "I feel terrible," he finally said. "I shouldn't have gone behind her back."

Stunned, Calum slammed his hand on Zane's desk. His friend jumped.

"What the fuck is wrong with you?" Calum said. "Does she have something on you that I should know about?"

Zane frowned. "What the hell are you talking about?"

"The way you are with her. If you're not mooning after her with puppy-dog eyes, you're apologizing when absolutely no apology is required. Jesus, it's like she's the boss and you're the lackey." Calum straightened as a thought came to him—a very unwelcome thought that brought a burning sensation to his chest. "Are you fucking her?"

Zane's eyes widened. "Of course I'm not fucking her. I'm in a happy relationship, remember?"

Calum shrugged. "Well, something's going on, because your behavior is not normal."

Zane launched to his feet, his nostrils flaring. He poked a finger in Calum's direction. "It's *your* behavior that isn't normal. Ever since you came back, you've been picking fights with

Laurella. Grow up. Find a way to get along with her, because I'm telling you now, Calum, she's here to stay."

Calum kicked up his chin and glared at the man who'd been his closest friend for almost ten years. "Well, maybe I'll have to find alternative employment."

He didn't mean a word of it. He loved Necron. He had a vested interest in the company, both financially and emotionally. And he loved Zane as just as much as his brothers.

Zane folded like a balloon pricked with a pin. He sank into his chair, all the fight having left him. "That's not even remotely funny."

Annoyed at himself for upsetting Zane when he didn't deserve it, Calum took the seat opposite. "I'm sorry. And you know I don't mean a word of it. But there's something about that woman. She infuriates me, and I can't help behaving badly when she's around."

"Because she's challenging you. Everything you believe in, everything you've done freely and without question over the past five years, she's asking you to look at again, to maybe try a different way. And because you're a hotheaded prick, you're railing against her. Please, give her a chance. I've said this before, but it's worth repeating to get it through your thick skull: she will help us take Necron places. I know it."

Calum teased at his facial scruff and blew out a deep sigh. "Fine. I'll apologize for not speaking to her about the report before I sent it to you. And I'll *try* to get along with her a little better."

"Good." Zane reached into his desk drawer and took out a pair of airline tickets. He slapped them on the desk in front of Calum. "Because you and she are going to a conference in Chicago. You fly out Monday morning."

Calum jerked his head back. "You have *got* to be kidding me."

"Nope. It's a sales and marketing conference. A lot of the

35

contacts Laurella is targeting will be there. It makes sense to have the heads of both departments in attendance. So pull on your big-boy pants and try to make sure you don't kill each other."

"Does she know about this?"

Zane nodded. "And believe me, she's no more psyched than you are. She just hides it better."

With a sense of foreboding, Calum went back to his office. He started up his computer, immediately spotting an email from Laurella in his inbox. He opened it and read:

You really are a sorry excuse for a man, Calum Brook. Nasty, narcissistic, a complete and utter basterd—not a spelling mistake, but the real thing probably won't get through the security filters, and darn it, I want you to see this email. Know this—I am furious. *I hope you're happy.*

He sat back in his chair, expecting to feel a sense of exhilaration that he'd riled her so much. Instead, exhaustion swamped him. Work had always been the center of his world, a place he couldn't wait to come to, but the last few weeks had taken their toll. He needed to build some bridges. He'd promised Zane. It was time to deliver.

He headed down the hallway to her office. He rapped once on her door and walked in.

She looked up, and her eyes hardened. "What do you want?"

He pulled up a chair and crossed one ankle over the opposing knee. "To apologize."

Surprise flitted across her face, an emotion she didn't try to hide. "Wow. I didn't think your mouth was capable of forming the word."

There was barely a twitch to his lips. "I thought your email was a little harsh."

"Did you." A statement, not a question.

He palmed the back of his neck. "Look, I know my faults all too well. I can be brusque, at times a touch too candid, even audacious. But I care about the success of this company. And if

I tread on some toes in order to protect it"—he shrugged—"so be it."

"My idea will make money," she said doggedly.

"Okay, then, prove it. Review my findings, and see what needs changing in your proposal. I'll happily take another look when you're done, and if I'm wrong, then I'll back you all the way."

She gave a curt nod. "Fine."

He got to his feet. "I'll meet you at the airport on Monday morning."

"He told you, then?" she asked.

Calum nodded. "And by the expression on your face, you're as thrilled as I am."

"I can be professional about it." She cast a scathing gaze over him. "Can you?"

He set his jaw. "Don't push me, sweetheart."

CHAPTER 6

L aurella breathed a silent sigh of relief as the taxi pulled up outside their hotel in Chicago. It had been a tense flight in which she and Calum had barely spoken a word to each other. Finally, she'd be able to get some much-needed space. She unlocked the door and climbed out.

The bellhop wheeled his luggage rack to the back of the car and opened the trunk. "Are you checking in?" he asked politely.

"Yes," Laurella replied as he lifted out each of their bags. "Separate tickets, please." She pointed to her suitcase. "That's my bag."

He scrawled on a ticket and gave it to her. "Hand this in at the front desk, and they'll make sure your luggage is sent up to your room."

"Thanks, man," Calum said, taking his own ticket. He slipped the bellhop a ten-dollar bill.

"Have a wonderful vacation," the bellhop said, wandering off before Laurella could correct him.

"Wish I was on vacation," she muttered, drawing a cocky grin from Calum.

"Don't worry, sweetheart. I'll see to it that you have a good time."

She gave him a sickly smile. "Oh, you're going to make sure you stay the hell away from me? Then you're right—I *will* have a good time."

She spun on her heel and stalked into the hotel. Fortunately, a check-in assistant was free, and Laurella stepped forward. "I have a reservation—"

"*We* have a reservation," Calum said, appearing at her shoulder. "Laurella Ricci and Calum Brook."

Laurella bit down on her lip before she said something that would no doubt embarrass the lady serving them. But she did make sure to grind her heel right into Calum's foot.

"Jesus," he said, snapping his foot away.

Laurella allowed a small smile to creep across her face. "Oh, sorry. I really must be more careful where I step."

Calum glowered as the check-in clerk tapped away on her computer. After a minute or so, she hit them both with a bright smile. "Ms. Ricci, you're in room five thirty-three, and Mr. Brook, you're in five thirty-five."

"Well, look at that," Calum murmured in Laurella's ear. "We're virtually sleeping together."

"In your dreams," she hissed, swiping her key card off the desk. Without waiting for Calum, she hastened across the lobby and managed to get into an elevator without him. The doors closed, and she sagged against the wall. As if the flight to Chicago hadn't been bad enough, the next two days were going to be torturous. Zane had the best interests of his company at heart and thought that by forcing them together, they would find a way to get along, but Laurella's view was quite the opposite. After two days spent in her company, Calum Brook would be lucky to leave with his teeth intact, not to mention his *special parts*.

The elevator doors juddered open, and Laurella strode down the hallway. She craved a shower and some rest. After that, she planned to order room service, go over her notes for the following day, and crash.

She inserted the key card into the slot, and the green light fortunately came on. Too often, these things didn't work, which resulted in a trip back down to the lobby. The last thing she needed was to bump into Calum on his way up to his room.

She slipped inside and tossed her jacket on the bed. Poking her head into the bathroom, she flicked on the light and nodded her approval. A nice bathroom was a measure of a good hotel, and this one excelled, with a huge walk-in shower, twin sinks, and a deep tub that she would definitely be taking advantage of over the next couple of days.

Laurella switched on the nightstand lamp. A soft, buttery glow gave the room a relaxed feel. She perched on the edge of the bed and removed her shoes then massaged the soles of her feet. She loved her heels, but they definitely didn't love her, especially when having to traipse through two airports.

When a knock came at her door, she wandered across the room and peered through the peephole. *Excellent.* Her luggage.

She opened the door. "Thank you," she said, indicating for the bellboy to leave her bag by the entrance. Laurella handed him a tip and closed the door then flopped onto the bed. She lay back and closed her eyes. Exhaustion settled over her like a blanket. She'd rest for a just few minutes, and then she'd unpack and freshen up.

She began drifting off to sleep, so she forced herself upright. A shower would make her feel much better. She pulled her bag across the room and heaved it onto the bed, ready to open it, and paused. This wasn't her bag. It looked similar, but hers was slightly larger and a deeper blue. She read the luggage label. *Damn it all to hell.* It was Calum's bag, which meant he had to have hers. *Wonderful.* Just when she'd hoped to avoid speaking to him until the morning, it seemed fate had other ideas.

With a heavy sigh, she hauled his suitcase back onto the floor, dragged it into the hallway, and rapped on Calum's door. When there was no answer, she knocked again, harder this time.

"Hang on," he called from inside.

He opened the door, wearing only a towel slung low around his waist. His hair was ruffled and damp, and rivulets of water dribbled down his chest. As much as Laurella tried to focus on his face, her eyes seemed to have a mind of their own. Calum Brook might be the most frustrating and hateful person she'd ever had the misfortune to meet, but dear God, the man had the body of an Adonis: hard pectorals, broad shoulders, the most delicious deltoid muscles she'd ever laid eyes on… and tanned, smooth skin.

And as her disobedient gaze traveled farther south, she was treated to a set of defined abs that had her fingers twitching to explore, not to mention a too-sexy-for-words thin strip of hair that started at his navel and disappeared beneath the towel.

She forced a swallow past a throat that had narrowed considerably.

Calum rested his arm high above the doorjamb. "Missing me already, Laurella?"

She schooled her expression into a bored stare and dragged her gaze to his face. "You have my suitcase."

He raised one eyebrow then grinned. "Yes, I believe I do."

He wandered over to the far side of the room, where her suitcase stood. The rear view wasn't bad either. His broad shoulders tapered to a narrow waist. She'd bet he had a firm ass, too.

What the hell, Laurella? She tucked her chin into her chest and nibbled on her bottom lip. Something about seeing Calum in this setting, especially as he was barely clothed, unsettled her.

He set her case down in front of her, swapping it for his own. "Here you go. Get dressed. I'll call for you in a half hour and take you to dinner."

She scowled at him. "I'm having room service."

"No, you're not. We need to plan for tomorrow, and as you were morose on the flight over, you give me no choice but to put up with your scintillating company this evening. Believe me, sweetheart, I'd rather seek a more… willing party."

"Fine." She almost spat the word.

"Good. Thirty minutes," he reiterated.

She wheeled her suitcase next door and opened her door.

"Oh, and Laurella?" he called out.

She stiffened her spin and reluctantly turned around. "Yes?"

"Wear the blue lingerie."

She frowned and then figured out what he was getting at. She strode back to him, hands on her hips. "You opened my suitcase?"

"Of course." He smirked. "Color me curious. I must say, you've got great taste."

"You're *unbelievable*," she bit out, astonished at his invasion of her privacy.

He full-on smiled then, not a hint of embarrassment on his face. "I think that might be the nicest thing you've ever said to me." And without a backward glance, he kicked the door shut—right in her face.

Laurella let out a frustrated growl before entering her own room. She slammed her door so hard the frame rattled. How on earth was she going to survive the next two days with that man?

CHAPTER 7

Laurella was fastening the strap on her shoes when someone knocked. She assumed it was Calum. With a resigned sigh, she looked through the peephole then opened the door.

"Ready?" Calum asked, leisurely raking his gaze over her.

When his eyes returned to hers, she set her jaw. "Have you quite finished?"

He leaned in until his face was much closer than she would have liked, but there was no chance of her stepping away. That would signal defeat. If Calum Brook wanted to try to browbeat her, he could go right ahead. She was perfectly capable of standing her ground.

"I haven't even started," he said, his eyes boring into hers.

An irritated sound fell from her lips. She was tired, overwrought, and hungry. She didn't need this shit. "Why are you so combative? Is it because I intimidate you?"

Calum laughed, short and sharp. "*You* intimidate *me*? Sweetheart, keep dreaming."

"Well, there must be some reason you constantly want to pick a fight."

"Yeah, there is." He raked over her with a derogatory eye sweep. "I don't like you, but as I'm fucking stuck with you—at least for now—I might as well amuse myself in the meantime."

And with that, he walked away, hands buried in his pockets, humming softly to himself.

"*Stronzo*," she muttered.

"I heard that," he said, still strolling down the hallway. "I've been called worse. Now, move your ass, Laurella. We have work to do."

She considered ignoring him, going back inside her room, and slamming the door. But as much as it stuck in her throat to admit it, he did have a point. They should discuss the best approach to take at the conference. Zane was counting on them to act professionally, to present a united front and, hopefully, impress one or two potential clients. If they spent the next day shooting daggers at each other and constantly arguing and backbiting, they wouldn't achieve their aims.

She closed her door with a quiet click and followed him. She'd keep the conversation focused on work. If he strayed onto other subjects or made a nasty comment or observation, she would simply ignore him and draw the conversation right back to Necron.

She caught up with him by the bank of elevators. He paid her no attention as he pressed the call button. When the doors opened, Laurella breathed a sigh of relief. Two other people were inside. At least they wouldn't be alone. The close confines of an elevator wasn't where she needed to spend time with Calum Brook—although the small space would make it harder for him to avoid a kick in the balls. Her lips twitched. Now, *there* was a fantasy she'd enjoy playing over and over in her mind.

"Something amusing?" he said, stepping inside.

She smiled sweetly. "Private joke."

Neither said anything further as the elevator traveled to the first floor. When the doors opened onto the busy lobby, Calum strode forward, his long legs making it easy to leave Laurella trailing behind. Damn the man.

They arrived at the podium in front of the hotel restaurant, and Calum gave his name. Only then did she realize he'd already made a reservation for two.

"And if I'd changed my mind?" she asked, irked by his presumptuousness.

He pinned her with his gaze. "Then I'd have found alternative company. Someone a little… warmer." He followed the host to their table, tossing, "I knew you wouldn't change your mind, though," over his shoulder.

Laurella ignored his throwaway comment and held her tongue until they were seated. She took the menu from the host with a bright smile, but when he moved away, her smile fell.

"You think you've got me all figured out, don't you?"

Calum didn't even show her the courtesy of looking up. "Yep."

"Enlighten me, then."

He placed his menu on the table, his eyes sliding to hers. He crossed his arms over his chest. "You're a typical woman who's on the rise in her career, who thinks that to be successful, you have to win at all costs, and that includes selling your colleagues down the river."

Laurella widened her eyes. "Have you any idea how offensive that is?"

He shrugged. "The truth hurts, I find."

Laurella sucked in a deep breath and held it, because if she spoke right then, *professional* was the last thing she'd be. Luckily, the waiter chose that moment to appear. She quickly scanned the menu and picked the chicken salad. Calum ordered a large steak—bloody. *What a surprise.*

"It's so strange," she said after the waiter had retreated. She arranged the napkin in her lap then rested her linked hands on the table. "It's only you I have issues with. At my last company, I didn't have any problems with my male colleagues."

"That's not what I heard."

Laurella paused for a beat, and then her heart began to race so fast she feared it would explode through her chest, like a scene in a horror movie. *Keep cool. He's fishing. Don't bite.*

"What's that supposed to mean?"

"Two words, sweetheart. Alberto Vorino."

Laurella's insides collapsed. Her legs trembled, luckily hidden by the table, and a tightness spread across her chest. *Oh God.* She couldn't breathe. Her vision blurred, and white spots danced in front of her eyes as memories she'd worked hard to forget crashed through the fortress she'd erected in her mind. Vorino. A name she hadn't heard in four years. A man she should have been able to trust who had assaulted her, violated her body, crushed her soul.

She fisted her hands into her napkin to stop them shaking and forced herself to meet Calum's intense gaze. He couldn't know. Only two people other than her knew the truth about what Vorino had done to her.

Don't give anything away. Make him tell you what he means.

She feigned a bored stare, although her abdomen twisted with fear, and a trickle of sweat eased its way between her breasts. "I have absolutely no idea what you're talking about." Her voice was strained, a hint of a tremor in her tone. She prayed he didn't know her well enough to pick up on it.

"Really?" Calum raised his eyebrows. "Because from what I was told, you wanted a promotion, and Alberto Vorino made it clear he didn't think you were ready. Unfortunately for poor Alberto, he wasn't aware that your daddy and the CEO of the company, were bosom pals. Next thing Alberto knows, he's out on his ear, and you've settled your fine ass into his corner office." He paused as the waiter poured their wine. When they were alone once more, he lifted his glass to his lips. "This is a small industry, Laurella. People talk. But your daddy isn't going to help you here. If you think for one minute I'll be as easy to get rid of, you're sorely mistaken."

Laurella almost slumped in her chair. *Thank God.* He only knew Vorino's sorry excuse of a tale, because the man could hardly tell the truth. Her secret was safe. She could go back to how things were, put the memories back in the drawer, and make sure they were buried beneath all the good things that had happened since then. She wasn't that girl anymore. She didn't have to live in fear.

With a slightly amused expression, she rubbed her fingertips over her mouth. "As you've already made up your mind about what happened, there's no point staying on this subject." She drank a larger than advisable mouthful of wine.

He frowned. "You're saying the version I was told isn't true?"

Her pulse jumped. She'd shown too much of her hand. *Close him down, Laurella. Right now.*

"I'm saying that I think we should focus on the here and now. How do you want to handle tomorrow?"

A puzzled expression drifted across his face, and for the briefest of moments, his eyes softened. He quickly recovered, though, his trademark sneer making a comeback. "Seeing as you're the one with all the answers, you tell me."

Relief flooded through her. He'd backed off. Her heart rate slowly returned to normal, and the burning sensation in her lungs receded.

"Well, one thing's for sure," she said, leaning back to allow the server to put her plate down. "We have to pretend to get along."

"Wrong Brook brother for that." Calum placed his hand over his wineglass as the server went to fill it up. "Nate, my younger brother, is the actor in our family."

"How many brothers do you have?" The question slipped out. She was suddenly curious as to whether the whole family shared the same enormous chip on their shoulder that Calum carried on his.

"Three," he said, surprising her with his willingness to share. "One older, one younger, and a twin."

"You're a twin?"

He nodded and proceeded to slice into his steak. The juices oozed out, seeping into his mashed potato. Laurella eyed his fork, watching it travel to his mouth. While he concentrated on his food, she took the opportunity to appraise him. She couldn't argue—he was very easy on the eyes. Such a shame. So beautiful on the outside yet so ugly on the inside. Fortunately, he was more interested in eating than in her surreptitious appraisal.

"What does he do?" she asked, keen to keep the conversation going, hoping that Calum would drop the bitter sarcasm he always spoke to her with. It'd be nice to have a few minutes of peace and relaxation, even if it wouldn't last.

"He's a cop. NYPD."

"Tough job," she said.

His chin lifted. "You have no idea," he said, but not in a horrible way, just in a way that suggested only someone close to a cop would understand the half of it.

"I'm sure," she said, tucking into her dinner as her appetite returned.

"So, we have to get along, huh?" he asked, bringing the conversation back to her earlier statement. He stared at her over the rim of his glass. "I guess I could give it a go for one day. Might call Nate tonight and get some tips."

Laurella laughed. She held up her glass, surprised when he clinked his against hers. "To Necron's success."

"To success," he said, which made Laurella wonder what he'd meant by leaving out the name of the company. Necron's success… or his own in getting rid of her?

They finished the rest of their dinner, their discussions centering on the strategy they'd adopt the following day. As their dessert plates were being taken away, a tall, willowy woman with waist-length straight red hair appeared tableside.

"Calum Brook," she said. "I thought it was you."

"Vonny." He rose from his chair to give the woman a more than friendly peck on the lips. "I didn't expect to see you here. You look great."

"So do you. Handsome as ever." She set her gaze on Laurella then. "You're a lucky girl, but enjoy him while you can. He's almost impossible to pin down for long."

"Oh, we're not together." Laurella almost fell over the words in her haste to spill them. "I'm a work colleague."

"So was I," Vonny replied with an exaggerated wink. "Never stopped me."

A smile tugged at Calum's lips. Laurella's face heated. "I assure you, it's not the same at all," she said in a curt, no-nonsense tone.

Vonny shrugged then seemed to lose interest. She turned her attention back to Calum. "What are you doing in Chicago?"

"Conference. Zane's got big plans for Necron. Hence, he's expanded the workforce." He cocked his head in Laurella's direction. "Brought in a big-shot marketing expert from a global player."

The way he spoke about her as if she wasn't there sent a loud message that the truce was over. The derision in his tone didn't seem to have been missed by Vonny, who looked at Calum, then Laurella, then back at Calum.

"Well, someone has to hold the sales department to account," Laurella said in a sickly-sweet tone.

"And someone has to bring home the bacon," Calum hit back. "If we left it to marketing, we'd have a nice logo and some half-assed advertising and nothing in the bank."

Vonny threw back her head and laughed. "Still a renegade, I see, Calum." She gripped his tie then let it slip through her fingers. "What are you doing later? I'm free for the evening if you are."

His eyes darkened with desire. Laurella shifted uncomfortably as she observed what was clearly two lovers—or at the very least, former lovers—having a silent conversation. Then Calum seemed to make up his mind. He picked up his cell, slipped it into the inside pocket of his jacket, and inserted his middle finger into Vonny's ample cleavage, using her bra as leverage to tug her toward him.

"Looks like I'm doing you." He bent his dark head and captured Vonny's mouth, but his eyes were on Laurella rather than his soon-to-be bedfellow. Transfixed, she tried to avert her gaze but found the simple action impossible.

And then, as quickly as the kiss had started, Calum drew back. He scrawled his signature on the check, snaked an arm around Vonny's waist, and walked away, throwing a casual, "Dinner's on me," over his shoulder before he disappeared from the restaurant.

Laurella sat alone for a few minutes, quietly fuming. She barely acknowledged the waiter, who'd returned to collect the check. When Calum had spoken about his family, she'd dared to hope—for one stupid, unbelievable moment—that they might have had some sort of a breakthrough and maybe, just maybe, he'd stop looking at her as the enemy and see her as an equal. But no, he'd simply lured her in and then, at the first opportunity, turned his bitter, evil tongue on her once more—the very tongue that he would no doubt be using in a different way on Vonny in the next few minutes.

A tightness stole across Laurella's chest, almost as if she were wearing a sports bra two sizes too small. She didn't want to think about Calum Brook and his tongue. She wanted to go home. And not to New York. To Italy. His mention of Vorino had stirred up all sorts of horrifying memories, and she craved the chance to curl up in Papa's arms and have him make it all go away, just as he had four years earlier.

She trudged to her hotel room, engulfed in loneliness—and then she gave herself a good shake. *Get a grip, Laurella.* One stray comment from Calum Brook should not send her careening back to a time in her life she'd worked hard to leave behind. She was a different person now, more worldly-wise in the art of life —and business—which was why the likes of Calum could go fuck himself if he thought for one moment his bully-boy tactics would scare her off.

Still, she had an urge to touch base with home. She picked up her cell to call Caterina then remembered Italy was seven hours ahead. She glanced at her watch. Ten in the evening. In another hour or so, her sister would be up. She'd call then. In the meantime, she'd go for a soak in the bath and forget all about Calum 'Evil Bastard' Brook.

An hour later, with her skin wrinkled and pruned, Laurella finally got out of the bath. She swaddled herself in a huge towel and trudged into the bedroom. She glanced at the clock beside the bed. She had a good chance of catching Caterina if she called right then. She dialed the number and crossed her fingers.

After three rings, her sister answered. "Ella," Caterina said, using the term she'd always used for her older sister from when she was a baby and couldn't say Laurella's full name. "*Mia cara*, how lovely to hear from you."

"It's not too early, is it?" Laurella asked.

"Not at all. The children are still asleep, so I'm getting a head start on packing for school."

Despite her earlier resolve, self-pity made a roaring return at the mention of her two nieces. God, she missed home. Her brothers, her sisters. Mama and Papa. The warmth of being in the bosom of her loving family. Hot tears scorched the back of her eyes, and her throat burned. "I've made a terrible mistake, Caterina," she blurted. "I should never have come here."

"Whatever do you mean?" her sister said.

Laurella could almost picture Caterina's frown, her eyebrows drawn low over her dark-chocolate eyes. "I hate it. I hate New York, I hate the job, and I hate Calum Brook."

"Slow down," Caterina soothed, her soft tone like dabbing aloe vera on a nasty burn. "Tell me from the beginning."

Laurella briefly recapped the last few weeks since Calum had returned to work. How she'd loved her first six weeks, and then *he'd* blown in and done everything possible to make her life a misery. She told Caterina the vile things he'd said, how he'd made it clear he would have her out of Necron the first chance he got. She even mentioned how he'd kissed that woman, while his eyes had mocked her as he'd met her startled gaze.

After she'd finished, she lay back on the bed, closed her eyes, and waited for her sister's advice.

"Well," Caterina said. "Sounds like someone's got a crush on my rather beautiful and talented sister."

Laurella frowned. "You mean Calum?"

"Who else?"

"Oh no. You're wrong. He hates me. You can see it in his eyes every time he looks down his nose at me. He takes every opportunity to sneer, to be mean and cruel."

"Hmmm. Reminds me of when we were at school and Diego Conti used to pick on you by putting slugs in your sandwich and telling everyone you were a witch just because you had black hair. Yet the truth of it was he adored you, but because you were too busy studying to notice him, that's how he courted your attention."

"Ah, Diego," Laurella said with fondness. "I wonder what happened to him?"

"Last I heard, he ran away to try to fix his broken heart over you, got married, had four kids, and put on a hundred pounds."

Laurella laughed. "I knew you'd cheer me up. But you're wrong about Calum. The only person that man has a crush on is himself."

Caterina snorted a laugh. "Honestly, *bella*, don't let him get to you. For years, you sacrificed everything to study, to work hard, to get your break. You always dreamed of getting into a company that was about to take off so you could be part of driving the growth. Don't let this *stronzo* take all that away."

"That's what I keep calling him. He says he's been called worse."

Caterina chuckled. "From what you've said, I can believe it. Look, keep your head down, do your job, and if things do get out of hand, then speak to the owner."

"Who happens to be Calum's best friend."

"*Merda.* It's almost incestuous."

Laurella smiled. "I have to go. It's late here, and I've an early start tomorrow. Give the kids a kiss from me, and say hello to Papa and Mama when you see them later."

"I will. Love you, Ella."

"Love you, too."

Laurella hung up. Even though her sister hadn't offered any earth-shattering advice, just hearing her voice had bolstered Laurella's spirits. She could handle Calum Brook. From now on, she'd be polite, professional, and refuse to rise to his gibes. She brushed out her hair, got dressed for bed and, after setting the alarm on her cell for six the next morning, snuggled under the sheets.

Laurella drifted off to sleep but was awoken sometime later by soft moans that bled through the wall, gradually growing in volume. Her eyes sprang open.

Oh no. How much shittier could her night get? Mortified, she grabbed her pillow and slammed it over her ears to try to drown out the increasing ecstasy from next door. Vonny was not to be silenced. But from Calum? Not a sound. No groaning, no panting—nothing.

She grabbed a blanket and stomped into the living area of her suite. After a mere ten minutes, the hard sofa gave her terrible backache. *Dammit.* She had no choice but to go back to bed.

She hadn't been there long when the sounds on the other side of the wall started up again. Vonny screamed Calum's name, and Laurella tightened her hands into fists, heat flushing through her body. She pulled the covers over her head and squeezed her eyes closed. As she lay alone in the dark, though, it wasn't the sexual noises from next door that kept her awake. The quickening heartbeat, the dry throat, and the tugging sensation in her gut led her to one conclusion: she was envious of the woman on the other side of the wall.

CHAPTER 8

C alum waited for Vonny to fall asleep before he slipped out of bed and crept next door into the living room of his suite. He felt around in the darkness, eventually happening upon the bottle of whiskey he'd brought back with him after leaving Laurella in the restaurant.

After pouring a healthy amount into a glass, Calum went to sit by the window. Sweeping a hand over his face, he stared at the closed bedroom door. He must have had rocks in his head to bring Vonny back here. When she'd told him she was moving to Chicago two years before, he'd pretended to be disappointed that their on-off relationship would have to come to an end, but in reality, he'd been thrilled. She'd saved him the job of finishing it between them, whatever 'it' had been. And yet, in order to stick it to Laurella—figuratively speaking—he'd stuck it to Vonny. The sex had been average, although Vonny would have disagreed, if her screams were anything to go by. He'd come only because he'd closed his eyes and pictured a dark-haired vixen who was invading his thoughts far too often of late.

Laurella… why did she get under his skin so much? How could he be so attracted to a woman he abhorred? How did that fucking work?

He tossed back the whiskey, the burn in his throat a welcome distraction from the fire in his gut as he thought of the woman sleeping next door. The walls at this hotel weren't exactly sound-proof so, no doubt, she'd have heard his nocturnal activities. And that bothered him. He didn't have a clue why it would, but facts were facts.

Vonny appeared at the bedroom door, naked, bleary-eyed, hair a holy mess, mascara smudges beneath her eyes. She yawned then stretched her arms overhead, the movement thrusting her breasts forward. He waited for a twinge in his groin. Nothing.

"Baby, what are you doing up? Come back to bed." She held out her hand and beckoned to him.

"Can't sleep." He ignored her invitation, and her hand fell to her side. It didn't stop her from walking over to him, though. He ground his teeth. She never could take a fucking hint.

"Who said anything about sleeping?" She began to straddle his thighs until he stopped her.

"Not now," he snapped.

Vonny scowled. "Same old Calum, I see. Gets what he wants and then casts you aside like trash."

Calum raked her with a cutting gaze. "Believe me, I most certainly did not get what I wanted." *Because what I want is on the other side of that wall.*

"Charming." Vonny sneered. She tossed her head and stomped back into the bedroom.

Calum huffed then got to his feet and followed her. *She'd better be getting dressed.* He opened the door. Vonny had burrowed back underneath the covers and was staring at him, a painted-on expression of hurt tightening her face.

Fuck's sake.

"Get out, Vonny," Calum said. "I've got an early start in the morning."

"You're kicking me out?" She frowned and glanced at the clock on the nightstand. "It's two in the morning."

"You're staying in the goddamn hotel. It's hardly forcing you to sleep on the street." Irritated when she didn't move, he sighed. "Why are you behaving differently? This is how it's always been between us, Vonny. You had an itch. I scratched it for you. Now it's time for you to go."

She paused for a second, probably wondering whether he'd change his mind. He wouldn't. Even when Vonny had lived in New York, they'd never spent the whole night together, and she knew that.

He kept his gaze trained on her, and eventually, she pouted and flung the covers to one side. "I thought it might be different this time."

He frowned, genuinely confused. "Why would it be?"

"You can be such a bastard, Calum."

He ignored her, his shoulder propped against the doorjamb, arms folded, watching as Vonny pulled on her panties, followed by her dress. She shoved her feet into her shoes and slung her purse over her shoulder.

"Do me a favor," she said. "Next time you fancy a quick fuck, pick on some other idiot."

Oh, darling, now *you're pissing me off.* He yawned and scratched his cheek when he could have ripped into her. Hell, in the past, he *would* have ripped into her. "Are you still here?"

Vonny's jaw tightened, and she pressed her lips together. When she passed by, she made a point of jolting her shoulder into his chest. Calum didn't react, and when the door slammed behind her, he let out a huge fucking sigh of relief. Taking Vonny up on her offer of emotionless sex had been a mistake— one he wouldn't be repeating.

His gaze fell on the rumpled sheets, and a sudden urge came over him to strip the bed. He tossed the sheets on the floor then opened the closet door, took out the obligatory blanket all hotels kept on the top shelf, and spread it over the mattress.

He lay in the dark, listening to his own breathing, and reached a hand behind his head to touch the wall. Beyond the thin layer of drywall and paint was Laurella, probably fast asleep, her thoughts and dreams far from him.

If only he could say the same.

CHAPTER 9

Calum scanned the restaurant, searching for Laurella. He couldn't see her. She must not have made it down for breakfast yet. He slipped into a booth with a view of the entrance and ordered coffee and juice. As the waitress brought his drinks over, he spotted Laurella chatting to the greeter. She'd pulled her hair into a high ponytail, leaving her long, elegant neck bare. It gave her a younger look, one he found extremely appealing.

He raised his hand and pointed to the spare seat opposite. He wouldn't have put it past her to go sit somewhere else but, ever the professional, she headed on over.

"Good morning," she said, the politeness in her tone setting his teeth on edge.

"Coffee?" he asked.

She nodded.

He signaled to the waitress then turned his attention back to Laurella. "All set for today?"

"I am," she said. "Not sure about you, though. You seem a little tired, if you don't mind me saying."

Calum scowled. "I'm fine."

"Late night?" She stared at him innocently, but the minutest curve to her lips gave her away.

"Carry on like that, Laurella, and I'll think you're jealous."

She snorted. "Of you and that woman you picked up? Hardly."

"If you're not jealous, why are your cheeks flushed?"

"I wasn't aware they were." She fanned her face with the menu. "It is a little warm in here."

Her calm demeanor increased his irritation. He wanted to get a rise out of her, to have that fiery Italian temper aimed in his direction. Her casual indifference would soon wear thin.

He leaned forward, his forearms resting on the table. "You don't fool me, sweetheart. You can lie to yourself but not to me. You virtually turned green last night when I left with Vonny." He grinned. "Just say the word, and I'll make you scream like I did with her."

She laughed, the sound brittle and tinged with derision. "Not even if you were the last man on Earth. You may think you're God's gift, but I prefer my men a little more humble and a lot more self-aware."

He opened his mouth to respond but was curtailed when the waitress brought Laurella's coffee.

"Can I get this to go?" Laurella asked her.

"Sure thing," the waitress replied. "I'll be back in two."

Laurella stood. With her fingers pressed to the table, she bent forward, showing the merest hint of cleavage. He lowered his gaze before dragging it back up to her face.

"Enjoy the view," she said. "It's the closest you'll ever get. So, before we head into the day, let me make one thing clear: I'm not interested."

Calum leaned away and draped his arm across the back of the booth. He looked her up and down while tonguing his teeth then lifted his eyes to hers. "Say it enough times, and you might even convince yourself. But you won't convince me, sweetheart."

With a frustrated huff, Laurella set off after the waitress.

Calum grinned to himself. He loved getting the last word. He'd won that battle. *Bring on the next.*

~

Her stomach rumbled, forcing Laurella to grab a pastry from the deli in the lobby. She would have liked something a little more filling, especially as it might be the last thing she ate before dinner. Calum had ruined that plan. The worst of it, though, was that he'd been right. She was jealous. Not that she'd ever admit such a thing. Hell would freeze over first. Calum's high opinion of himself did not need any stroking from her.

She returned to her room, grabbed her notebook, and headed down to the conference room, thinking she might as well get an early start. It was never too soon to begin networking. With any luck, she'd avoid Calum for as long as possible.

The large room was set up classroom style. Laurella entered, spotting a couple of other people milling about. She wasn't the only early bird, then. She introduced herself, glad to have someone to stand with while she waited for the conference to begin.

The room rapidly filled up. Laurella sat beside the people she'd already introduced herself to. Still no sign of Calum. Well, too bad. There weren't any seats left near her, so he'd have to sit elsewhere. She wasn't complaining.

A glance at the schedule showed that the first speaker was someone she couldn't wait to hear. Daryl Hudson was CEO of an online clothes company that he'd started from scratch. Even though Necron operated in a very different field, she could still learn a lot from his perspective on growth. Daryl, too, had begun his career in marketing, and she was hoping that by listening to the lecture, Calum might at least begin to understand that having a robust and growth-focused marketing strategy was key to taking Necron from a small to a medium-sized business. Without that type of game plan, they'd be unlikely to achieve their goals.

She reached for the water and unscrewed the bottle top. A cool finger trailed across the back of her neck. She jumped, spilling the water all over her notebook.

"Oh, shoot," she said, dabbing the soaked paper with a napkin. She glanced over her shoulder and scowled. *Calum!* "What are you doing?"

"I got us seats over there." He pointed across the room.

"I'm fine here, thank you."

Calum reached over her shoulder and picked up her note-book and pen. He walked away without saying another word. *Damn the man.* She had two choices: either stalk after him and snatch her stuff back, or meekly follow and look like a complete pushover. Actually, strike that. She only had one choice—and Calum knew it. Murmuring apologies to the person sitting next to her, she gathered her purse and bottle of water and trudged across the room.

Calum ignored her as she sat beside him, choosing instead to chat with the woman on his right. He murmured something under his breath, and the woman giggled, her body automatically leaning toward his. Laurella gritted her teeth. She had to hand it to him—Calum could turn on the charm when he wanted. She was the only one who seemed to feel his wrath.

After the initial presentations were over, the first breakout session began. Now, *this* was the main reason she'd wanted to come to this event—the chance to network, to swap thoughts and ideas, and to learn from others. She slipped away while Calum was deep in conversation with his seat neighbor. *Probably negotiating the route into her panties*, Laurella thought uncharitably.

She joined a group of marketers, and soon they were sharing their experiences. There was a broad mix. Some worked at companies such as Necron—up-and-coming small and medium-sized enterprises—and others at the large conglomerates. But the one thing they all had in common was regular conflict with the sales department.

"I got on fairly well with the sales director at my last place," Laurella said to a young guy standing to her left who was having a particularly bad time. "It's been my experience that sales teams are like abusive spouses. When things are tough, they want to blame, to take it out on the marketing department, to beat up on them. But when they want something, they're as sweet as pie."

"That's an interesting concept," an all-too-familiar voice drawled behind her. She inwardly groaned as Calum muscled his way into the gathering. His arm brushed hers, and she thought about stepping to the side, but that would have meant getting far too close and personal with the man on her left. "Calum Brook," he said, layering on a charming smile. "The abusive spouse."

A guy standing across from her sniggered. Deciding it was time to find a new bunch of friends, Laurella stepped away. She didn't get far, though. Calum's hand shot out, and he gripped her elbow, holding her firmly in place.

"It's been *my* experience," he said, parroting Laurella's words, "that sales teams are hunters. They're agile predators who act fast, bring home the prize, and then quickly move on to the next kill. Whereas marketers"—he turned to Laurella with a devious grin—"are much more interested in setting a trap and simply hoping their prey takes the bait."

A few people snorted with laughter, which, considering Calum had basically insulted their profession, showed once more how he could charm a snake when the mood took him.

"As fascinating as that theory is, Calum," Laurella said, her tone dripping sweetness, "the fact remains that without marketing, the sales department wouldn't have any prey to hunt."

"Oh, I don't know about that," he said. "I found plenty of prey to hunt before I met you. And I had a lot of fun pursuing them, too."

His double entendre wasn't lost on her. The man even had the gall to wink. Laurella managed to free herself from his grip in a subtle way without drawing any extra looks from the group, who were already watching the exchange between her and Calum with barely veiled fascination.

"How lovely for you," she murmured. "Now, if you'll excuse me…" She stepped away, half expecting Calum to follow, but instead, he simply turned his back and carried on chatting as though the spiky interchange hadn't happened at all.

With her heart pummeling against her ribcage, Laurella headed outside for a breath of fresh air. She sat on a bench right by the front entrance, her chin trembling with suppressed anger. She'd hoped that by being away from the confines of the office in New York, she and Calum might find a way to work together, but it seemed that particular hope was little more than a pipe dream. He was toying with her, and she didn't have a clue about how to fight back. She'd faced worse than him, so why did he get to her so much? How did he burrow beneath her skin and lay his poison, making her throat burn and her hands inadvertently form into fists?

"There you are."

She lifted her chin, shielding her eyes from the sun. Calum wandered over and sat beside her. He handed her a coffee. Their fingers brushed as she took it from him, sending an unwanted shiver down her spine.

"Thank you." She peeled off the plastic lid, the welcome smell of coffee tickling her nostrils. For a second, she considered throwing it all over Calum's pristine white shirt. It would serve him right for the way he'd behaved. Instead, she blew on the hot liquid and sipped, her attention locked on a point in the distance.

"I know I'm a bastard," he said, drawing her gaze to him.

"Yes. You are."

"How about a cease-fire?" he said.

She eyed him with suspicion. "What's brought this on?"

When he shrugged one shoulder but didn't answer her, she added, "For how long?"

His genuine laugh made something funny happen to her insides. She didn't like the sensation one bit.

"At least until the conference is over or you do something to piss me off. Whichever comes first."

"And what if you do something to piss me off?"

He clasped a hand to his chest. "Me? Never."

Despite her deep-seated irritation with her nemesis, her lips twitched, but as she gazed into his green eyes, the bright sunshine highlighting flecks of gold around the edge of his irises, a tremor sent shockwaves through her body. She recognized the sensation, of course. Lust. Desire. Longing. Any of those words would suffice. But she could not let the bane of her life know her innermost feelings. They were hers and hers alone. She needed to concentrate on how he made her working life a misery. That should be more than enough to keep the unwanted hankering at bay.

"I guess we should go back in," she said.

"You sound almost disappointed." Calum grinned. When she scowled, he gave her shoulder a playful nudge. "Kidding, Ricci."

His jokey manner by using her surname was so different from the Calum she'd come to know, warmth flooded her body, and her heartbeat thundered in her ears.

Oh hell. What do I do now?

CHAPTER 10

C alum kicked off his shoes and flopped onto the bed. Two very successful days were at an end, and he couldn't help a pinch of sorrow nibbling at his insides. They were headed back to New York in the morning—but did that also mean he and Laurella would return to being at each other's throats? Since their impromptu truce, they'd worked really well together and secured some useful leads. Even if those leads didn't come off, they'd made several key contacts, and some influential people had definitely taken notice. Necron's name wasn't unknown any longer.

He was on his way to take a shower when his cell rang. He turned back into the bedroom. Jules. With a frown, he answered.

"What's up?" he asked his second-in-command.

Jules chuckled. "I'm starting to get a complex. One of these days, you'll sound happy to hear from me."

"I will sound happy—when you stop bringing me bad news every time you call."

Jules laughed again. "How did the conference go?"

"Good. We've come away with some more leads that we can add to the ones we're already working on—thanks to Laurella."

Jules let out a low whistle. "Has the glacier melted?"

"Very funny. I wouldn't go that far, but we decided to stop fighting over every little thing, and it's been beneficial both to our working relationship and to Necron."

"Well, hold on to your hat, because you're not going to like what I have to say."

His skin prickled, and he sat on the edge of the bed. "Go on."

"You know how we've always cleared our overstocks through Ben Davies at Weston's?"

"Yeah."

Jules hesitated. She heaved a breath—and then dropped the bombshell. "So, he calls me today, saying he's received an email telling him he can only have half the usual amount—at a fifteen percent increase on the price he normally gets."

"What?" Calum bellowed. "Who sent the fucking email?"

"Guess."

Calum clenched his jaw so tightly he could have sworn a tooth cracked. "Laurella."

"Got it in one, boss."

I'm going to fucking kill her. She has been the one ranting on about team players and then she goes and does this. If Weston's decided Necron had reneged on a longtime deal—albeit an informal one—and decided to back out from taking any future overstocks, it'd hit their cash flow badly, not to mention their reputation.

He took a deep breath and held it deep in his lungs. He needed to try to calm down before he self-combusted. After two or three long pulls of air, he'd regained control of the murderous feelings racing through his body.

"What do you want me to do?" Jules said.

"Call Ben. Tell him to ignore the email. Get onto the warehouse and ship the stock. Then get accounts to send him the invoice at his usual price."

"Got it." She paused. "Try not to kill her. You're too pretty to go to prison."

Despite his utter fury, Calum smiled. Jules knew just what to say to talk him off the ledge. "I can't promise."

"I'll start stockpiling cigarettes, then, and see if I can't negotiate a cellmate with a small dick."

Her joke coaxed a laugh from him. "What would I do without you?"

"Try to remember your current gratitude when annual reviews are being discussed. Night, boss. See you tomorrow."

Calum cut the call and threw his cell on the bed. He stormed into the bathroom and gripped the sides of the sink, staring into the mirror. Rage burned in his eyes, turning them from a warm jade to almost black.

Truce over. Time to make her pay.

Calum knocked at Laurella's door. He had a plan. It was a cruel one, but he didn't care. At least, after he'd executed it, she'd think twice about interfering in his business again. He'd best nail the point home with a fucking big hammer.

She opened the door with a bright smile. "Hi. Come on in for a second. I just need to grab my shoes, and then we can go."

"You look nice." Calum glanced around her room. It was neat and tidy, unlike his own, which could've had a tornado blown through it.

"Thank you." She slipped her feet into a pair of four-inch heels. They instantly elongated those amazing legs.

He gave her a leisurely once-over. When their eyes finally met, a pink tinge had crept over her cheeks.

"Let's go," Calum said, sticking out his arm.

She slipped her hand through, and they walked to dinner in companionable, if false—at least on his part—silence. Once settled in the restaurant, they ordered their food, and Calum put his plan into action, starting with… charm offensive.

"You've really impressed me these last two days," he said.

"The contacts we've made seem positive, and added to the ones we're already working on, I'd say you've definitely earned your place in the company."

For the second time that evening, warm color flooded her cheeks, and she dipped her chin, glancing up at him with a shy smile. "Thank you, Calum. It just shows what we can achieve when we work together. I think, in time, we'll make a great team."

You won't be around long enough, sweetheart.

"I agree. I can only apologize for my behavior since you started." He circled the rim of his wineglass and gazed at her with as much intensity as he could fake. "I've been so used to going my own way without having to consider others. I guess it's been a tough change for me."

Her eyes softened. "Apology accepted."

Time for a different subject before he choked on his own lies. "Tell me more about you," he said, even though his research had already told him most of what he needed to know.

She clutched the pendant on her necklace and zigzagged it back and forth along the chain. "There's not much to tell, really."

"Do you have any family?"

She nodded. "Three brothers, two sisters."

He chuckled. "I thought my family was big."

"That's Italians for you. We like our big families."

"Parents still alive?"

"Yes."

"And together?"

"Happier than ever," she said. "My mama is English. She met Papa when she was on vacation in Milan and never left." She tucked a lock of hair behind her ear and fiddled with a silver stud earring. "You never mentioned your parents when we were chatting the other night."

"They're dead," he said in a flat tone, familiar agony spearing his chest. *Close it down, nice and quick. Move on.* The last thing he wanted was to let *her* see his pain and loss. "Car crash. More than twelve years ago. Jax, my eldest brother, brought us up until we were old enough to strike out on our own."

Wearing a sympathetic expression, she reached across the table and squeezed his hand. "I'm so sorry. That must have been terrible for you all."

Calum shrugged. "Jax is the one who lost the most."

His clipped responses stopped her questioning him further. Instead, she withdrew her hand, possibly fearing she'd over-stepped the mark by touching him. In response, he took it back and folded it between both of his. "What about boyfriends?"

She squirmed a little and tried to pull away. He tightened his grip. When she relaxed, he gently brushed his thumb back and forth across her knuckles.

"No one serious. Not for a while anyway."

"So there was, once?"

She nodded. "I was engaged to be married, but I was far too young. It worked out as it was meant to in the end."

Sounds to me like the guy had a lucky escape. "What happened?"

Her answering smile was stiff. "I wasn't enough for him. Affairs aren't too out of the ordinary in Italian culture. I antici-pated it would happen sooner or later, but I did rather hope he'd at least wait until after we were married."

A twinge of empathy for her surprised him, but he bit down on that fucker damn quick. She didn't deserve compassion. She deserved payback. "That's too bad."

"Not really. Like I said, I was young. Smitten. Even if I'd gone ahead with the wedding, it wouldn't have lasted."

"All the same, not a fun experience."

She sipped her wine, and the minute she replaced her glass on the table, Calum filled it up.

She giggled. "Are you trying to get me drunk?"

He raised an eyebrow. "Maybe."

That faint flush made another appearance. If he didn't hate her guts, he might have found it appealing.

"For what purpose?" she asked, her chin slightly curved into her chest from where she looked up at him through long, thick eyelashes.

Calum's groin tightened. His stupid dick clearly hadn't gotten the memo. "Maybe I need you to relax."

She blinked several times. "Again, for what purpose?"

He slowly grinned. "Why do you think, Laurella?"

Before she could respond, their food arrived. Calum didn't know whether to curse the timing or celebrate it. It couldn't do much harm to have her chew over how to respond to his question.

She cut into her steak. She had this rather adorable way of holding her fork in her right hand and seesawing at the hunk of meat with her left. It was both awkward and cute. He gave himself a metaphorical slap. *Don't get caught in her web.* She'd shown her colors, and they weren't pretty. She deserved everything coming at her.

"Good?" he asked, nodding at her plate.

Her tongue swept over her full lips. "Delicious."

Another twinge in his groin. He considered slamming his fist into his crotch, but as that would probably hurt like fuck, he focused on her backstabbing email instead. She hadn't even mentioned it to him, yet she must have sent it while they'd been at the conference. All this time, she'd been pretending to bury the hatchet. Well, he'd bury the hatchet all right—between her fucking eyes.

"I've been meaning to ask you, what's that book you keep on the corner of your desk back at the office?"

"You mean my memory book?" She grinned. "I started it when I got my first job. It's just things I've collected over the years that I find inspirational, bits and pieces of ideas. Could be an article in a magazine or a picture I've seen in the subway. Anything I find interesting or inspiring or that might be useful in the future."

"That's really cool," he said.

"Yeah. It means a lot to me. Irreplaceable really."

"I'm sure," Calum murmured, the stirrings of a subplot forming in his mind.

When they left the restaurant, Calum caught hold of her hand. He wasn't sure what her reaction would be, but when she tightened her grip and leaned her head on his shoulder, he internally high-fived himself. *Easy pickings.*

He led her along the hallway, stopping outside her room. He lifted her purse from her shoulder and removed her key card.

"I'm a little drunk," she said, giggling.

He dropped her purse on the floor and slipped the key card into his pocket. "I like you drunk." He tucked a lock of hair behind her ear, and when her lips parted in anticipation, he curved a hand around the back of her neck. "Say it, Laurella," he murmured.

"Kiss me."

Exactly the words he'd been hoping for. He moved into her body. His hard-as-a-baseball-bat cock played along, a state she couldn't fail to notice. *Hadn't* failed to notice, if the flare in her eyes was anything to go by.

He tugged at her chin, opening her mouth farther. She inclined her head, readying herself for what was to come. He pressed his lips to hers and slid his tongue inside the warmth of her mouth. A soft groan eased from her throat. Her hands came around his neck, but instead of allowing her to knit her fingers into his hair, he captured her wrists and pushed her arms over her head. He penetrated her mouth, mirroring the movement of his hips with his tongue.

As fast as he'd begun, he stepped away. Her eyes glistened. He knew desire when he saw it. There was no doubt in his mind that Laurella Ricci wanted him. *Time to up the ante.*

"What do you want, Laurella?"

"You," she said, her mouth swollen and glistening from their kissing.

He swept his thumb over her lower lip, removing the moisture. "Tell me more. Be specific."

"I want you to fuck me," she said.

He tilted his head to the side and caressed her cheek with the back of his hand. "What about our professional relationship?"

She tongued her teeth, her gaze sliding over his body. "We're both adults, Calum. I'm sure a mutually beneficial tussle between the sheets won't be detrimental to our working relationship. It might even enhance it."

He suppressed a smile. This was going better than he'd imagined. He removed her key card from his pocket and handed it to her.

"Better open up, then."

She took it from him, her soft smile full of promise. In a way, it was a shame he wouldn't get to enjoy the fruits of his labor. Laurella crouched and picked up her purse from where he'd dropped it on the floor, then she opened the door. She stepped a couple of feet inside and turned around. Only then did she realize he hadn't moved. She crooked her finger.

"Come on, lover."

Calum breathed in then formed his expression into a cold, hard stare. "I think I'll pass."

A quick frown drew her eyebrows low, and then she laughed. "Playing hard to get?"

He sneered, his lip curled with just the right amount of disgust. "Trust me, sweetheart, I'm not playing. I realize you like to use your feminine wiles to seduce men of power, to get them on the back foot. Use sex as a tool to win whatever shitty little game you're playing. Sadly—for you, that is—I won't be dipping my wick in your poisonous pussy tonight or any other night."

A flash of raw pain crossed her face, as though her skin had been peeled back and the nerves exposed to the elements. It gave him a moment of pause—only a moment, though, before he brushed it aside. She'd been caught out—that was all. She hadn't earned one second of hesitation.

He gripped her chin, forcing her head backward.

She gasped. "What are you doing?"

He loomed over her. "Next time you want to play games, sweetheart, make sure you have a winning hand. Ben Davies is, right now, enjoying our overstock, a deal I've done with his company for the last *five fucking years*. In the future, if you decide to piss off one of our best clients, remember there will be fucking consequences." He dropped his hand.

She stumbled backward. "This was a play?" she asked in a stunned tone.

"Yeah. What, you thought I actually *wanted* you? Oh no, sweetheart. What I wanted was to teach you a lesson. Don't fucking mess with me, because I guarantee you will lose."

Her face blanched, and she blinked rapidly as though trying to hold back tears. An uncomfortable spasm flared in Calum's chest. He spun around on his heel and slammed Laurella's door behind him.

CHAPTER 11

L aurella finally gave up trying to get any sleep at four a.m.
She padded around her hotel room, carefully folding her
clothes, hoping that focusing on something practical would
diminish the awfulness of the previous evening. After Vorino,
she'd sworn to never allow herself to be disempowered by a man
again—yet Calum Brook had cruelly broken through her armor
and stripped her bare, leaving her raw and exposed.

She recalled his awful, brutal words, and a spear of pain had
her wincing. He thought she'd actually been trying to use him
sexually so she could get ahead on the career ladder. Was that
the kind of vibe she emitted? Bile rose in her throat, and as she
swallowed, it burned.

She'd been a fool, a gullible idiot who'd failed to see through
his charade. He'd clearly misunderstood the context of the
email she'd sent Ben Davies, although she cursed the fact she
hadn't taken the opportunity to talk to him about it first. She'd
made a mistake, and now she'd have to pay a heavy price.

All the progress they'd made to improve their working relationship had been blown to pieces with his hateful taunts. She
should have trusted her earlier instincts about Calum and seen
through his fake charm offensive. People didn't change that

quickly. She'd been correct in her first impressions of him. He was beautiful on the outside, but the inside was ugly and heartless.

She finished packing then opened her laptop and went to the airline's website. There was no way she could face flying back to New York with Calum Brook sitting beside her. She'd rather fly in the cargo hold.

She pulled up her reservation. *Yes!* It allowed changes—for a fee. She didn't care about the money. They could charge her a month's salary, and she'd willingly pay it. As luck would have it, there was an earlier flight than the one she was booked on. She glanced at her watch. If she hurried, she could make it.

She changed her reservation then quickly showered and dressed. The lobby was deserted, with only the night manager on duty.

"Checking out. Room five thirty-three."

"Of course, madam. Early start?"

She nodded. "Could you call me a cab? I'm going to O'Hare."

"Certainly."

Five minutes later, having spent every one of those minutes looking over her shoulder, half expecting Calum to appear, Laurella was on her way to the airport. As the hotel disappeared from sight, she let out a relieved sigh. She'd have to face him in the office, but being away from the scene of the crime and on her own turf would make it easier. She wouldn't bring up what had happened, and if he did, she'd brush it aside as if it meant nothing.

Liar. It *had* meant something. He'd sucked her in with his charisma, his come-to-bed eyes, his pretend interest in her and her life. And she'd dropped her guard in a spectacularly embarrassing way. It had been a long time since she'd found herself attracted to a man, and that was why she'd responded so favorably to his touch, his kiss.

Her stomach flipped as she recalled the feel of his mouth on hers. Calum Brook was an outstanding kisser, probably because of all the practice. A twinge of jealousy bit at her insides—a feeling she immediately pushed away. He didn't deserve jealousy. He deserved antipathy.

Laurella entered the departures hall, checked in her bag, and headed straight through security, still glancing over her shoulder from time to time. What would she do if he suddenly appeared? Thoughts of her knee and his balls came to mind. A night in jail would be a small price to pay to have the permanent memory of Calum writhing in agony on the floor.

Only when the plane doors closed did Laurella properly relax. At least she'd reach the office before him, which would give her time to brief Zane on the success of the conference— and her part in securing the leads. It was time she took a leaf out of Calum's book and played dirty.

The flight to New York was uneventful, and Laurella found herself outside her building at eleven. Calum wouldn't be arriving for at least another two hours. She left her bag in her office and strode down the hallway. She tapped on Zane's door and peered inside. He glanced up from his computer and gestured to her.

"Morning," she said as brightly as she could manage, despite the inner turmoil and lack of sleep.

"Hey, you're back." He pointed to the seat opposite his. "And you're early."

"Yeah," she said, folding her skirt beneath her as she sat. "I couldn't sleep, so I grabbed an earlier flight. I'm excited to get started on what I learned. I already have a meeting planned this afternoon with someone I met who could be a good contact. I think he'll be able to get me an introduction into one of the leading supermarket chains on the west coast."

"That's great. Exactly what I was hoping to get out of the conference." A frown drifted across Zane's face. "Calum called this morning, though, worried about you. Said you didn't let him know you were leaving early?"

Worried? Pah!

"I didn't want to wake him. He looked pretty tired after dinner last night."

"Very thoughtful of you." He smiled. "So, tell me everything, and then I'll let you get to work."

As the clock ticked closer to one-thirty—the time she and Calum were originally expected to arrive back in New York—Laurella couldn't stop her leg from bouncing, and nerves flooded her stomach. She'd never been the type to seek conflict, yet Calum was forcing her to take a crash course just so she could keep up with *him*—the master.

But when she left for her meeting at three, he still hadn't turned up. She thought about asking Zane if he'd heard from him, but she didn't want Zane wondering why she was so concerned. No doubt, Calum would appear when she least expected and cause her more misery and heartache.

By the time she got back to the office, it was seven o'clock. The floor was in darkness apart from a strip of light bleeding from underneath the door at the end of the hallway. *Calum's office*. On tiptoes, she crept into her own office and quietly shut the door. She'd only returned to the building so she could grab her memory book. She had a few ideas she wanted to work on that night.

She turned her attention to her desk and frowned. The corner where she kept the book was empty. It had definitely been there when she'd left for her meeting. Perhaps the cleaning staff had knocked it to the floor. She bent down to look under her desk. Nothing.

She crossed over to her filing cabinet and opened each drawer, cringing when one squeaked. Sound traveled in silent places. She'd dreaded facing Calum earlier in the day, let alone this late in the evening when everyone else had gone home.

Her search proved fruitless. The book was nowhere to be seen. She clenched her jaw. Only one answer to the conundrum remained: Calum was playing more of his childish games. *I'm going to have to face him after all.* Well, that was fine by her. The night before, she'd been hurt. Right now, she was downright furious. That bastard wanted conflict and chaos? She'd damn well give it to him.

She straightened her spine, took a deep breath, and marched down the hallway to his office, her heels clipping on the tile. He'd hear her coming, for sure. A knot formed in her stomach the closer she got to the door, but she rammed it down and brought what he'd done to the forefront of her mind. It steeled her resolve. Without knocking, she launched his office door open.

"Calum, what the hell are you—"

His office was empty. The lamp on his desk had been left on. Laurella glanced around, searching for her book. It wasn't there. She was about to start searching through his drawers and cabinets when a folded-up piece of paper propped up against the printer caught her eye. She moved closer. Her name was scrawled on it in his black, spidery writing.

She snatched up the note and opened it.

Interesting book. Want it back? Then come get it.

Underneath he'd written the name of a hotel—the Miller-Brook—and an address.

Her hands shook as rage surged through her body. Goddamn the man. He was purposely taunting her. She briefly wondered if the hotel had something to do with his family—not that she really cared. For the sake of his own safety, it was good he'd chosen a public space—because she wanted to kill him.

Maybe she should simply ignore the note and go home… then again, knowing Calum, he'd taken her book to force her into facing him, and until she did that, he wouldn't return her prized possession.

With a resigned sigh, she left his office. She'd better get it over with, go toe-to-toe with the man who'd demeaned her, embarrassed her, *kissed her*... and demand that he return her book. Then she'd stop by the liquor store, buy a large bottle of gin, and blot out the disaster of the last three days.

She slipped the piece of paper into her pocket and, after fetching her purse, left the building. Subway or cab? Exhausted, she decided on the latter. Twenty minutes later, the taxi stopped outside the hotel. She paid her fare and stepped onto the sidewalk. Straightening her posture, she walked as steadily as she could manage up the front steps.

The noise coming from inside drew her into a huge lounge area with comfy chairs and sofas dotted about. A large modern-looking wood-burning stove threw out welcome heat, and at the far end was a bar, busy with patrons. What game was Calum playing now?

Behind the bar, a man and a woman were serving drinks, chatting with the guests as though they were long-lost family. As Laurella drew closer, there was something familiar about the man, but she was sure she'd never seen him before. She slipped onto the only free bar stool and held up her hand. He nodded to show he'd seen her, finished serving his customer, then wandered across.

He put down a napkin along with a small bowl of peanuts. "What can I get you?" he asked with a broad, welcoming smile.

"Some help," she said, returning his smile. "I'm looking for someone who gave me this address."

"Well, if they're staying here, I'll definitely know them. We get a lot of regulars."

Hence the familial atmosphere.

"Calum Brook."

The man grinned. "Oh, I definitely know him." He stuck out his hand. "You must be Laurella."

She frowned but shook his hand anyway. "Should I be worried?"

"I'm Jax. Calum is my younger brother."

So *that* was why he looked so familiar. Now that she knew who he was, the similarities stood out: the same thick, dark hair, although Calum wore his longer than Jax's, and the same emerald-green seductive eyes and angular jaw. Jax was clean-shaven, though, in contrast to the constant designer stubble Calum favored.

"Is he here?" She glanced around.

"He's in the basement."

She frowned in confusion, although keeping Calum in the basement was probably where he should be. Somewhere cold, dark, without food or light.

"Our living quarters," he further explained.

"Ah," she said. "Well, he has something of mine, so would you mind awfully telling him I'm here to collect it?"

"Yeah, he said you might drop by. That's how I knew who you were. Well, that and the fact he mentions you a fair bit."

Her heart stuttered, but she clamped down on the excited tingle that spread to her fingertips and brought his callous behavior to the fore. "Is that right?"

"Yeah." He winked. "But don't tell him I said that." He stepped out from behind the bar. "Come on. I'll take you down."

"Oh, you don't need to do that," she said, determined to make the bastard come to her. She might need people around to stop her from punching him. "You look busy."

Jax waved away her protestation. "It's fine. Indie," he called to the woman who'd been serving with him. "Five minutes, babe, okay?"

Indie nodded and smiled as she expertly poured a cocktail into a triangular glass.

"My girlfriend," Jax said proudly by way of explanation. "Financial whiz kid by day, bartender by night."

He walked ahead, giving her no option but to follow him. Halfway down the hall, he opened a door marked Private.

"Watch your step," he said, flicking on a light that illuminated a twisting stairwell. At the bottom, the space opened out into a large open-plan living area. Calum lay sprawled on the couch, which was positioned in front of a large-screen TV affixed to the wall. A football game was playing, a sport Laurella had never understood.

Calum clearly hadn't heard them. His attention was fully on the game. He suddenly sat bolt upright. "Touchdown!" he yelled, punching the air with his fist.

"Bro," Jax called out. "You've got a visitor."

Calum glanced behind him and gave her a derogatory once-over. "You took your time," he said before turning his attention back to the TV.

"Calum!" Jax berated.

"It's fine," Laurella said, her tone suitably cold. "That's polite compared to how he spoke to me last night."

Her barb got Calum's attention. He muted the TV, clambered off the couch, and glared pointedly at Jax. "Don't you have thirsty guests to serve?"

Jax shook his head, muttered "Asshole," and with a final apologetic smile in Laurella's direction, took off upstairs.

"Seems I'm not the only one who regularly uses that nickname for you," Laurella said.

"I prefer your version." He strolled across to the kitchen and bent down to grab a beer from the fridge. He didn't offer her one—not that she would have accepted it anyway.

"Where's my book?" she said, deciding that getting straight to the point meant she wouldn't have to spend a second longer than necessary in his personal space.

He ignored her. "Why did you leave without me this morning?"

Astounded, she glared. "Are you joking?"

"Does it sound like I'm joking?" he snapped. "When I couldn't get an answer from your room, I started imagining all sorts of shit."

"Oh, Calum." She clasped a hand to her chest. "Anyone would think you cared."

He snorted. "Don't flatter yourself. I didn't want the hassle of explaining to the police why you'd slashed your wrists in the bathtub because I'd turned down a chance to share bodily fluids with you."

Now it was Laurella's turn to snort. "As if. You kissed me as punishment. I stupidly fell for your false charm. I should have known better. It's hardly the end of the world."

"Your face told me a different story. As did your body."

He raked her with a gaze, warming her insides in a very unwelcome way. She dug her nails into the palms of her hands. Calling on her inner bitch, she curled her lip disparagingly and planted her hands on her hips.

"You really are a shitty excuse for a human, aren't you? You say I'm flattering myself?" She strode across the room until she was standing right in front of him and poked a finger in his chest. "It's *you* flattering *yourself*. You're attractive enough on the outside, I suppose, but so are dragon fruit, yet bite into one of those pretty little things, and they're the biggest disappointment." She looked him up and down. "No doubt as you would have been."

His eyes flared, and he crossed his arms. "Oh, the gloves are coming off now, huh, sweetheart?"

She let her smile build slowly, tapping her fingers against the side of her leg as she prepared for a putdown. "We'd have been a terrible fit anyway. I'm too *Italian* for you. Too passionate, too controlling. You want a woman beneath you, who'll let *you* be in charge." She let her gaze travel the length of his tanned throat, down over his hard chest muscles, past his impossibly flat stomach, eventually ending her cold appraisal at his groin. "Besides, it looks like I'm not the only one of us who's attracted to the other."

He straightened his spine, adding a few inches to his already considerable height, and loomed over her. Anxiety clawed inside her gut at his icy stare. Maybe she'd gone too far, but it was too late to back down. She widened her stance, holding her position firm.

A sneer curved his lips upward. "That's the thing about men, Laurella. They can get a hard-on with very little stimulus. I wouldn't want you getting the impression you're irresistible, because, sweetheart, you ain't—as I proved all too readily last night when I found it easy as pie to walk away from you when you were gagging for it."

Her lungs flattened, and she found it hard to breathe. It seemed she wasn't the only one who could hit the bull's-eye with vicious words. She forced herself to maintain eye contact. She would *not* back down. "My book," she said, sticking out her hand, palm up. "Give it to me."

"Why did you tell Ben he couldn't have the overstock?"

Laurella let out an impatient sigh. The bastard wanted his pound of flesh. "I didn't tell him that. I said he couldn't have the full amount, and I also disagree with the price you're offering. He's getting it far too cheaply."

Calum glowered at her. "What the fuck do you know about it? Ben is one of our original customers. Five years ago, he took a chance on a startup company with an unproven supply chain. He's been loyal, and he's a good outlet to bring quick cash into the business. He pays immediately, whereas our other customers are on sixty- or ninety-day payment terms."

Laurella crossed her arms. "Have you seen a copy of the latest accounts?"

His scowl deepened. "Do I look like the fucking chief finance officer?"

"I have," she said, ignoring his outburst. "We're cash rich at the moment. We don't need to sell stock virtually at breakeven. I am developing an online presence where we'll make considerably more than your *friend* Ben is paying."

"Are you suggesting—"

She shot her hand into the air, cutting him off. "If we were cash poor, your strategy would be the right one. But you're out of touch, Calum. You've taken your eye off the ball. You're so focused on making sales you've forgotten the small issue of profit. When your cash flow is healthy, it's time to make plans for growth, for investment."

She paused for breath. The heavy atmosphere created by Calum's fury zinging off the walls had kicked her fight-or-flight instinct into action. And right then, her body was screaming *Flee!* But she wasn't going to let him intimidate her. She jutted out her chin and waited for him to make his next move.

After what felt like hours—but in reality was only seconds—he started to pace while chewing on his thumbnail, a frown scoring two deep lines between his eyebrows. He shot the occasional glance her way and then, without saying a word, crossed over into the kitchen, opened the freezer, and took out a bottle of vodka. After grabbing two tumblers from a cupboard, he poured a healthy amount into them, dropped in a few cubes of ice, topped them off with tonic water, and added a slice of lime to each.

"Here." He held a glass toward her. When she hesitated, he let out a curt laugh. "You watched me make it."

"I don't trust you."

He went to sit on the couch, a glimmer of a smile curving his lips upward. "Glad to see I'm keep you on your toes, Ricci."

Her breath caught. That was the second time he'd called her by her surname—once in Chicago and now here—and hearing it on his lips set off a fluttering in her abdomen. To quell the growing flames, she sipped her drink, but all the alcohol did was stoke them. Well, she'd certainly discovered something about herself: it was possible to desperately want to go to bed with a man who pushed all of her buttons—and not in a good way.

Calum swept a hand over his face. "You're right. I have taken my eye off the ball."

The astonishment must have shown on her face, because he laughed, the sound sharp and cold. Like him. "I might be an asshole, but I'm an honest one. When I'm wrong, I'll say I'm wrong. But I'm giving you fair warning. Next time you get the urge to send a 'Dear John' email to one of our oldest clients, you'd better come talk to me first. Otherwise, I won't be held accountable for my actions."

He said the latter with the hint of a smirk playing around his mouth, which, after the latest sparring match, she was too exhausted to try to figure out.

"Deal. Now, give me my book."

Calum rose from the couch and wandered over to a dresser on the far side of the room. He opened the top drawer, reached inside, and took out her book. He set it on the arm of the couch.

She picked it up and cradled it in the crook of her arm. She skated her fingers over the do-it-yourself covering she'd put on it when she was only twenty-two. It was torn slightly at the edges, but she wouldn't replace the covering. It reminded her of the ideals and dreams of the young girl who'd created it, even though the farther she went in her career, the more cynical she became.

"Thank you."

He shrugged. "It was childish to take it, but I knew it would get you here. The way you spoke about it in Chicago told me it was important to you. Maybe don't take up poker anytime soon."

The sound of heavy footfalls on the stairs had her glancing over her shoulder.

"That'll be Cole. My twin."

A replica of the man sitting in front of her appeared. His hair was a tad shorter and his beard slightly longer than Calum's, but the eyes were just as absorbing.

"What a crap shift," Cole said, dropping his bag at the foot of the stairs. "Two shootings, one domestic assault that made me want to rip the guy's arms out of his sockets, and an attempted rape on a sixteen-year-old. Sixteen, for Christ's sake. What the hell is wrong with this god-awful society?"

A shiver stole over her at the mention of the attempted rape, but as Cole spotted her and smiled, the feeling receded. There was a warmth about Calum's twin that drew her in and somehow made her feel safe. Very different from how she felt about Calum, which, even on good days, bordered on murderous.

"Sorry, bro. Didn't realize you had company."

"This is Laurella Ricci," Calum said.

Cole's eyebrows shot up, almost disappearing into his hairline. His reaction told her he'd definitely heard of her, which added credence to Jax's earlier comments. The thought that Calum had spoken about her with his family was oddly thrilling.

Cole recovered quickly, and he thrust out his hand. "Nice to meet you." He winked at Calum, who rolled his eyes. "I'll leave you to it."

Laurella waited for Cole to leave before she turned her attention back to Calum. "When you said twin, I expected some differences, but you really are identical."

"Almost." Calum pointed to the faint silver scar under his left eye. "A fight in high school. Guy wore a ring. Hurt like a bitch. Other than that, yeah, we're pretty identical physically. Best way to tell us apart, though, is to remember that I'm the asshole and Cole's the nice one. That is, unless someone he cares about needs protecting. Then he has a hell of a dark side. It's probably what makes him such a great cop."

"I don't envy him that job." She turned away and walked toward the stairs.

Calum caught up to her. "You're leaving?"

She nodded. "I got what I came for."

Was that a tinge of disappointment that crossed his face? She couldn't work the guy out. One minute, he was spoiling for a fight, and the next, he seemed loath to let her go.

"I'll get you a cab," he said.

She shifted the weight of her memory book. "I can get my own cab, thank you."

"Suit yourself." He folded his arms like a sullen teenager.

She suppressed a grin. She'd been right about Calum liking to be in charge. Well, too bad for him, because so did she. And she'd definitely won that round, even though he'd probably deny it.

Leaving Calum sulking, she jogged upstairs. As she crossed the main hallway, she caught Jax's eye and returned his friendly wave. Outside, she flagged down a passing cab.

As they pulled away from the curb, something made her look out the backseat window. Her breath caught in her throat. Calum was standing with his shoulder propped up against the wall outside the hotel, an unreadable expression on his face. He might not have argued with her getting her own transportation home, yet he'd still made sure she'd done so safely.

A warm feeling stirred in her chest. She turned back around, rested her head on the window, and smiled.

CHAPTER 12

A couple of weeks later, Calum stepped into the boardroom and took his seat on Zane's right. Laurella hadn't sat there, apart from that very first meeting. He wasn't sure whether it was out of a growing respect for him professionally—even if she couldn't stand him personally—or because she couldn't be bothered with the ensuing argument. He didn't care either way. He still chalked this up as a minor victory. Yeah, he was that much of a dick, as those who knew him well would testify.

Since their last sparring match—which he begrudgingly conceded she'd won—on the night he'd taken her memory book, he'd found his mind turning to the fiery Italian more and more. Lesser women would have buckled under the pressure of what he'd put her through, but Laurella seemed to thrive on the conflict he had purposely created. As much as he hated to admit it, he knew he was falling more and more under her spell as the weeks went by, and despite his cruel and unusual punishment in Chicago, they'd begun to rub along without too much bickering.

Calum watched the door every time it opened, a flutter of excitement ending in disappointment when the person who entered wasn't her. When she finally walked into the board-room, he got a full-on punch in the gut. She was wearing a soft gray silk dress that clung to every single curve. It rose high on the neck and fell well below the knee. She'd topped it off with a pair of black patent-leather high heels that made her calves as slender as a thoroughbred horse. Her trusty notebook was clutched in her left hand, the Montblanc pen attached to the back cover.

Calum had always been more attracted to obvious women. He'd never subscribed to the argument that it was better to keep the goods hidden. He preferred to see what he was getting to make sure it was worth the effort. But Laurella's classy style made him question his preferences. He liked the fact she kept her assets hidden, that her boobs weren't constantly spilling over the top of a dress cut too low. Maybe her classiness came from her Mediterranean roots. Weren't Italians known for their style and fashion sense?

She caught him checking her out, and a soft smile inched across her lips. She pulled out the seat directly opposite and smoothed her hands under her dress before sitting. Her gaze moved to his. Pleasure rushed through him as those dark-chocolate eyes almost stripped him bare.

"Okay, shall we start?" Zane said, oblivious to the fact that his sales director was surreptitiously trying to rearrange his junk under the table.

They followed their usual agenda. Calum barely paid attention. He'd already been through the deck. But when it was Laurella's turn to speak, he sat up in his chair, his eyes refocusing, his ears on full alert.

And that was when World War III broke out.

It all started so well. Two of the contacts from the conference had come through and had told her they intended to place large orders. It remained to be seen whether their promises turned into hard cash, but the fact they'd called her, without her having to chase, was a positive sign. She went through a campaign she'd designed, alongside the new branding the board had signed off on the previous week. It looked good—a real step in the right direction.

"There is one more thing," she said, her gaze falling on his. She seemed almost apologetic. "I don't think you're going to be happy, Calum. But please, hear me out."

His skin prickled, and the hairs on the back of his neck stood on end. He didn't like the sound of this already—and she hadn't told him what was going on yet.

"Let's hear it, then," he said, giving her a tight smile.

"I think we should remove the exclusivity from the raspberry gin you gave to Haltons when the contract comes up for renewal next week."

He straightened in his chair. Haltons was one of their big clients. Rob Halton owned a string of cocktail bars across the US. He purchased in huge quantities, albeit at a very preferential discounted rate. But still…

"And why would we do that?" His tone might have been bland, but his stare was cool.

She got the message loud and clear, squirming under his intense scrutiny. She'd avoided coming to him with this because she knew he'd be pissed, choosing instead to share it at the weekly board meeting, where she knew he'd be more likely to temper his reaction. When would the damned woman learn?

"I've been warming up a couple of potential clients. They like the product. I get the feeling they'd place huge recurring orders and at a better price than Haltons currently enjoys."

"You have a 'feeling'?" Calum said, using air quotes to press his point home. "Come back when your feelings are facts, sweetheart."

Her lips pressed into a firm line, and she glared at him across the table. "I didn't say I *had* a feeling, I said I *get* the feeling. Please don't twist my words, Calum."

"Sounds the same to me," he snapped.

"Well, it would to you. Because you don't damn well listen."

Calum rose to his feet and slammed his fist on the table.

Everyone jumped—except *her*. He leaned menacingly forward, rage burning through his veins. "When you stop pissing all over my territory, I might start to listen a bit more. Your job is to find the leads. *My job* is to talk to potential clients."

She folded her arms. "Pissing on your territory? I suppose an analogy to a dog suits you perfectly."

"Now, now, children," Zane said, his eyes crinkling as he grinned. "As much as I love the Laurella-and-Calum show that has turned into a regular feature at these board meetings, let's keep it friendly."

Their chief financial officer sniggered, while their IT director looked out the window, his shoulders shaking with barely contained laughter.

"Perhaps if you'd talked to me about this first before bringing it up in front of everyone, we could have had a sensible chat. When will you learn, Laurella?"

Her eyes flashed with defiance. "Learn?" She snorted. "I doubt there's much to learn from you, unless annoying the hell of out of people ever becomes useful in the world of business."

"I see my control over this boardroom is rocking it today," Zane said, using his usual relaxed style in an attempt to keep things calm. "Here's what's going to happen. You two"—he poked his finger at each of them in turn—"are going to make a decision on the right approach. Only when you're both in agreement will I listen to any more of this."

"Zane—"

"But—"

Zane's hand shot into the air. "I don't want to hear another word. I suggest you both take this discussion off the premises. Go for a drink, a meal, somewhere neutral where killing one another would have too many witnesses for either of you to get away with it."

The CFO gave another snigger. Calum shot him a glare, but all that did was make the man's grin wider.

Laurella let out a resigned sigh and got to her feet. "I have some things to do, but I could make myself free in an hour." She looked over at Calum, her eyes hard, a stark contrast to the way they'd stroked him at the start of the meeting. "If you can?"

"No, I can't. But I'm free tonight," he said, surprising himself as much as her. Even though they'd had yet another falling-out, he didn't want a rushed lunch before they both had meetings to get to. He wanted to take his time, to spar at length. Because if his rock-hard cock told him anything, it was that sparring with Laurella turned him on more than any other woman had ever managed.

Laurella's forehead wrinkled. Then she nodded curtly. "Fine. Let me know when and where." With a smile for the other board members and a scowl for him, she picked up her notebook and pen and left the room.

When Calum went to follow, Zane stopped him. "Thanks, folks," he said to the rest of the team. Chairs scraped backward as one by one the other board members left the room. Once they were alone, Zane pointed to a chair. "Sit down."

Calum reluctantly obeyed. "Whatever you're about to say, save it." He leaned back and laced his hands behind his head as he stared at the ceiling. "We've been getting along better recently. After the Ben Davies debacle, she agreed she'd talk to me about this kind of shit first." He made eye contact with Zane. "And then she goes and does this. The woman infuriates me more than any other person I've ever met."

Zane thoughtfully tapped his forefinger against his lips. "You want her," he stated bluntly. "Your arguments suggest intense sexual frustration rather than a mere disagreement about the way each of you does business. And if her responses are anything to go by, I'd say the attraction is mutual."

Calum chewed on his bottom lip. He and Zane had always been completely honest with each other. He wasn't about to start lying to his best friend now.

"You're right. I do want her. Although more often than not,

I'd like to put her across my knee and give her a good, hard spanking."

"Same outcome." Zane laughed. "Look, what you get up to in your own time is your business, but you two have got to work this out. I don't care whether that's done in the boardroom or the bedroom. You're both fantastic assets to Necron, and if I could just get you to work together, I think we'd have world domination in our sights."

Calum expelled a breath. "I can't even say it's all me. Honestly, that woman gives as good as she gets."

Zane chuckled. "I know. Like I said, we all get the show at the weekly board meeting."

Calum's lips twitched. "Good thing my boss is so laid-back he's horizontal."

"He's also your best friend who wouldn't want you any other way. Your forthright persona is what makes you, *you*. If you're going to stab someone, it sure as hell won't be in the back. They'll see that blade coming from a mile off."

"True enough." Calum rose from his chair. "Wish me luck tonight."

Zane grinned and gestured with a flick of his wrist. "Get out of here."

Calum unfastened the button on his single-breasted jacket and straightened his tie. He'd considered going casual, but as his strategy that evening was going to be all business, the sensible choice was a suit and tie. He had made one decision, though: the time had come for them to work through their shit once and for all. And that meant he had to start behaving like an actual human being.

Blessed with a sixth sense that had only awoken since Laurella had started working at Necron, Calum lifted his head at the precise moment she entered the restaurant. He watched her speak to the host, who nodded, helped her remove her coat, and handed it off to another employee. She'd also gone for formal wear, but as with everything Laurella wore, she did it with style.

The host indicated for her to follow him, and they began to make their way over. Calum got to his feet, seating himself again once Laurella had taken her chair. He gestured to the waiter.

"I took the liberty of ordering wine, but did you want anything else?" he asked Laurella.

"Some still water, please," she said.

"Certainly, madam." The waiter gave a brief nod before retreating.

"I wasn't sure you'd turn up," she said.

He tapped a finger against his bottom lip. "You really do have a low opinion of me, don't you?"

She forced a smile. "It's been well-earned."

"Ouch." He grinned. "I guess I deserved that."

She licked her lips as if her mouth was dry. He moved his gaze south. She really did have the most wonderful full lips. Kissable lips. He shook his head of those thoughts. They'd only lead to trouble.

"I don't understand you at all," she said, scrutinizing his face. "One minute, you're the epitome of charm. The next, you're like a venomous snake ready to sink your fangs into me. It's like you have a split personality."

"You have fangs of your own, Laurella," he said, ignoring her insult.

"Mine are only used for self-protection."

He paused as their server came across with her water and the wine. Calum shook his head at the offer to taste it then leaned back in his chair until their glasses had been filled. When they were alone once more, he bent forward, his forearms resting on the table.

"I'm not sure that's true. Yes, I'm a complicated man, but

you're a complicated woman. If you're being honest with yourself, you'll admit at least partial responsibility for our constant arguments. Take today, for example. You should have come to me first before sharing your ideas in front of the whole board. I don't know how things worked in Italy, but here in America, you don't embarrass your colleagues in front of their peers and their boss without giving them the courtesy of telling them what you're planning to do."

Her eyes slid away from his, and she nibbled on her lower lip. "You work so differently from the way I did at my last company. There, all ideas were welcome. We just wanted Spirito to succeed."

He drummed his fingers on the table to attract her attention. When she finally lifted her chin, he said, "It's the same here. Of course your ideas are welcome, Laurella. You're really creative, and I have no doubt you'll push Necron forward, but you've gone from working in a much larger company to a significantly smaller one. You can't apply the same rules. They simply won't work. All you'll do is piss people off. Small companies are like families in a way. They're extremely close-knit. They fight, they argue, but they also pull together toward a common goal. I don't want to crush your creativity, your flair, your spirit. But for God's sake, woman, fucking talk to me."

Her eyebrows shot up at his outburst. "You've basically described an Italian family. We fight and argue all the time, but we'd also die for one another."

"Then you shouldn't have too much trouble adapting, should you? Although I draw the line at dying. It's only work." He grinned. "Seriously, though, I owe it to Zane to find a way for us to get along."

She offered him a faint smile, picked up her wineglass, and held it toward him. "That sounds remarkably like you're offering me a more permanent truce. A real truce this time."

Calum lifted his own glass and touched it briefly to hers. "I am."

She sipped her drink, those melted-dark-chocolate irises studying his face. Eventually, she let out a resigned sigh. "I don't know about you, but I'm tired of fighting. I just want Necron to succeed."

"Sounds like we both want the same thing."

"Indeed," she murmured, although the way she was looking at him made him wonder if they were still talking about Necron's success.

"Let's order," Calum suggested, as much to distract himself from drowning in her eyes as from a desire to eat. He perused the menu. "What would you like?"

"You order for me."

He nodded, still keeping his gaze averted. He needed a couple more moments to gather himself. Now that they'd gotten the thorny issue of their working relationship out of the way— at least for the night—this felt much more like a date.

"Anything to avoid?" he asked.

"No. I'll eat most things."

His abdomen clenched at the way she'd said 'eat.' He glanced up. The look in her eyes scorched him, and his pulse thrummed. She circled her middle finger around her wineglass before dipping it inside. With her finger covered in wine, she inserted it into her mouth and sucked.

Fuck. His insides did a triple fucking salchow, and his cock hardened. "Are you flirting with me?"

The briefest of smiles touched her lips. "I'm not going to embarrass myself by lying. You already know I'm attracted to you. But given the appalling way you have behaved toward me, the fact remains that I'm still not sure how much I *like* you. You said and did some very hurtful things in Chicago. I can't simply push them aside as though they don't matter, because they do."

A hot flush crept across his cheeks. *Jesus.* He never blushed, never got embarrassed or felt the need to apologize for his behavior, yet with that dressing down, he could have been back in high school, standing outside the principal's office, awaiting punishment for picking on someone half his size.

"Well, fuck," he said, a tight ache spreading through his chest.

"Your actions have consequences, Calum, and not everyone has the hide of a rhinoceros. Not even me, despite your beliefs to the contrary."

"You've made your point," he muttered. "If it means anything, it didn't feel good… what I did in Chicago. You pissed me off, and I retaliated. It was cruel, not clever, and I shouldn't have done it. The professional thing to do would have been to speak to you about the email. I'm sorry."

Whoa, where did that come from?

Laurella must have been as surprised as he was by the confession and subsequent apology, because her eyebrows almost disappeared into her hairline, widening her eyes. "I didn't expect that, but I appreciate it. And I accept your apology."

"Don't worry. It won't become a habit," Calum said, teasing.

Laurella smiled. "Shall we move on? Put it all behind us?"

He nodded. "Let's. I'm not exactly in my comfort zone here."

She tugged on her bottom lip, drawing his attention. He wanted to do that—with his teeth.

"Hmm. Then maybe I'll make you grovel a little longer."

He dragged his gaze away from her mouth. "Too late, sweetheart. Show's over."

"In that case, you might as well feed me. I'm ravenous."

The way she said *ravenous*—a replica of *eat* earlier—gave the impression she wasn't only referring to food. He swallowed hard and gestured to their server, who came scurrying over.

Keeping his eyes fixed on Laurella, Calum barked out their order. "Two New York strips. Rare. Peppercorn sauce. Dauphinoise potatoes. Asparagus. Another bottle of wine, and the check."

He held out the menus. The waiter tucked them under his arm. He furiously scribbled down the order then dashed away.

"Someone's in a hurry. What if I want dessert?" Laurella said.

Time to test the waters. "You'll get dessert."

She blinked slowly. "What if I only want a sample?"

He repressed a triumphant grin. "Then I'll have to make sure it's tasty enough for you to want to try the full-sized portion."

She giggled, a girlish sound that took years off her. She might only be thirty, but sometimes she acted much older, as though life had kicked her in the teeth one too many times, making her defensive and cautious.

"If it's anything like the first sample, I might be inclined to take a bite," she said, obviously referring to their kiss in Chicago.

"Oh, I can guarantee it'll be better than that."

Her teeth grazed her bottom lip, and she looked up at him from beneath her eyelashes. *Holy shit.* Flirty Laurella was sexy as fuck.

"How so?" she asked.

He stroked his beard. "Because this time, I'll mean it."

Another flash of hurt crossed her face. He winced. She might have agreed to leave it all behind them and accept his apology, but feelings cut deep, and he'd drawn blood. It would take a while for the wound to heal.

"How will I know?" she asked bluntly.

He reached across the table and took her hand in his. Lifting it to his mouth, he pressed a soft kiss to the inside of her wrist. "Believe me, you'll know."

She shivered, and his pulse raced so fast that when their food arrived, he found he could barely get it down. Every mouthful seemed to take forever to swallow, and he drank more wine than he should have, trying to force the food past his dry throat.

Laurella fared little better, toying with her steak, pushing it around the plate with her fork.

When they'd both eaten enough to avoid the waiter asking if there was something wrong with their meal, Calum tossed some money on the table, waving away Laurella's offer to pay her half. "I'll put it on expenses. It was Zane's idea we come out to dinner, so he can pay."

Outside the restaurant, Calum captured her hand in his. When she didn't pull away, a thrill rushed through him.

"Shall we walk?" Laurella asked "I only live a few blocks away, and it's quite mild."

Calum nodded. "Spring's finally on the way."

"Thank goodness. It gets much colder here than in Milan. Even though I spent my college years in Boston, I've never enjoyed the cold that much."

"I can't say I mind it, although summer in New York is a great time of year. Too hot for some, but I like it that way."

"I'm looking forward to it, especially now that I don't have to leave my job because of the annoying sales director."

Her sassy grin quickened his breath. He nudged his shoulder against hers, thrilled at this surprising turn in their relationship —one he certainly hadn't anticipated. "Yeah. He's a real asshole."

"*Stronzo*," she said, outright laughing now.

He drew to a stop and threaded his hands into her soft, silky hair. He paused, giving her the chance to move back or to tell him to get his hands off of her. She did neither.

He tilted her head backward. "I know it's supposed to be an insult, but said in your beautiful accent, it makes my cock hard."

Despite the street being full of people, as they stood there, staring into each other's eyes, they could have been completely alone. Even when jostled, neither of them moved from their spot. And then slowly, so slowly, Calum lowered his head.

The second their lips touched, Laurella wound her arms around his neck. He deepened the kiss, unconcerned by the fact they were in the middle of Fifth Avenue. This was New York. No one cared what anyone else was up to. A kiss, even one as passionate as this, would barely catch a glance from passersby.

A soft moan broke from her throat, and she pressed herself closer to him. Her arms dropped from around his neck, and she buried them inside his coat, beneath his jacket. The warmth from her palms soaked through his shirt as her hands roved over his back.

And then, without warning, she tore herself away. She stepped back once, then twice. Her chest rose and fell in time with his.

"What's the matter?" he asked, concerned.

She blinked slowly. "If I taste any more of the sample, I'm going to want to eat the whole pie, except I'm worried it will give me indigestion."

Calum chuckled, even though the pain from his erection straining against his zipper wasn't remotely funny. "As much as I'm loving these food analogies, I need to translate to make sure I've understood. Can I?"

She nodded.

"Okay, so you liked kissing me, and you want to take it further, but you think it might be too soon, especially as just a few hours ago, we were close to killing each other. And after what I did to you in Chicago, you're not sure you can trust me, despite my earlier apology."

She breathed in then grimaced. "That's about it."

He cupped his hands around her face and pecked her softly on the lips. Slipping his arm around her waist, he began to walk. "Let me take you home." She stiffened, and he gave her a squeeze. "I heard you. Loud and clear."

"And you're not mad?"

The uncertainty in her tone annoyed the hell out of him. His irritation wasn't aimed at her but at what her anxiety signaled. He stopped again, forcing her to do the same. "I know there are men out there who believe no means yes. I'm not one of them. I like my women willing and agreeable."

She blushed, and he found it fucking adorable.

"Thank you," she said. "I think there's a good person hidden in there somewhere, despite your determination to show the world the complete opposite."

Calum gave her a wolfish grin. "Who are you, and what have you done with Laurella Ricci?"

She dug him in the ribs with her elbow, and he fake groaned.

"I could say the same about you," she said.

They walked the rest of the way in a companionable silence, his arm around her waist, hers around his. Too soon for his liking, they arrived at her apartment building.

"Well, this is me." She looked up at him. The light from the street lamps cast her face half in shadow.

"Want me to see you up?" he asked.

"No, I'm good."

You got that right, sweetheart.

"We didn't talk about the proposal."

"No, we didn't," she said, pinning him in place with those soulful eyes. "What do you think we should do, Calum?"

"I think we should meet in your office in the morning and come to a mutually beneficial agreement."

Her mouth creased in thought. "Does such a thing exist?"

He gathered her in his arms. Already, it felt as though she belonged there. "Believe me, Ricci, I can make it worth your while."

Her lips twitched. "I drive a hard bargain."

He circled his hips. "So do I."

She grinned. "Then bring your A game, Brook, and we'll see who turns out to be the winner."

Calum bent his head until his lips were an inch from hers. "I have a funny feeling we'll both win," he said before he pressed his lips to hers.

CHAPTER 13

Laurella and Calum managed to get through the next few days with barely a crossed word. They compromised on the raspberry-gin deal. He conceded the exclusivity with Haltons, and they came up with a six-month transitional pricing deal, which the client had agreed to. They found time to grab coffee, but nothing more intimate.

It was a crazy week, and even though peace had been declared, by the time Friday afternoon arrived, she was ready to drop. She was terribly excited about the upcoming weekend, though. Her youngest sister was arriving on Sunday for a few days before she started college. The downside to Alessia's visit was that Laurella wouldn't be able to see Calum. Still, she couldn't wait to catch up with her sister.

She had her head buried in a client proposal when her concentration was broken by a knock at her door. Laurella looked up with a frown, but that soon turned into a smile when she saw who'd knocked. So much had changed in such a short space of time that it made her head spin and her belly do weird flips.

"What are you doing tonight?" Calum asked, stepping into her office.

"I was planning a quiet night curled up with a good book. I won't get much free time when Alessia arrives on Sunday."

A flash of disappointment crossed his face. "Oh yeah. I'd forgotten she was coming. Even more reason to spend the next couple of evenings with me. My brother, Nate, is visiting from California, but it's a short trip. We're having a family dinner tonight, and I want you to come with me."

She widened her eyes. "Me? Why?"

He shrugged. "Why not? I warn you, though, things are a bit touchy between Jax and Nate. My younger brother has been a little difficult of late, and Jax is getting pissed off with his attitude. I can't promise there won't be fireworks."

"More hotheaded brothers. That's quite a family you have there."

He grinned. "We're all quite different, and if it weren't for Jax, we'd probably only get together for holidays and the occasional birthday. But when our parents died, Jax was insistent we stick together. That's the whole reason he bought the hotel with our inheritance. It's a family business—a place for us all to gather and work toward a common goal."

"He sounds like an amazing guy."

Calum stared off into the distance, a slight curve to his lips. "Yeah. He is. Not sure what would have happened to us if he hadn't stepped up to the plate." He looked back at her. "You'll come?"

"I'd love to."

"Great. Shall we say seven? I'll pick you up on my way back from the gym."

She shivered with pleasure at the thought of Calum lifting weights, all hot and sweaty. She passed it off as a chill, rubbing her arms as if cold. "It's okay. I'll make my own way there."

Calum didn't argue. "If you're sure," was his only comment.

He turned to leave, and she dropped her gaze to his ass. He sure filled those pants well. A soft sigh fell from her lips, barely audible, but Calum must have heard. He glanced over his shoulder and caught her checking him out.

He laughed. "Now, *that's* made my day."

Laurella picked up a paperclip and threw it at him. It bounced harmlessly off his jacket. "Get out of here."

Calum's continued laughter still reached her ears long after he'd left her office. *Goddamn irritating male.* Even with that thought, she couldn't seem to wipe the smile from her face.

Laurella didn't see Calum for the rest of the day, but as she made her way home, her excitement began to build. She'd met Jax and Cole, of course, but that had been under very different circumstances. Calum inviting her for dinner signaled a shift in their relationship. Not that she'd go so far as to admit they were dating, but since their dinner a few nights before, and their subsequent compromise on how to manage the exclusivity deal, peace and harmony had reigned.

The way he'd kissed her on Monday evening had set a fire within her, the flames burning out of control. Yet Calum exhibited remarkable self-restraint and hadn't touched her after that. She'd expected him to want to move things along much quicker. In one way, she was glad. Since Vorino, she'd barely let a man come anywhere near her. In another way, the ease with which Calum was able to wait was driving her insane. She was ready to eat the whole pie. Calum wasn't even offering a sniff of the pastry crust.

You really need to stop thinking in food analogies.

Later that evening, after sorting through her entire closet— most of which ended up in a heap on her bed—Laurella finally settled on a mulberry-colored pleated crossover dress that didn't show too much cleavage and finished just at the knee. With the addition of black high-heeled sandals and a rhinestone clutch by an up-and-coming Italian designer, the whole ensemble fit nicely into the smart-but-casual bracket.

After a short subway ride, she found herself outside the Miller-Brook hotel, nervous tension nibbling at her insides.

Stupid really. Dinner with Calum's family was hardly anything to get worked up over. The younger brother intrigued her. From what Calum said, he didn't buy into the whole close-family thing Jax had going on. Laurella had instantly taken to Jax the one time she'd met him, as well as Cole. Calum was a different prospect altogether. He wasn't someone who gave out a warm-and-fuzzy feeling, but the two of them seemed to be working out the kinks.

She stepped onto the sidewalk, dodged around a throng of people spilling from the bar next door, and entered the hotel. Inside, the atmosphere buzzed, just as it had the last time. She glanced around for Calum but couldn't spot him. Heading into his living quarters seemed an invasion of privacy. She'd begun to walk toward the bar when an arm curved around her waist. She jumped.

"So skittish, Laurella," Calum's deep-baritone voice murmured in her ear. Before she could respond, he twisted her in his arms and slanted his mouth over hers. "You taste as good as you look." His hot gaze traveled from her toes to the top of her head.

Her skin flushed at his appraisal. "Am I suitably dressed?" She smoothed her hands over her hips.

"No," he replied bluntly. Her eyes widened until he went on to say, "You're wearing far too many clothes for my liking."

"Calum." She lightly tapped his arm in reprimand. "I thought you were being serious when you said no."

His scorching gaze left burn marks on her skin. "I was."

She swallowed hard. Something had changed between them. The dynamic was definitely more sexual, as if both were waiting for a… release.

He captured her hand. "Come on."

They walked into the living area, and Laurella instantly recognized three of the people: Jax, Cole, and Indie, Jax's girl-friend. The fourth, she guessed, had to be Nate, a beautiful if rather sullen man who gave her a quick once-over before he returned to tapping on his cell.

Jax, though, was as welcoming as he had been the first time they'd met. He beamed when his gaze fell on her hand inside Calum's. "Laurella," he said, walking toward them. He kissed her cheek. "So glad you could make it."

"Thank you for having me."

Calum eased her coat off her shoulders and hung it inside a closet on their left.

"This is Indie," Jax said, sliding an arm around his girlfriend's shoulders.

Laurella couldn't miss the darkening of Calum's expression as he glowered at Jax's girlfriend. Laurella glanced at him, puzzled, but he answered with a brief shake of his head.

"Lovely to meet you," Indie said, hugging Laurella warmly. "Any friend of Calum's is welcome here."

"Unlike you," Calum muttered. Either Jax and Indie didn't hear him, or his obvious contempt for her was normal behavior and they had stopped paying attention.

Laurella made a mental note to ask him about it when she got the chance.

"You've already met Cole," Calum said. "And that sour-faced dick over there is Nate. The youngest."

"Welcome, Laurella," Cole said while Nate raised his hand in greeting and gave a glimmer of a smile, which faded when he went back to his cell phone.

They settled down to dinner, and Laurella immersed herself in the warmth around the table. The banter that was usual in large families began. Coming from a big family herself, she missed the noise, the arguments, and the love. Usually, her evenings consisted of a meal for one and her laptop. She didn't regret the move to New York, and at least she and Calum were no longer at each other's throats, but she missed her family terribly. Even though Alessia's visit would detract from moving her relationship with Calum along, she couldn't wait to spend time with her sister.

"You're quiet," Calum murmured in her ear, his hand sliding up her leg beneath the heavy tablecloth.

"A little homesick," she said. "This reminds me of family dinners back home."

His hand moved farther up. He slid it between her thighs and applied pressure, daring her to open her legs. She clamped them shut, trapping his hand, and hoped her eyes gave him a clear message.

"Stop it," she whispered.

His breath caressed the shell of her ear. "Make me."

Laurella glanced around the table. Cole was chatting to Indie, his expression holding none of the hatred of Calum's, so whatever his problem was with Jax's girlfriend, his twin didn't feel the same. Jax was busy uncorking another bottle of wine, and Nate was still staring at his cell as if it held the answer to world peace. Did the man ever talk?

"No one is watching," Calum said, correctly guessing why she'd been checking out the others around the table. With his palm flat against her inner thigh, he applied enough pressure that her legs opened a couple of inches. That was enough for Calum to go exploring. Laurella caught her breath. She couldn't deny that the game excited her. He curved his free hand around her neck, the other one feathering at the very top of her thigh, so close to her sex that she had to clench her inner muscles to control the need that grew by the second.

"Tonight, you're mine, Laurella." His tone held a command that dared her to deny him. "Mine. No more pretending I don't ache for you every second of every day. No more games that push us apart instead of bringing us closer. I know it's happening quickly, but I don't want to wait any longer. If you feel the same, nod."

She dampened her lips and swallowed then nodded. Calum hissed. He slipped a finger inside her panties and swept it over her sex. Only once, but it was enough to drive her crazy. Her eyes briefly closed. She almost moaned. Almost. But as quickly as he'd started the game, he withdrew.

Mourning the loss of intimacy, Laurella lifted her eyes to his. He winked then inserted his middle finger into his mouth and sucked, mirroring her actions when she'd flirted with him in the restaurant the other night. Except it wasn't the taste of wine on his fingers. It was the taste of her.

"*Merde,*" she muttered.

"Only the beginning, sweetheart," Calum said.

"The beginning of what?" Indie asked.

Laurella and Calum both looked across at her at the same time, but before Laurella could make up a lie, Calum answered for her. "None of your fucking business."

Laurella flinched at the hatred in his tone. A furious expression crossed Jax's face, whereas Indie simply painted on a polite smile.

"Apologize," Jax snapped.

"To *her*?" Calum almost spat. "Not a fucking chance."

"It's fine, Jax," Indie said, putting her hand on his arm.

Jax pounded his fist on the table. "It is *not* fine." He poked his finger in Calum's direction. "Stop grinding this axe. Indie is my girlfriend, and she's going nowhere. This vendetta stops now." He snorted. "You just love acting as though *you* were the wronged party, don't you, Calum? Well, you weren't. And Indie was as much of a victim as I was. We've moved on. You'd better find a way to do the same. Otherwise, we're going to have a serious problem."

Laurella held her breath as the atmosphere switched from light to very dark in a split second.

"Here we go," Nate drawled.

Jax's head swiveled around so fast that he surely must have cricked his neck. "I'll deal with you in a minute."

"What the fuck have I done?"

"Absolutely nothing, Nate. That's the problem. Ever since

Mom and Dad passed away, I've tried to do everything to keep us together, to put this family first, yet you'd rather live on the other side of the country than spend time with us. You don't answer your phone. You don't visit unless one of us uses emotional blackmail. You won't reply to emails. Well, you know what? You can all fuck off."

He shoved a hand through his hair, his face blotched with fury. Calum had warned her it could all kick off. He'd been right.

"Take a fucking chill pill," Calum said in his usual completely unsympathetic manner.

"Jax." Indie touched his hand. "Your brothers appreciate you, as do I."

"Really?" he said, his voice full of bitterness.

"Yes." Indie glared across the table at Calum then flashed a hard look in Nate's direction. "Isn't that right?"

After a few seconds of silence, Nate was the first to speak. "I'm busy, that's all. I'm trying to build a career. I can't be flying across the country every five minutes."

Jax turned to his younger brother, his face softening. "I know. I'll try not to nag."

A brief smile brought a couple of dimples to Nate's face. They disappeared all too quickly. That was a shame. They'd made him appear much less moody.

When Calum remained silent, Laurella squeezed his knee— not in a sensual way but in a way that said if he didn't apologize, she would break his kneecap.

He sighed. "Of course I appreciate you, dickhead."

Laurella squeezed harder. Calum winced.

"And as my girlfriend seems to be giving me a clear message she's going to break my fucking leg if I don't apologize to you, India, I guess I'd better. I'm sorry."

Shock rolled through her at the speed of a bullet, and she loosened her grip. *Girlfriend.* She was having enough trouble managing the transition from hating him to flirting with him.

And now he'd basically announced to his family on their very first dinner together that they were in a relationship.

Calum seemed oblivious to her stupefied state as he held his hand out to Indie. "I can't say I completely forgive you for what you did, but give me time."

She shook his hand. "I can do that," she said, her voice muted.

"Thank Christ for that," Cole piped up. "At least I can take a break from the role of peacemaker."

"And on that bombshell, let's call it a night," Calum said. "Laurella and I have an early meeting on Monday morning that we need to prep for."

Laurella frowned. She didn't have an early meeting, because she was taking a few vacation days to spend with Alessia. Maybe he wanted out of the heavy atmosphere, which had only receded a little after the tentative truce. She couldn't say she was sorry he'd called time, although until his dig at Indie, they'd been having a lovely evening. The dinner-table drama reaffirmed her determination to ask him about Indie at an appropriate time.

While Calum said goodnight to his brothers, Indie sidled up next to Laurella. "I don't know how you've managed to tame him, but well done," she said with a grin.

Laurella chuckled. "I wouldn't say I've done that, but I have a mean grip. I simply put it to good use. Sometimes physical discomfort is the only thing a blunt instrument like Calum understands."

Indie didn't get to respond because Calum appeared at Laurella's side. "Ready to go?"

She nodded. "Thank you for having me over," she said to Jax.

"Anytime," Jax replied. "And who knows—next time, the evening might even be argument free."

"Don't count on it," Calum said, groaning when Laurella gave him a dig in the ribs.

When they reached the top of the stairs, out of earshot of the rest of his family, Laurella frowned at him. "We don't have an early meeting to prepare for."

"Correct," Calum said. "But I definitely have a blunt instrument that you'll be getting very well acquainted with."

CHAPTER 14

Laurella struggled to keep up with Calum as he strode into her apartment building. Another couple was just exiting the elevator. Calum urged her inside.

"What floor?" he asked.

"Seventeenth."

Calum moved his body into hers before the doors had time to close. Pinning her to the wall with his hips, he gathered her hair into a ponytail and gently tugged. Her head fell back, and his mouth came down on hers with a groan.

She'd barely given in to his kiss when the pinging sound of the elevator arriving at her floor interrupted them.

"Couldn't you live in a taller building?" he muttered.

Laurella giggled as she walked down the hallway, Calum's arm clamped around her waist as if he couldn't bear to let her go. Excitement began to build, pooling low in her belly. It had been far too long since she'd reveled in a man's touch, although none of her previous lovers had set her skin on fire the way Calum did with the simplest touch.

They turned the corner, and Laurella stopped abruptly. Sitting outside her apartment, knees pulled up to her chest, arms curved around them, was her youngest sister, Alessia. Her face was tearstained, and when she looked up and saw Laurella, more tears fell.

She scrambled to her feet and came charging down the hallway. She flung her arms around Laurella's neck. "Oh, Ella. Thank goodness. I thought you were never coming home."

Laurella took hold of her sister's shoulders and eased her back. "Alessia, what on *earth* are you doing here? You're not due until Sunday."

Alessia sniffled then wiped her nose with the back of her hand. "I had a fight with Papa, so I caught an earlier flight. He wants me to go to college in Milan, but I won't do it, Ella. I won't. Gianni is going to Rome, and I want to go with him. You have to help me. You have to talk to Papa."

Gianni was Alessia's childhood sweetheart and the crush Papa hoped would simply fade away. From the desperate, pleading look in Alessia's eyes, Laurella knew Papa's hopes weren't going to come to fruition anytime soon.

Laurella opened the door to her apartment. "Go inside, Alessia. I'll be in shortly." She gently shoved her sister through the door and pulled it closed behind her, a wry grimace twisting her lips. "Do you think the fates have conspired to keep us apart?" she asked, wrapping her arms around Calum's neck.

Calum's hand curved around her face, and he bent to kiss her softly. "Go deal with your sister."

Laurella huffed. "I'm so frustrated."

Calum laughed and glanced down at the unmistakable bulge in his jeans. "You're not the only one."

She grinned. "Cold shower?"

"Or a hot one," he said, winking. "I've got a pretty good imagination. It'll have to do for now."

"I'm going to kill her," Laurella said, more to herself than to him.

Calum kissed her again. "I'll see you next week."

Laurella watched him until he disappeared from view. She sighed, then went inside.

Alessia had already made herself at home—shoes cast aside, feet curled beneath her on the sofa. Her suitcase, bursting at the seams, was set on top of the chair by the window.

"He's hot." Alessia cocked her head at the closed door.

Laurella ignored her. "Does Papa know you changed to an earlier flight?"

Alessia shook her head sheepishly.

"Alessia!"

"I thought you could tell him. You know he loves you the best. If you talk to him, he'll listen. I know he will."

"Where does he think you are? He'll be going out of his mind, as will Mama."

Alessia shook her head. "It's okay. They think I'm staying at a girlfriend's house tonight. They won't worry for a few hours yet."

Laurella breathed out through her nose. "You are so irresponsible. You're eighteen now, Alessia—an adult in the eyes of the world. When are you going to start acting like one?" She was being overly harsh with her baby sister, but that was because of the thwarted night of sex with Calum.

Alessia's eyes filled up once more. "I thought you'd understand."

Laurella sat beside her. "I do understand. I know that Gianni is important to you, but don't you think Papa also knows what's best? He probably thinks some distance will allow you to spread your wings before committing to Gianni for the rest of your life."

In defiant mode, Alessia folded her arms across her chest. "I don't need to spread my wings. I know what I want."

Laurella stroked her sister's hair. "Why don't you go and get some rest? You must be exhausted after the long flight. I'll call Papa and talk to him."

Alessia's face flooded with relief. She flung her arms around Laurella's neck. "Love you, Ella. I knew you'd make it all better."

Laurella kissed the top of Alessia's head. "Love you, too. Now scoot."

Happy now that she'd gotten her own way, Alessia grinned, grabbed her suitcase, and wheeled it into the one and only bedroom. Laurella shook her head affectionately. Alessia was incorrigible but adorable.

She put on a pot of coffee. Papa wouldn't be up for a couple of hours. It was going to be a long night. She flicked on the TV, more for background noise than any interest in watching, sipped her coffee, and replayed the evening's events. The Brooks were certainly a complicated lot, although her family wasn't dissimilar.

She touched her lips, still able to feel Calum's kiss in the elevator. If Alessia hadn't arrived two days early, they'd be in bed together right at that moment. What would he be like? Proficient, certainly, but she also got the sense he'd be adventurous. His inappropriate touching of her at the dinner table was testament to his lack of care for rules or etiquette. Calum took what he wanted when he wanted it.

A delicious shiver crept up her spine. They'd had to delay, not cancel. It would make their eventual coming together all the sweeter.

On impulse, she grabbed her cell and sent him a text: *How was the shower?*

He didn't take long to reply: *Lonely.*

She smiled to herself and was wondering whether she should respond when he sent another: *How's your sister?*

His interest and concern surprised her. The more she got to know him, the more she realized she'd misjudged him initially, although he had more than his fair share of culpability for her original beliefs.

She texted: *Hormonal. Alessia likes to overdramatize everything.*

When he didn't reply, she sent another: *I'm sorry the evening ended the way it did.*

She stared at her cell, willing a reply. When it came, she

knew it was a text she'd keep forever: *It might not have ended with me buried deep inside you, but you're still mine, Ricci.*

She hugged herself and tapped out a response: *Noted. Goodnight, Calum.*

Night, beautiful came the reply.

A couple of hours later, Laurella shook off her tiredness and dialed her father's number. He answered immediately, and the moment she heard his voice, her homesickness became almost unbearable.

"Laurella, *tesoro*. How are you, my girl?"

"I'm good, Papa. You sound very chirpy this morning." *That won't last long.*

"Your voice would brighten the lowest of spirits. But it's late there now, no? Why aren't you in bed?"

She decided to plunge straight in. Delaying tactics would only make her dread grow. "Papa, when I came home this evening, I found Alessia waiting for me."

There was a gasp down the line. "But she's not coming to you until Sunday."

"She changed her flight."

"Put her on the phone," he demanded. Her father's tone had grown deep and serious, his earlier levity blown away like a leaf on a breeze.

"She's sleeping. I'll get her to call you in a few hours. She wanted me to talk to you about college."

"Pah," her father said. Laurella could imagine him slicing his hand through the air in a dismissive fashion. "She thinks she can't survive without that boy, Gianni. But she hasn't *lived*. How can she possibly know what she wants?"

"Papa, I know you want to protect us, but sometimes we have to make our own mistakes. Otherwise, how will we learn?"

"I allowed you to make your own mistakes. And what did that bring? Alberto Vorino. I couldn't protect you then, but I can protect Alessia now."

Laurella sucked in a breath and doubled over as if she'd

been punched in the stomach. She squeezed her eyes closed, memories Calum had stirred up with his questioning in Chicago coming to the fore. "You can't compare a young boy like Gianni to *gentaglia* like Alberto Vorino."

"Maybe not," he replied. "But Alessia isn't ready to forge her way forth on her own yet."

"Papa, she's eighteen."

"A *young* eighteen," he said firmly. "You were born thirty, yet still things happened."

"Papa, please," she whispered. "I don't want to talk about that time."

Especially now, when I've found a man who might have a chance of repairing my shattered soul.

"And even if Alessia goes to college in Milan, you can't be with her every minute of every day. Just consider letting her go to Rome. Maybe compromise on the first year until she proves you can trust her. You could get her to call you every night. If you smother her, she'll fight. You know how headstrong she is."

Silence greeted her, but then her father let out a soft sigh of capitulation. "Okay. She can go, but I don't like it, Laurella. And you tell that girl to call me when she wakes. It's a good job she's staying with you for the next few days. It will give me chance to calm down."

Laurella chuckled. "No doubt that was part of her plan, Papa."

He grunted. "I miss you, *tesoro*. So does your mama. Come visit us soon."

"Yes, soon," Laurella said. "I love you, Papa."

"I love you, too. Hold on. Your mama wants to talk with you."

After she'd spoken to her mother, Laurella expected her homesickness to be much worse. But talking to her parents had given her comfort, peace. And her burgeoning relationship with Calum helped bring on a sense of belonging in her new home, in New York.

Exhausted, she crept into her bedroom. Alessia was fast asleep, her hair a dark, tangled mess, the sheets tossed to one side. Laurella quietly dressed for bed and slipped under the covers beside her sister. Alessia may have won this round, but no doubt, her ears would be ringing from the dressing down she'd get from Papa as soon as she called him in the morning.

Laurella entered her office the following Thursday with a spring in her step. She'd had an enjoyable few days with Alessia, and her batteries were well recharged. Her sister was heading back to Milan the next day, which meant that Laurella and Calum could carry on where they'd left off before Alessia's untimely arrival.

Juggling a coffee, her laptop bag, and her purse, Laurella nudged open the door to her office with her hip. Inside, Calum was sitting in her chair, his feet resting on her desk.

"Morning," he said, his wide smile tugging on her heart and flipping her stomach.

She kicked the door shut. "Out of my chair, Brook," she said, setting her stuff on the desk. When he didn't move, she knocked his feet to the floor. In an instant, she found herself sitting in his lap. He drew her head down to his and kissed her. He tasted of minty toothpaste and that morning's caffeine fix.

When he flicked his tongue inside her mouth, she pulled away. "What if someone comes in?" she said, trying—and failing—to get off his lap.

"Unless it's Zane, they'd better knock first, in which case, I'll do the gentlemanly thing and let you go. If they don't knock, I'll fire their ass."

She bent her head to the right. "And if it *is* Zane?"

Calum shrugged. "He's seen worse from me."

An uncomfortable feeling stirred within her. "I'll bet he has," she said quietly as she gripped his wrists and unwrapped his arms from around her. She stood, walked around to the other side of her desk, and removed the plastic lid from her coffee.

Calum chuckled. "Are you *jealous?*"

"No," she said, a little too quickly.

"You are," he said, laughing harder. "Oh, this is priceless."

Laurella pretended to ignore him. Instead, she nonchalantly strolled over to her filing cabinet and took out a thick manila folder. She dropped it on her desk, but before she could open it, Calum got out of her chair and pulled her into his arms.

"I like this side of you." He brushed his lips against hers. "It means you care."

She snorted. "You think a lot of yourself, Calum Brook."

"That goes without saying," he said, grinning boldly. "The question is, what do you think of me? Based on that green tinge to your skin, I'd say quite a lot."

"Don't you have something you need to do?" she snapped.

He bent his head, his lips touching the shell of her ear. "Only you, Laurella. I need to do you, desperately."

A hot flush rushed through her body. She'd never been so turned on by a man using words alone. As she remembered where they were, her professionalism made an unwelcome return. She twisted out of his arms and put some distance between them.

Calum laughed.

How has he figured me out so quickly?

"Did you enjoy your time off with Alessia?"

A smile came to her lips. "I did. We both had an amazing time, but it's definitely made me want to plan a trip home to see the rest of my family. Speaking of family, I meant to ask you after the dinner at your place: what's your issue with Indie? She seemed nice enough to me."

His lips curled in a menacing manner. "She almost got Jax killed."

Laurella's skin tingled at his obvious malevolence. "What do you mean?"

Calum shook his head. "It's a long story. Suffice it to say, she and her brother had a vendetta against my family, and Jax was the one they decided to target. Indie's brother died. Jax didn't. I'll tell you the full story sometime."

She read his abrupt end to her questioning as a signal to drop the subject, evidenced by the fact that he wrapped her in his arms once more. "When's your sister flying home?"

"Tomorrow afternoon."

"Tomorrow night it is, then."

She frowned. "What do you mean?"

"Tomorrow night is when I truly make you mine."

CHAPTER 15

Laurella checked—again—that she'd changed the towels in the bathroom. Not to mention that every time she passed the bed, she smoothed the sheets. She'd primped, preened, shaved any and all unwanted hair, slathered on body lotion, and dabbed perfume on her neck, behind her ears, and even in her cleavage. She'd spent time on her hair and makeup and tried to pick something to wear that ticked all the boxes, the most important one being *easy access*. In the end, she'd gone for a simple wrap dress with a tie at the waist. The last thing she needed was to be wearing some complicated outfit that took Calum forever to break into.

Oh hell. Anyone watching her would think she was desperate and easy. *Desperate* was certainly a good description. She was still smarting from their thwarted attempt a couple of nights earlier. She'd even gone so far as to stay at the airport until she was sure Alessia's flight had taken off. Her other family members were safely in Italy—of that she was sure. Nothing stood in their way now.

This is happening. Tonight.

Her pulse jolted, her heart thudding against her ribcage. She'd never been a casual-sex kind of girl, but she didn't know how to describe this thing with Calum. He kept using words like *mine*, and he'd called her his girlfriend at the family dinner. They certainly hadn't rushed into anything—not least because they'd spent ninety percent of the time since they'd met at each other's throats. But still, after tonight, would she need to change her Facebook status to 'In a relationship'?

She glanced at her watch. He was late. What if he didn't turn up at all? After all, he'd tricked her in Chicago. Maybe that was all this was—an elaborate ruse to cause her even more hurt.

She paced. Every few steps, she stopped, checked her cell, saw he hadn't texted, then tossed it aside. When the anticipated knock at her door finally came, she jumped. Her mouth dried up, and she had to grab a towel to wipe her damp palms. With a glance in the mirror, she smoothed a hand over her skirt and went to the door. She drew to a halt, took a deep breath, and opened it.

In direct contrast to his usual business attire, Calum had gone for a completely casual look. If he intended to turn her on without even touching her, he'd succeeded. A pair of faded denims clung to his thighs and his white shirt was unfastened at the neck, giving her a peek of smooth, tanned skin. He smelled amazing, of bodywash and designer cologne. She took a deep breath through her nose. Her stomach vaulted, and she swore her heart actually skipped a beat.

"Are you going to let me in?" he asked, a curve to his lips telling her she'd probably been standing there gawking for some time. He held up a bottle of red wine. "I brought supplies."

She stepped back, heat rushing to her cheeks. "Of course."

He came in and curved a hand around her neck. He drew her in for a kiss—a long, lingering kiss that had her toes curling and her heartbeat racing.

He released her. "Where's your corkscrew?" he asked, wandering into her kitchen.

"Top drawer. There on your right," she said, still trying to recover from that panty-busting kiss, whereas Calum seemed completely relaxed and unaffected.

He set the bottle of wine on the countertop and fished about in her kitchen drawer. "Got it." He opened the wine. The cork popped as he pulled it out.

"Here, let me get some glasses," she said, finally working out how to put one foot in front of the other.

Calum poured the wine—a rather nice merlot—into both glasses and held one out to her. After she accepted it, he tapped his against hers. "To us," he said.

A delicious tingle crept up her spine at the comment. She gulped down more than she really should, but her nerves were going crazy. She needed something to take the edge off. Unlike the other night, this date wasn't spontaneous, which was giving her time to panic. When she simply stared at her wineglass, Calum removed it from her and placed it on the countertop next to his.

He captured a lock of her hair between his fingers and twisted it. "Where's my always confident, sometimes quarrel-some woman gone?"

There he goes again. 'My woman.'

She swallowed and licked her lips. His gaze fell to her mouth before he looked back into her eyes.

"She's still here," she said. "Just taking a break."

Calum laughed. "I hope she isn't on vacation too long."

She frowned. "Why? Don't you like this one?"

His arms went around her waist, and he tugged her close. "I like every single one. The crabby one. The combative one. The shy one. They're all you, Laurella. And they're all damned fine."

Her breath caught in her throat. "See, you can be a nice guy."

He cocked a brow. "Use the word 'nice' about me again, and I'll show you just how un-nice I am."

Before she could hit him with a comeback, he captured her mouth. The sound of her heart thundered in her ears—so loud, so strong she half expected her ribs to crack. She wound her hands around Calum's neck and held on for dear life. Out of all the men she'd ever kissed—which wasn't a whole lot—Calum easily won first prize. She didn't want to think about how much practice he must have had to learn how to kiss so well.

"Laurella Ricci, you might well be the death of me," Calum murmured against her swollen lips. He dipped his finger into his glass of wine. "Suck," he said, placing it to her mouth.

Without hesitation, she drew his finger deep into her mouth. His eyes fell shut, and he groaned. She clenched her thighs together at his husky sigh.

He withdrew his finger, dragging the tip over her lips, her neck, before settling briefly between her breasts. Her breath snapped on a gasp of anticipated pleasure, but instead of exploring further, he picked up his wineglass and took a mouthful. His hand cupped her chin, and he kissed her, pouring the wine into her mouth. It was quite possibly the sexiest thing anyone had ever had done to her.

She swallowed the wine, and a plea fell readily from her lips. "More."

Calum slowly blinked, his Adam's apple bobbing as he swallowed. "God, you're fucking perfect, woman." He drank the wine again and repeated the action.

This time, it was Laurella's turn to groan. "Let's go to bed," she said, her eyes half-closed. "I want to see if you're as good as you think you are."

Calum chuckled. "Now, there's a challenge."

When they walked into her bedroom, the smell from the scented candles she'd lit earlier filled the space, and the flickering light added sensuality to an already highly charged atmosphere.

Calum kicked the door shut. "Turn around," he said softly. "Face the bed."

Her pulse stuttered, but she did as he'd asked. She held her breath, so very ready to feel his hands on her. A few seconds passed. Her chest rose and fell rapidly while she waited. And waited. Frowning, she glanced over her shoulder.

"I said turn around," he ordered, his tone low and commanding. Impossible to resist.

She closed her eyes, straining her ears for any rustling of clothes or quiet steps that would mean Calum had moved closer. Nothing. The speed of her breathing grew until she was almost panting, and *still* he didn't put his hands on her.

"What are you doing?" she whispered.

"Building the anticipation." His lips touched her ear unexpectedly, and she jumped. "I want to savor every single second of this evening."

Frustrated, she huffed. "The anticipation has been building for over two months, Calum."

"Then it can't hurt to wait another few minutes."

She couldn't see him, but the smile was there in his voice, his tone. He was teasing her, raising the stakes between them, seeing how far he could push before she snapped. She tensed, desperate for his touch but knowing if she begged, he'd make her wait even longer.

"Untie your dress and let it slip to the floor," he said.

Tingles broke out all over her body. Whatever she'd thought sex with Calum would be like, she hadn't expected this slow seduction. When she'd tried to imagine it, her mind had conjured up images of a wild, raw coming together—a man who would take her quickly, roughly even. She'd thought that the minute they walked into her bedroom, he'd have made his move.

She couldn't have been more wrong. And a small voice, one she kept under lock and key because it reminded her of a girl she refused to be, whispered that she was glad. She needed tenderness, not animal sex. Not yet at least. Trust was a commodity very easily broken and almost impossible to repair— as she'd found out in the most brutal of circumstances.

She tugged on the tie, her fingers trembling. Her dress

parted at the front, and she slid it from her shoulders. It fell in a heap on the floor.

He hissed. "You have the most amazing legs." He swept her hair over her shoulder.

His tongue traced a path across the nape of her neck. She quivered in anticipation of pleasure that was almost within her reach.

Standing in her bra and panties, she waited. Again. Involuntarily, her head twitched to the side.

"Don't move," he demanded.

There was no doubt in her mind: Calum Brook was a master at seduction. Since walking into that room, he'd barely touched her, yet her panties were soaked with evidence of her arousal. Her mind boggled at what he'd make her feel when he finally put his hands on her bare skin.

His breath feathered the back of her neck. The hairs there stood on end, and she tensed, craving his touch.

"Turn around. Look at me."

She slowly pivoted. Heat licked through her veins as she stared into his eyes, those dark pools of intense green that had somehow touched her heart and given her hope that she might, in time, be capable of having a normal relationship.

His gaze tracked over her, scorching her already heated skin. "I knew you'd be stunning, but my imagination didn't do you justice." His fingertips grazed her sides, feathering up and down while those hauntingly beautiful eyes locked on hers.

"Calum, please," she groaned.

His answering smile was crooked, teasing. Annoying. "So impatient."

He kicked off his sneakers, simultaneously unfastening the buttons on his shirt. He tossed it to one side. Although Laurella had seen Calum's naked chest before, she'd been so furious and full of hatred that she hadn't wanted to admit to his perfection. But now, this close, near enough to touch, she simply stared. He was like a work of art. Firm, hard chest muscles. Defined deltoids and broad shoulders—she'd always been a fan of shoulders—and biceps big enough to make any girl feel safe and protected.

She placed her palm flat against his pecs. He closed his eyes and swayed a little. His hand came over the top of hers.

"I want to explore," she said.

He made a noise in the back of his throat. "Go ahead."

She stepped closer. She clutched his biceps, and bent her head, flicking her tongue over his nipple. She sucked it into her mouth.

"Laurella." The word came out on a breath, more sighed than spoken.

When she moved to the other nipple, his hands gripped the back of her head, his fingers knitting into her hair. She inserted a finger into the waistband of his jeans, and her nail scraped the blunt head of his cock. Oh, that had promise.

His hips jerked, and he groaned loudly. "Take 'em off," he ground out.

She smiled against his chest. With each passing second, her confidence grew, and the woman she *now* was came out to play. He'd tortured her. It was her turn. *Payback time.*

She straightened and curved her hands around the back of his neck. "So impatient," she said, mirroring his earlier words.

"Fuck's sake, woman," he said, his jaw clenched. "Either you take them off, or I will."

Taking pity on him—at least that was what she told herself —she unfastened the button on his jeans and unzipped the fly. She slid her hands around his back and dipped inside, cupping his ass. *Oh yeah.* She'd been right about how firm his butt would be.

She eased down his jeans, gradually revealing taut thighs covered in a dusting of dark hair. She crouched down and, unable to resist, kissed his thick erection through his boxers. It jerked as though it had a mind of its own.

"Fuck. Me." Calum stepped out of his jeans and bent his

knees, his hands cupping her ass. He picked her up and laid her gently on the bed. Crawling after her, he parted her thighs, leaning on them with his forearms. He pressed warm, gentle kisses to the soft skin on the insides of her legs, slowly inching upward. Unable to take her eyes off him, Laurella watched as he kissed her through her panties. Her legs twitched when he eased the delicate material to one side. With those wicked green eyes focused on hers, his tongue swept over her slit—and then he slipped it inside her.

Laurella arched her back and groaned. *Jesus*—the man knew how to go down on a woman. Not that she had a whole range of other men to compare him to, but she knew *good* when she saw it—or rather, felt it. He applied just the right amount of attention to her clit, his fingers and tongue moving in perfect harmony, and when he sensed her getting closer, he increased the speed and pressure.

"God help me." She fisted the bed sheets as, like a wave coming into shore, she peaked and then crashed. Calum had taken her over the edge with so little effort. Surely that was the fastest orgasm she'd ever had?

He gently slid her panties down her legs and dropped them on the floor. He crawled up her body, his lips searingly hot and damp with her arousal. His mouth touched her hips, her stomach, then he turned his attention to her breasts. He tugged down both cups of her bra, and once her breasts were sitting proud, he began licking, sucking, biting, bringing her close once more, even though her body was still recovering from the last climax.

She gripped his cock through his boxers. It wasn't enough, though. She needed to properly feel the silky-smooth hardness beneath the thin cotton. She pushed his boxers down as far as she could with her hands then bent her knees and shoved them the rest of the way with her feet.

Once he was free, she sighed with pleasure, wrapped her hand around the base, and gripped him. She skimmed over the head with her thumb, capturing the moisture that had gathered there.

She put her thumb in her mouth, tasting the very essence of him, as he had done with her, and reached for him once more.

"Don't make me wait any longer," she said. She needed this so badly. Needed *him*. Needed their coming together to chase the bad memories away.

As she guided him to her entrance, he froze. "Condom." He leaned down, grabbed his jeans from the floor, and removed a square packet from the back pocket. Calum ripped the packet apart with his teeth then rolled the plastic sheath onto his erection.

He parted her thighs, entering her slowly, carefully, pushing inside an inch at a time. His large hands with those slender fingers gripped her wrists, planting them either side of her head. His mouth came down on hers, his tongue surging inside—and then he thrust in all the way.

She buried her head in the pillow and squeezed her eyes shut, memorizing exactly how he felt. And then he shifted his hips. *Oh boy*, her man could move. He thrust inside, massaging her with every forward push, demonstrating an expertise she hadn't believed existed until that moment.

"Okay?" he gritted out, releasing her hands.

She forced her eyes open. He was staring down at her with concern—but also tension, probably because he was trying to control his climax. She melted, turning into a puddle of need and want and desire at the fact that he cared enough to ask.

"More than okay," she whispered, wrapping her arms around him to pull him close.

Calum buried his face in her neck, his breath hot on her skin. He pushed into her again and again. Their bodies, slick with sweat, moved easily against each other. Unbelievably, another swell began within her, and as it erupted from her core, spreading to the very tips of her fingers and toes, she groaned. "*Dio mio.*"

"Fuck." Calum gave a final hard thrust then stilled.

She hooked her legs around his hips and tilted her pelvis, holding him deep within her, drawing out his pleasure—and hers—while she watched pure ecstasy cross his face.

He cupped her face and kissed her, slower now that their respective needs had been met. When he raised himself up on his elbows, she gazed into those captivating emerald-green eyes and wondered how she'd ever despised this man.

"I knew it would be different with you," he murmured before rolling to the side.

She turned over, her hand propping up her head. Was that good or bad? She frowned. "How so?"

He brushed his thumb over the deep crease that had formed between her eyebrows, smoothing the skin. "Maybe because we started off hating each other. Or maybe because we were hindered by your sister's arrival last week, increasing the frustration." He shrugged. "It meant more. I felt you, everywhere. It was… intense."

Her heart flipped. It actually felt as if it had been turned upside down in her chest, stopping it from beating normally.

"So you don't hate me anymore?"

He smiled. "Do you still hate me?"

"Sometimes," she said, drawing a bark of laughter from him.

"I guess I deserved that."

She leaned forward and pecked him on the lips just to make sure he knew she was only joking. "Will you stay the night?"

He wrapped his arm around her, pulling her into his side. His lips grazed her temple. "I'm going nowhere, beautiful."

CHAPTER 16

C alum turned up the heat on the stove. Once the pan was sizzling, he poured in the pancake batter. Thank goodness Laurella believed in the ready-made variety, because he didn't have a clue how to prepare the mixture from scratch.

He made a stack, along with a pile of bacon. He poured them each a glass of orange juice, his mind turning to the previous evening. His head spun with the speed at which he'd switched from thinking of Laurella as *that damned woman* to *my damned woman*. And the sex… *holy hell*.

"That smells amazing."

Calum turned toward the bedroom. Laurella was leaning against the doorjamb, her hair piled high in a messy bun. She looked sexy as hell in a cream camisole top and a pair of short shorts. He raked his gaze over her. She really did have the sexiest legs. His stomach clenched as his mind replayed how she'd wrapped them around his waist. Next time, he'd see if he could persuade her to wear heels.

"Come and eat, then. Before it gets cold." He set the plate of pancakes and bacon in the center of the small table and pulled up a chair. "What do you normally do on a weekend?" he asked, pouring maple syrup over his pancakes.

She shrugged. "Work."

"Not the whole weekend, surely?"

Another shrug. "I don't have anything else to do. I haven't really had time to make friends."

"But you went sightseeing with Alessia, right? I mean, you've seen New York."

She shook her head. "I walked up and down Fifth Avenue. Several times. And I know every inch of Bloomingdales. Alessia likes to shop."

"Sounds like my idea of Hell," he muttered.

"It might surprise you, but it's also mine."

He chuckled. "That settles it, then. I'm taking you sightseeing today. I don't know how far we'll get, but I'm sure we'll see a few of the main touristy bits." He reached across the table and captured her hand. He lifted it to his mouth and kissed her knuckles. "And just so you know, from now on, you'll be busy on weekends."

He refrained from adding "sucking my cock" as he would have if speaking to a woman like Vonny. Laurella was too classy for that. Not to mention that he had an inkling that if he did add such a crude comment, she'd probably cut off his favorite body part.

They finished eating breakfast. Laurella insisted on clearing the dishes while Calum shot home to change. He was back within the hour. He'd worked out a sightseeing route, although because it was already past ten, they wouldn't be able to see a whole lot. Manhattan might only be thirteen miles long and two miles wide, but it packed masses into that small space.

"So, my personal tourist guide," Laurella said, drawing a grin from him, "what do you have planned for me?"

"I thought we'd go from south to north. First stop: Statue of Liberty. For the rest, well, you'll have to wait and see."

"Oh, this is going to be so good." She stood on tiptoes and kissed his cheek. "Thank you, Calum. I hope this won't be too boring for you, especially as you're a native."

"It won't be boring," he said, slipping his arm around her waist and tucking her into his side. "I'm with you."

~

While they waited in line for the ferry to Liberty Island, Calum could barely take his eyes—or keep his hands—off Laurella. She kept pushing away the wisps of almost-black hair that the springtime breeze blew around her face.

"How long does it take to get there?" she asked.

"Only fifteen minutes or so."

She smiled up at him, her eyes shining with excitement. "This is the best day I've had since coming to New York, and it's barely started."

He kissed her temple. "I'm offended. I thought a night in bed with me would beat most things."

Her cheeks reddened. "Shush." She glanced over her shoulder before looking back at him. "People might hear."

He shrugged. "So? You're worth shouting about. You're a fireball in the sack, sweetheart."

"Calum!" She dug him in the ribs, but he just laughed.

The gates opened, and people shuffled forward onto the ferry. Calum caught Laurella's hand and, keeping a tight hold, walked up the plank. He went straight to the back, securing a good spot to watch Manhattan Island from a distance as the ferry headed out.

Within minutes, they'd set off. The wind picked up, and Laurella wrapped her jacket closer around her.

"C'mere." Calum wrapped her in his arms. He rested his chin on her shoulder and pointed out various landmarks as they set sail from Manhattan. He watched her animated expression, and answered her questions, and an alien feeling stirred within him. Making Laurella smile was like winning a coveted award— except he wasn't satisfied with just one prize. He wanted them all.

They docked at Liberty Island, and Laurella slipped her hand through his arm, her excitement palpable as they melded into the crowds that flocked there in the thousands so that they could tell their friends and family they'd visited the symbol of freedom. The statue had been familiar to Calum his whole life —but seeing Laurella's enthusiasm for what had become a mundane monument, he felt he should have been more appreciative.

"I heard you can climb it," Laurella said. "Is that true?"

Calum nodded. "It's quite a climb, though."

"Have you done it?"

"Yes. A long time ago."

"Oh." Her face fell. "I guess you've done everything you're going to show me today. There's nothing new about it for you."

He slipped his hands around her waist. When she tilted her face up to his, Calum brushed his lips over hers, the now familiar rush of desire thickening his cock, which pressed, almost painfully, against his zipper. "It's all new, because I'm seeing it with you."

"Oh, Calum." She wrapped her hands around his neck and drew his mouth down to hers. They only broke apart when another tourist jostled them. The stranger muttered an apology before shuffling off.

"Do you want to climb to the crown?" Calum asked.

Laurella nodded enthusiastically. "I really do."

"Good job I made reservations for us, then." He'd had to call in a favor. Tickets to climb to the crown sold out weeks in advance. Luckily, he had a contact who'd pulled a few strings. It had only cost him a night's stay in the penthouse, and dinner. Jax had offered the place for free, but Calum had refused. His brother was running a business, not a charity. Paying the significant sum was worth every penny to secure Laurella's happiness.

Her forehead wrinkled. "You can't just climb it."

"Nope."

She squealed with excitement and threw her arms around

his neck, tucking her head under his chin. "You thought of everything."

"Well, I wouldn't be a very good boyfriend if I didn't spoil you this early on in our relationship."

She drew back and studied his face. "Is that what this is? A relationship?"

Calum bent his head, stealing another kiss. "I told you, Laurella. You're mine. I'm never letting you go."

The words tumbled out of their own accord, but before she could say anything in response to such a revelation, he clutched her hand and headed over to the entrance, which would take them inside the statue. She *was* his. And he had no intention of letting her escape his clutches. But he wasn't yet ready for a discussion about it. He was still struggling to get his head around how fast they'd moved from animosity to this strong connection they'd forged.

By the time they reached the top, both were out of breath, but the views were worth every agonizing step, especially when Laurella swept a hand over his ass, squeezed it, and whispered, "You are so getting laid tonight."

"Where now?" she said when they stepped off the ferry back onto Manhattan Island. "I feel like a real tourist."

"You are a tourist," Calum stated. "You can't say you live in New York until you've been here at least five years."

She frowned. "Really?"

"No." He laughed. "I didn't take you for someone so gullible."

She dug him with her elbow, catching him just underneath his ribs.

He grunted and rubbed the offending area. "Careful, now. If you damage me, I won't be able to perform to the best of my abilities later."

"If you accuse me of being gullible again, you won't get the chance to perform," she said, her tone teasing and light.

"Oh no you don't." He caught her around the waist and held her flush against his body. "You've made a deal with the Devil. No backing out now."

All frivolity left her. She looked up at him with those dark, long-lash-framed, soulful eyes and blinked slowly. "I wouldn't back out even if I could."

A surge of desire flushed through him, and his cock thickened. She noticed and, instead of pulling back, wriggled closer.

"Carry on like that, and instead of the tourist hot spots of New York, the only sight you'll see will be my naked body covering yours."

She giggled. "You are such a *man*. Restraint, Calum. It'll make tasting the honey all the sweeter."

"Oh, believe me, sweetheart, I'll be tasting *your* honey. Repeatedly. And if I remember rightly, it was *you* who couldn't control yourself last night. Four times was a challenge even for me."

Her eyes twinkled. "A gentleman shouldn't remind a lady of such things."

He gently flicked the end of her nose. "I love the way you speak. It's so… not American."

"That's because I'm Italian."

He laughed again. "That's stating the obvious. Come on. If you thought the view from the top of the Statue of Liberty was good, it's even more impressive from our next stop."

"The Empire State Building?" she asked.

He shook his head. "Somewhere even better."

After they'd walked all around Top of the Rock several times and Laurella had spent a while peering through the scenic viewer that magnified the city landscape, she straightened and beamed at him.

"I know I haven't been to the top of the Empire State Building, but it'd be hard to beat this view. It's magnificent."

Calum took her hand, cold from the keen wind at that high elevation. He rubbed it between both of his. "It's very much a personal choice, and there are those that argue either way. In my opinion, the view from here is better than the Empire State Building, because you're more central. I'll take you there another day, and then you can make up your own mind."

"I'd like that," she said, smiling up at him.

"Seen enough?"

"I'm not sure I'll ever get sick of this view, but yes, we can go now if you like."

He checked his watch. "The next thing I have planned is a must-do for a tourist such as yourself. We have just enough time before our dinner reservations."

She punched his arm. "Stop teasing me."

They strolled up Fifth Avenue, past the gaudy Trump Tower on the right, before turning left alongside the Plaza Hotel.

"We must go to the Palm Court sometime," Calum said with a nod toward the Plaza. "I assume you haven't been yet?"

She shook her head. "I've never heard of it."

"It's iconic. You have to go at least once." He drew to a halt and pointed across the street, where a long line of horses and their adorned carriages were waiting for the next fare. "Want to take a ride with me?"

Her eyes lit up, and she stood on tiptoes to kiss him. "I'd love to."

They crossed the street, and Calum helped her inside the back of a bright-red carriage. He briefly spoke to the driver and paid him for thirty minutes. He wished they had more time, but New York was one of those places that took much longer to get around than people thought.

Calum climbed in. He opened out the blanket, placed it

around Laurella's shoulders, and tucked her into his side. As they set off to the clip-clop of the horses' hooves on the road, their driver began to point out areas of interest, but when they paid more attention to each other than to what he was saying, he simply smiled and left them to it.

"Good day?" Calum asked, nuzzling her neck.

She tilted to the side to give him better access. "The best day." A sigh fell from her lips, a contented sound that swelled his chest.

"I'm sorry we couldn't see more, but there's always next weekend or the one after or the one after that."

She grinned. "So you meant it before when you laid claim to all my weekends?"

"Yep." He nibbled on her earlobe, and she sucked in a sharp breath.

"Calum," she said in a warning tone.

"I like to hear my name on your lips." He traced his tongue from the soft spot beneath her ear down the long column of her neck. "Especially when I'm inside you," he added in a low voice.

"You're getting me all hot and bothered," she whispered.

"That's the idea, beautiful."

When the horse and carriage drew to a halt in the same place they'd set off from, Laurella pulled a sad face. "That was over so quickly."

"We'll do it again another time," Calum said, jumping down onto the sidewalk. After helping Laurella from the carriage, he paid the driver, adding a healthy tip. The man deserved it after he'd picked up on the cue to keep quiet.

They rode the subway to a French restaurant in Soho, a longtime favorite of his. It was cozy without being clichéd, and the food was out of this world.

He stopped outside, and Laurella glanced up, squinting as she read the restaurant name. "Balthazar. Wasn't he an angel in the Bible?"

Calum winked. "A fallen angel, actually."

She rolled her eyes. "Figures."

Such an American phrase spilling from her perfect Italian lips made him laugh. "We'll make a Yank out of you yet."

She stared at him in mock horror. "My papa would disown me."

He pushed open the door and, with his hand at the small of her back, eased her inside. They were seated quickly, and once the waiter had taken their drinks order, they were left alone to peruse the menu.

"Have you been here before?" Laurella asked.

Calum nodded. "Many times."

"Then what would you recommend?"

He waggled his eyebrows. "Oysters."

Laurella shook her head. "I'm not sure your libido needs any more stoking."

"I like it hot, and from what you showed me last night, so do you."

Her eyes burned into him, hauntingly beautiful. Mesmerizing. He found he couldn't look away, almost as though she'd trapped him in that moment with her gaze alone.

"I do like it hot. And varied."

Fuck. Me.

He fidgeted in his chair, surreptitiously reaching beneath the heavy linen covering on the table to rearrange his junk before the damn thing bust through his jeans.

"Oysters it is, then," he said, clearing his throat several times.

She dipped her chin, glancing up at him through those unbelievably long lashes, one of the first features he'd noticed about her all those months ago.

Her foot rubbed against his leg. "Are you turned on right now?"

He'd been sipping water when she asked that. He almost spat it out but managed to swallow. "You know I am."

That foot crept upward. Sometime between sitting down

and right then, she'd removed her shoes. Damn. When had she slipped them off? Her toes curled over his erection, and he almost leaped out of his chair. A quiet groan eased from his throat. Then her foot was gone.

"Why—"

She jerked her head. The waiter was patiently standing by their table, his face as red as the window banner advertising the name of the restaurant. Their wine was in an ice bucket by the side of the table. Calum had been so entranced by what Laurella had been doing to him that he hadn't even realized they weren't alone.

"Are you ready to order, sir, madam?" the waiter asked, unable to make eye contact. His pen was poised over his pad, and his face had the look of someone who wanted to be anywhere but where he was.

Calum grinned at Laurella and mouthed, "Busted."

She giggled. "Yes, we're ready. He'll order for both of us."

Calum gave the menu a cursory glance, even though he knew it by heart. "The oysters du jour and two portions of the braised short ribs." He held the menus out to the side.

The grateful waiter took them and scurried away.

"That poor man," Laurella said, still chuckling.

Calum poured them each a glass of wine. "That was all you. And here I was thinking I'm the badly behaved one."

She sipped her wine, and her foot began exploring once more. "Now, where were we?"

By the time they'd finished dinner, both of them were running hot. The second they got outside, Laurella dragged Calum down a side street where the crowds were less thick. There were still plenty of people around, although she didn't seem to care. She pushed him up against the wall and kissed him. The control was all hers. He was simply a passenger along for the ride. And what a ride it was.

His cell buzzed, but he ignored it. Nothing could be more important than tangling tongues with the hottest girl he'd ever met. He'd always thought being in charge was the turn on, but how wrong he'd been. Giving control to someone else, especially one as sexy as Laurella, stirred him up something fierce inside.

When his cell buzzed again, he inwardly cursed. His lips were still connected to hers as he took it from his pocket and glanced at the screen. Zane. What the hell did he want?

"Who is it?" she murmured, her red, swollen lips urging him to put his mouth on her again.

"Zane." He swiped to answer. "What?" he snapped into the phone.

"Where are you?" Zane asked, sounding mightily pissed off.

"Why?"

"Because we're all sitting in Fred's like a bunch of dicks, waiting for you."

Fuck. He'd forgotten. The first Saturday of every third month, he and his old college buddies met up for a night of pool and beer.

"Shit." He looked down at Laurella, whose eyes were misty with desire, an undoubted mirror image of his own. "Sorry, Zane, I need to bail."

"Are you sick?"

"No."

"Is Jax okay?"

Calum frowned. Where the hell was he going with this? "Yes."

"Cole? Nate? All good?"

Realization crept in. "Yes," he said in a resigned tone.

"Then you're coming. Unless you're in a life-or-death situation, you don't bail." He paused. "Are you with a chick? Because if you are, put her in a cab and get over here. Bros before hoes, remember? That's the code."

Calum let out a frustrated breath. "No, I'm not with a *chick.*"

"What's the matter?" Laurella whispered.

"Hang on," he said to Zane before putting his cell on mute.

"Every few weeks, Zane and I meet up with the guys we went to college with. I completely forgot it's tonight."

Laurella hid her disappointment behind a wry grin. "Then you must go."

Calum curved a hand around her neck and pecked her lips. "I'd rather be with you."

She shook her head. "Bros before hoes, remember?" When he showed his surprise, she laughed. "Tell Zane he's got a loud mouth."

"Shit. Are you sure?"

"Of course I'm sure. You go. Have fun with your friends. I don't want to come between you and your life, Calum. If we were in Milan instead of New York, and it was me going out with my girlfriends, I'd still go. Sisters before misters, right?"

He laughed. "Okay, but I'm coming over tomorrow, and we're spending the whole day in bed."

Her smile built slowly. "That's what Sundays are for."

CHAPTER 17

Calum saw Laurella safely into a cab then rode the subway to Fred's bar. For the past six years, he'd looked forward to these get-togethers, yet right then, standing outside the place where he and his buddies had shared many a great night, he could easily be heading for the gallows. *Jesus.* Had he been whipped into shape by Laurella so quickly? He needed to slap a smile on, and damned quick, because Zane and the others would see through him in a fucking heartbeat.

He walked into Fred's and glanced around. A loud cheer came from the back, over by the pool tables. Zane, Jacob, and Leron all started clapping as he walked over.

"The prodigal son arrives," Zane said, standing to slap him on the back.

"You're a bunch of dicks," Calum said, shaking hands with the other guys. A bottle of beer was pressed into his hand, along with a pool cue.

"So, how come you forgot?" Zane asked, leaning across the baize to set up the balls.

Not exactly the balls Calum thought he'd be playing with that night. *Or rather, Laurella would be playing with.*

"No particular reason. It's been a busy day is all."

Zane tossed a coin. "Call."

"Heads," Calum said, his mind totally on how many times he could go down on Laurella the following morning before she begged him to stop.

"You win," Zane said.

Calum lined up the cue ball and broke. Two balls immediately went into the far left and right pockets. "Stripes," he said, moving around the table to take his next shot.

Zane's keen gaze cut into Calum. "We've been doing this for six years, Calum. You've never forgotten or missed a night. Want to talk about it?"

Calum hit a bad shot and cursed. "What are you, a woman? There's nothing wrong, and even if there was, I'm not going to sit around the table drinking homemade lemonade and knitting scarves while I pour out my troubles."

Zane bent over the table and easily knocked in his first solid. He went on to sink the next two before he missed a tricky shot. He straightened and leaned on his cue while he took a swig of beer. "I meant to ask, how are you getting along with Laurella? You two manage to iron out your differences yet?"

Calum wasn't sure whether Zane was fishing or not. He schooled his expression into cold, no-nonsense stare. "For now."

"Well, try to keep the peace," Zane said, laughing. "With all the schmoozing she's been doing with that big client, I need the girl operating on top form."

"I'm sure that won't be a problem," Calum drawled.

"You haven't talked her into bed yet, then?"

"Jesus, what is this—twenty fucking questions?"

Zane held up his right hand. "Christ, what did I say?"

Calum hit another ball into the pocket. "Too fucking much." He needed to get this game over with, and quickly, before Zane tied him to a chair and shined a light in his eye, torturing him until Calum spilled every detail.

Zane frowned. "I don't know what's eating you, Calum, but either shake it off or fuck off. We don't get much downtime, and what little we do get shouldn't be spent taking chunks out of one another."

Calum ignored him. He hit another shot and missed, and to add insult to injury, the white ball slowly trickled into the corner pocket.

Zane laughed. "Jeez, you're on shitty form tonight."

"You taking your shot or what?" Calum growled.

Zane's mouth twisted, but he didn't respond. He did, however, pot the remaining balls without giving Calum a chance at a comeback. Zane's triumphant grin grated on Calum's one remaining nerve.

"If you're going to play so badly, then feel free to turn up in a foul mood next time, too."

Calum laid his cue on the table, and Jacob wandered over ready to play the next game. They'd been following this routine for years. Calum and Zane always started off, then the winner played one of the other guys. And so on. Except normally, Calum was the last man standing. Not tonight, though. His mind wasn't on the game—well, not this game anyway. He flopped into the chair next to Leron.

"You okay, man?" Leron asked. "You seem out of sorts, if you don't mind me saying."

Calum swung his beer bottle by the neck before taking a long pull. Unlike Zane, who could be as blunt as Calum, Leron had a quiet way that made it difficult to be obnoxious around him.

A cheer came from the pool table. Zane was winning the second game of the night.

"Not really in the mood for a get-together is all."

"That's not like you. Normally, we have to drag you home at the end of the night."

"How's Kayla?" Calum asked when the gold band on Leron's left hand caught the light, giving him a perfect reason to change the subject.

Leron's face lit up. "She's great. I never thought I'd say this, but marrying her is the best decision I ever made."

Calum nodded. "You snagged a good one there."

"Yeah." Leron laughed. "Better than I deserve."

Calum stared into the distance. His insides felt all wrong, like a jigsaw puzzle that had been put together and was found to have missing pieces.

"I can be discreet if you want to talk."

"Not really my thing," Calum said, his smile fleeting.

"Is it a woman?"

Calum briefly nodded.

"A special woman?"

He blew out a heavy breath. "If you'd asked me a couple weeks ago, I'd have told you I hated her."

"And now?"

He stroked his beard. "Well, let's just say I don't hate her anymore."

"And that's who you were with when Zane called?"

Another nod. "On my way back to her place."

"Ah." Leron chuckled. "No wonder you're in a bad mood. Blue balls will do that to you."

For the first time since he'd walked into the pool hall an hour earlier, Calum's mood lifted. It was difficult to remain crabby around Leron.

"Can I ask you something?" Calum said.

"Sure."

"When you asked Kayla to marry you, how did you know she was the one? I mean, how could you be sure you wouldn't meet someone you were more attracted to the following week?"

Leron laughed. "And there speaks a man who's never been in love."

Calum nodded. "True."

"I'm sure it's different for everyone, but for me, it was simple. I couldn't imagine living even one day without her. When we were apart, it was like I'd lost an arm. When we were together, I felt whole. She's my safe place to fall, my soul mate."

He laughed again. "And if you tell Zane or Jacob I just told you that, I'll nail your nuts to the wall."

Calum grinned and placed a finger over his lips. "Not a word."

"Leron," Jacob called over. "You're up."

Leron got to his feet. He started to walk over to the pool table then paused and turned around. "If you like this girl, then don't be afraid to tell her. Because if you don't, someone else might get there first."

He ambled toward Zane, aiming a high five at Jacob as he passed. Jacob flopped into the seat next to Calum. "He's killing it tonight," Jacob said, referring to Zane's pool-playing prowess. No doubt, Zane would remind them of this night repeatedly over the coming months.

"He must be. He beat me." Calum got to his feet. "Another beer?"

Jacob drained the last dregs from his bottle. "Yeah."

Calum sauntered to the bar rather than call the waitress over. It gave him five minutes alone. While he waited for the beers, he lifted his cell from his pocket. The need to text Laurella consumed him. He craved that jolt of excitement when she replied. With Leron's words of advice at the forefront of his mind, he typed a quick message.

I'm missing you.

After he pressed Send, a funny sensation came over him, sort of like the one he'd had earlier in the evening. If someone had asked him to describe it, he'd have said it was like standing on the edge of a precipice. He had to decide whether to jump and potentially crash onto the rocks below or to back away and never know whether someone would catch him at the bottom.

His cell vibrated, and her name appeared on the banner. He swiped to the left to read her message: *Miss you more.*

His stomach vaulted, and a warm feeling spread through his midsection. Calum paid for the beers and headed back over to his friends, but for every step he took, it was like an invisible thread kept tugging him back, urging him to go to her.

He forced himself to keep going. He'd set the beers on the table when Zane and Leron joined them.

"That was quick," Calum said.

Zane blew on his fingertips. "The master has arrived."

Calum snorted. "Keep dreaming."

The four of them bantered, and the evening began to feel more normal, but when his cell buzzed again and he spotted another text from Laurella, his pulse jolted: *I'm off to bed. Wanted to say goodnight. See you tomorrow.*

He glanced at his watch. Ten-thirty. Normally, these get-togethers went on well into the small hours. He faked a yawn.

"Fuck, look at Granddad over here," Jacob teased.

"Sorry," Calum said, even though he was anything but. "It's all Zane's fault. He works us like slaves."

"Bullshit," Zane said. "And even if I did, you've got more stamina than anyone else I know."

Calum yawned again. "You're right, but I'm still helping Jax out at the hotel." *Liar.* "Must be taking its toll, even on me."

Zane offered an understanding nod. "Sorry. Of course you are."

"Jax is okay, though, yeah?" Leron asked.

A twinge of guilt pinched at Calum's insides. Using his brother to further his own ends was low—but necessary. "Oh yeah. He's well. Fully recovered. I want to make sure he doesn't overdo it, though, so I try to fit in a few shifts a week."

Yep. I'm going straight to Hell. But it'll be worth it. He got to his feet. "I'm going to call it a night."

He expected Zane to give him a hard time, especially as these get-togethers were infrequent, but instead, his best friend stood and clapped him on the shoulder. "Take it easy, okay? Can't have you burning out on me."

"It's all good." Calum shook hands with Jacob and Leron. "I promise I'll be bring my A game next time."

His friends waved away his apologies, and ten seconds later, Calum found himself on the street. He paused outside the subway, removed his cell from his pocket, and sent her a response:

You're not going to bed without me. I'm on my way.

She replied instantly:

I'll be waiting.

CHAPTER 18

Laurella overslept on Monday morning, probably because Calum hadn't left until the early hours. Her mind turned to the last couple of days, and a smile stole across her face. This weekend had been the best, by far, since she'd moved to New York. After Calum had come over late on Saturday night, they'd only left the bedroom to eat or use the bathroom. Or shower —together.

They'd both agreed to keep their burgeoning relationship under wraps at work, so it was with her professional veneer fully in place that Laurella tapped on Calum's door upon arriving at the office.

"Yeah," he called out.

She poked her head inside. "Oh, sorry," she said as her gaze fell on Julie. "I didn't realize you were busy. I'll come back later."

"No need," he said. "We're done here anyway."

Julie frowned. "No, we're not. I still need to go over last week's sales figures with you."

Calum glared at her. "I said we're done. Put another meeting in my calendar for later today. We can go over the figures then."

Julie looked from Calum to Laurella then back at Calum. She shrugged and climbed to her feet. "You're the boss."

"Correct."

Julie sidled past Laurella, who smiled apologetically. Calum could be overly brusque at times. She should know, having been on the receiving end of his venomous tongue on plenty of occasions.

Julie, however, seemed remarkably untroubled by his curt manner. "Good luck, Laurella," she said, stepping into the hallway. "Try not to stab the miserable bastard. I still need him to come to the McShorey meeting with me tomorrow."

Laurella giggled. Right there was why Julie still worked for Calum. She was one of the few people who refused to let his mood swings get to her, and she gave as good as she got.

The second the door closed, Calum strode across the office. His hands cupped her face, and pinning her with his hips, he kissed her. "God, I missed you," he groaned and kissed her again.

"You saw me a few hours ago," she said, tilting her head as he nipped along her jawline. "And I thought we were keeping it professional at work."

He drew back. "I am being professional. I didn't kiss you until Julie had left."

She fixed him with a stare. "There was no need to be so rude to her. I expect you to apologize. You basically threw her out."

"That's right. So I could do this." His mouth slanted over hers, his tongue slipping between her lips. He ground his groin into her, forcing a low moan from her throat. The sound must have spurred him on because he increased the pressure of his hips.

"Is it time to go home yet?" he murmured, pressing tiny kisses to her neck. He slipped the strap on her dress down her arm, moving her bra strap out of the way, which allowed him unfettered access to trace along her shoulder with his tongue.

The hairs stood up on the back of Laurella's neck, and her head began to spin with need. "Calum, stop." She didn't want him to stop, but if he carried on, she'd do something very unprofessional involving her mouth and his cock.

"What if I say no?" he said, smirking. "Because you might say the words, Laurella, but you don't mean them."

"Of course I don't want you to stop," she said, knowing there was no point denying it. Her flushed face and short, quickened breaths gave her away. "But you agreed we'd keep work and our personal lives separate."

Calum stroked his chin thoughtfully then stepped back, giving her space to recover her poise.

"I might have to renegotiate terms, because I'm having trouble keeping my hands off you for a few minutes, let alone an entire day."

Tell me about it.

"If I can't kiss you, what can I do for you?" he asked.

"I wondered if you had any free time this morning to come to the Sorensen's pitch with me."

Calum's eyes widened in surprise. "Last time I asked you about that, you made it very clear that you'd cut off my balls if I dared poke my nose into that account until you'd nailed the initial marketing pitch."

Her face heated. She'd uttered those exact words only two weeks earlier. So much had changed in such a short space of time that it had her head spinning.

"That was before."

He grazed his teeth with his tongue. "Before what?"

She narrowed her eyes. "Stop teasing me."

He folded his arms across his chest. "I'm not teasing. I found your words cutting and hurtful, so yeah, I'm going to make you work for that apology."

"Settle in for a long wait, then," she muttered, irritated. Then she saw the twinkle in his eye. "You are a mean man."

He laughed and slipped his arms around her waist then

dropped a quick kiss on the end of her nose. "Of course I'll come. With us working together, Sorensen's doesn't stand a chance."

Calum swung Laurella up in the air the minute they rounded the corner from Sorensen's offices.

"You nailed it." He planted a kiss on her lips.

"*We* nailed it," she said. "Zane is going to be thrilled."

"I can't believe the size of the order they placed. If the first month goes well, this could become a regular thing. And it was all down to your pitch, which was the most impressive thing I've ever seen."

She arched a brow. "Are you admitting Zane was right to bring me on board?"

He smirked. "Don't get too arrogant, sweetheart. That's my job."

She laughed and slipped her hand through his arm. They walked back to their building, chattering excitedly. Once inside, they headed straight to Zane's office. To land such an influential account—well, Sorensen's had businesses all over the globe. This triumph could be the start of a major growth spurt for Necron.

Calum knocked once on Zane's door then pushed it open. He gestured for Laurella to go on in ahead of him.

"Got a minute?" Calum asked, unable to keep a smile off his face.

Zane leaned back in his chair and steepled his fingers under his chin. "When I saw the two of you together, I was inclined to say no. But as you're both smiling, it shouldn't be too much of a risk to say yes."

Calum pulled up a second chair in front of Zane's desk, and he and Laurella sat. "We have some good news. Laurella, go ahead."

His heart stuttered at the grateful smile she sent his way.

"We got the Sorensen's account," she said.

Zane's eyes widened, and his mouth parted. "You're kidding?"

Laurella briefly frowned. "I'd never joke about such a thing."

Calum grinned. "He didn't mean it like that. It's an expression of surprise."

"Oh." She made a face. "I still get confused occasionally."

"How much did they take?" Zane asked.

"Twenty percent more than our projections," Calum said.

"Holy fuck." He grimaced. "Sorry, Laurella."

"No need to apologize," she said. "This is an exciting day. The beginning of a very exciting time for Necron. I just know it."

"This calls for a celebration. We haven't had a company get-together this year, so I think this is the perfect excuse." Zane pressed the intercom that went through to his PA. "Ellie, grab your party planner and that little black book of yours. I've got a job for you."

CHAPTER 19

Laurella climbed out of the cab, careful not to trap the thin heel of her stiletto in the hem of her evening gown. Ellie, Zane's PA, had worked miracles in the last two weeks to put this event together. It had started out as a way of thanking the staff for their hard work, but in the end, Zane had expanded it to include their most treasured customers. Poor Ellie had to scale up from a gathering of between fifty and a hundred, depending on whether employees brought partners, to the eventual guest list containing close to two hundred names.

Her relationship with Calum grew by the day, but Laurella wasn't yet ready to go public. Calum had gone along with her wishes, even though he didn't like it very much. His agreement to do something he didn't want to said more about his feelings for her than any words he might utter.

She found the event room and handed her coat to the cloakroom attendant then slipped the ticket into her purse and stepped inside. She sought out Calum but couldn't spot him. She did, however, see Julie. Laurella waved.

Julie waved back, held up a glass, and mouthed "Prosecco?"

Laurella nodded and headed over to the bar area. By the time she got there, her glass of prosecco was waiting.

"You look stunning, Laurella," Julie said, giving her a quick hug. "I wish I had your Mediterranean skin tone. You can get away with much more vibrant colors, and that red looks amazing on you."

"It can be a curse," she said. "I can't wear pastels at all. They look awful. Your sky-blue dress is beautiful, and the cut is perfect for your figure."

Julie smoothed a hand over her hips. "Hides a multitude of sins, more like. My mother had what they call childbearing hips, and she passed them down to me. Bitch."

They burst out laughing. A couple of girls from finance joined them, and Julie regaled them all with stories of her parents. Laurella listened with half an ear. She continually scanned the room, waiting for Calum to appear. When he did, her breath caught in her throat.

The black tux and crisp white shirt fitted him to perfection. His hair was a little longer than his usual preferred style. It grazed the collar, and all Laurella could think about was pushing her hands through it later when she kissed the hell out of him.

He hadn't seen her yet, so she could watch him unobserved. He shook hands with several guests, his smile warm and friendly, but he still had a reserved aloofness that she recognized from their early interactions. Calum might be a complex man, but he'd allowed her to peek beneath the public persona.

She spotted Zane heading toward Calum. They shared a quick word then disappeared. Cramming down disappointment that he hadn't immediately sought her out, she turned her attention back to the group.

"What are your thoughts on our gorgeous sales director, Laurella?" Sally, one of the finance girls, asked.

Laurella's heart stuttered. *Shit.* Had they noticed her checking him out? She decided to play dumb. "Sorry?"

"Nalini and I think he's hot. I bet he's amazing in bed."

"Urgh," Julie said. "Do you mind? That's my boss."

"Oh, come on, Jules," Sally said. "Don't tell me you haven't thought about it?"

"Not even once."

Julie winked at Laurella, who was desperately trying to figure out how she could retreat… fast.

"He doesn't have the right equipment to attract me," Julie said.

Sally's brow furrowed. "Huh?"

Julie leaned in. "I'm gay," she said, clearly enjoying the embarrassment she'd caused Sally, who flushed bright red.

"Oh, shit. Sorry, Jules. I didn't know."

Julie laughed. "No need to apologize. It's not like I walk around with a flashing neon sign on my head."

Awkward moment over, Sally turned her attention back to Laurella. "So, come on, Laurella. Calum Brook. Hot or not?"

With a sinking feeling, Laurella realized—too late—that Sally was one of those girls who latched on to a subject and wouldn't let go until she'd gotten her answer. All three girls laid their interested eyes on her.

She shrugged. "Italian men are hotter," she said, hoping that by not answering the question directly, she'd get away relatively unscathed.

"So you wouldn't, you know… not even if he threw himself at your feet?"

She inwardly groaned. "Not even if he got down on his knees and begged," Laurella said, hoping that would be the end of it.

"Ms. Ricci. A word, please."

Laurella froze as Calum's deep baritone voice rumbled in her left ear. Sally gave a horrified stare while Julie grinned. Nalini simply fixed her gaze on the floor as though she were praying for it to open up and swallow her whole.

"Of course," Laurella murmured. There was still a chance he hadn't heard… wasn't there?

He took her by the elbow and propelled her forward.

Laurella glanced up. His jaw was set, and a nerve jumped in his cheek. Yep. He'd heard. And by the looks of him, he wasn't happy.

"Calum—"

"Don't say a goddamn word," he said.

As they passed through the crowds, he murmured the odd greeting but didn't stop to speak to any of the guests. They stepped outside the event room, and Calum opened an adjacent door. Inside, laid out on a large rectangular table, were the prizes and awards Zane planned to give to the top-performing employees later that evening.

Calum ushered her inside and kicked the door closed. Before Laurella could say anything, his mouth crashed down on hers. He was already hard. Whether that was from desire or anger, Laurella couldn't know. Whichever of those emotions was most prevalent, it didn't matter, because she melted beneath his kiss. His tongue played with hers, a dance she was beginning to know well. Her breathing grew heavy as he rubbed his erection against her.

And then he pulled away. He took three steps back and glared at her with a flushed face and mussed hair where Laurella had shoved her hands through it. "From the looks of you, sweetheart, I won't need to be begging anytime soon."

Agitated, she glared at him. "Don't be so childish," she snapped. "You'd rather I spilled the truth? Because if I'd answered Sally's question honestly, I'd have told her that I find you so hot I want to turn the air conditioner up whenever you're near. I'd have said that when we're apart, I crave your touch. I'd have shared that when you're inside me, nothing else matters apart from you and me and how connected we are in that moment. Is *that* what you'd rather I'd said?"

By the time she'd finished her rant, her chest heaved, and she was short of breath.

"Christ, you're beautiful when you're angry," he said. "And, yes, I'd rather you said all those things. I don't want to hide our relationship any longer, Laurella. I thought I could do this. I wanted to go along with your wishes, but then a few minutes ago, I heard a couple of guys who work for McShorey's talking about you. They were saying how stunning you are, how they planned to steal a dance later. One of them said he was going to ask you on a date. And it made me furious. I wanted to put my hands around their throats and warn them that if they laid a finger on you, I'd fucking kill them. You're mine—and I want everyone to know it."

She hesitated, but only for a second. Closing the distance between them, she flung her arms around his neck and drew his head down toward hers. This time, she kissed him, pouring every ounce of what she was feeling into the kiss. She'd been wrong to make him wait, wrong to expect him to keep secrets from his best friend, wrong to hide their relationship so that everyone thought she was fair game, like a prized cow at a cattle market.

By the time they broke apart, her lips felt swollen and raw. Undoubtedly, she'd need to reapply her lipstick. But she didn't care. What did it matter if everyone in the room next door knew she'd been thoroughly kissed for the last few minutes?

"Okay, let's go public."

Calum's answering smile took her breath away. He captured her hand, and together, they walked back into the event room. During the few minutes they'd been gone, almost everyone had arrived, and the place was packed.

"Let's get a drink," he said, towing her toward the bar.

Julie, Sally, and Nalini were standing exactly where she'd left them a few minutes earlier, and as she and Calum drew closer, Julie looked over. Her eyes dipped to where Laurella and Calum were holding hands, and they widened in surprise.

"Well, well, boss. You sly old fox," Julie said. She turned to Laurella. "And as for you, all I can say is you're one hell of an actress. How long has this been going on?"

Calum kissed Julie on the cheek. "None of your goddamn

business, you nosy bitch." He added a grin to cushion his words. He definitely had a soft spot for Julie, and at least her sexual preference made it easier for Laurella to keep her jealousy at bay. However, Nalini—and even more so, Sally—were a whole other prospect. From the way Sally shot daggers in Laurella's direction, the young finance analyst clearly was not happy that Laurella hadn't been candid when questioned before.

"We hadn't exactly planned to tell anyone, and certainly not tonight," Laurella said, facing Julie, but her words were meant more for Sally's benefit. Necron was a small company, and Laurella could do without making enemies.

"That's true." Calum slipped his hand around her waist and kissed her temple. "But I got sick of sneaking around. And I wanted to stake my claim."

Julie laughed. "Piss on your territory, you mean. Watch this one, Laurella. He has a tendency to like to own things."

Laurella chuckled while Calum whispered, "She's right. You are mine," in her ear.

She shivered. There was something delicious about the way Calum said 'mine.' Even for an independent woman like her, being wanted was addictive.

"I guess we'd better go fess up to Zane," he said, picking up his drink from the bar. "He'll get pissy if he isn't told personally that his best friend is off the market."

He led her through the crowd once more with *off the market* playing on a loop in her mind. She metaphorically hugged herself. Calum was what Papa would call 'Quite the catch.' Smart, successful, hard-working, ambitious. She'd also add—although not for Papa's ears—handsome, hot-as-all-hell, and fantastic in bed.

Goodness, was she really considering telling her family about Calum? That was a big step. The second they found out she was in a relationship, they'd expect them both to fly to Italy so everyone could grill Calum and give him the seal of approval. Or not. It could go either way. Her family had never liked

Alessandro, her former fiancé. They hadn't quite come out and said as much, but they'd never made him feel welcome. When he'd cheated on Laurella, and she'd broken off their engagement, each and every member of her family had been quick to tell her how happy they were and that they'd never thought Alessandro was good enough for their Ella.

"Zane," Calum called out, holding his free hand in the air. He sidled through a couple more people, shaking hands with one or two. Finally, they reached Zane, who homed right in on where their hands were knitted together.

"Fuck me. Does this mean what I think it means?"

Brienne, Zane's girlfriend, rolled her eyes. "Smooth, Zane. Real smooth."

Calum hitched a shoulder. "No need to make a big fuss about it. Just thought you should know."

Zane grinned. "So this is why the white flag of surrender has been waved. I wondered why I hadn't had to dodge any bullets at our recent board meetings."

"Zane!" Brienne glared at him.

"It's okay, Brie," Calum said. "We're used to him. And now we'll say no more about it."

"Well, for what it's worth, I'm pleased for you both, although clearly you got the better end of the deal, Calum." He shook Calum's hand and gave Laurella a brief hug. "My commiserations to you, lovely lady, for having to put up with this asshat."

Her boss's approval removed the last vestiges of awkwardness that starting a relationship with a coworker could bring. *Phew.* One more worry put aside.

Calum led her into the center of the dance floor. He slipped one arm around her waist, taking her hand with the other. He touched her cheek with his and began to move.

"I didn't know you could dance," she said.

"There's a lot you don't know about me."

"I can imagine."

Calum drew back, studying her face. "Have I told you how stunning you look tonight?"

She smiled. "I think your words were that you thought I was beautiful when angry."

His hand traced up from her waist to curve around her neck. He brushed his thumb beneath her earlobe, traced the tip over her cheek, and caressed her bottom lip. He applied gentle pressure until she parted her lips. When she did, he slipped the tip of his thumb inside. Laurella sucked hard, taking him all the way in. He groaned. They were standing so close it would be virtually impossible for anyone to witness their seductive dance.

She released him. He lowered his head and touched his lips to hers. "For the record, I think you're beautiful when you're angry and when you're happy. First thing in the morning and last thing at night. When you're all made up, like tonight, and when your face is clean and clear. Whether you're in a ball gown or when you're wearing sweatpants. Your kind of beauty comes from the inside, Laurella. That's why every man in this room who is not in a relationship—and even some who are—is envious of me right now. Because I'm with you."

Her heart squeezed so hard she feared it might stop beating altogether. "Oh, Calum."

"I know being with me isn't easy. I'm a complicated man. I can be overly critical, blunt to the point of causing offense, hostile at times. I'm sure I don't need to tell you any of this, because you were on the receiving end during our first weeks and months of knowing each other. But I am loyal to those I love, and I put them first. Always."

Laurella's breath caught in her throat. Had he said what she thought he had? Had he just told her he loved her? Hope blossomed in her chest. Neither of them had spoken of love, but these last few weeks had been the happiest of her life. They hadn't had the most auspicious of starts, but it was *here and now* that mattered.

Her mouth went dry as she looked up into Calum's dark-green smoldering eyes. "I adore you. Even if you do push my buttons quite a lot and sometimes make me want to hit you instead of kiss you."

It was a hell of a risk. But she'd been humiliated before and survived. One more humiliation wouldn't kill her if he recoiled from her declaration.

He cupped both hands around her face and kissed her. "How long do we have to stay here?"

She laughed. "I think Zane expects us to stick around to the very end."

"Fuck that," Calum said. "He gets another two hours max. And that's pushing it, given how much I need to be inside you."

The rest of the evening turned out to be a great success. Zane played the part of master of ceremonies beautifully, and those who won prizes and awards went home happily clutching their gifts. Necron might only be small, but Zane had the right idea when it came to staff loyalty. An employee who felt appreciated would always do more than one who felt put-upon.

They said goodnight to a few stragglers who were clearly intent on stretching out the evening—not to mention the free bar—as far as they could. Then they climbed into the back of a cab, and Calum tugged Laurella astride his lap. When he gave the driver the name of Jax's hotel instead of Laurella's apartment, she frowned.

"Why there?"

Calum grinned. "I *may* have managed to get the penthouse for the night. Jax had someone cancel at the last minute, which meant they lost their fee. So being the good brother he is, he offered it to me."

"Oh, you are so going to get laid," she whispered.

"That's the plan, beautiful." Calum locked his lips on hers.

It took about twenty minutes to reach Jax's hotel. Calum paid the driver, and like a pair of teenagers, they spilled onto the sidewalk, still kissing.

Inside, the hotel was as busy as every other time Laurella

had visited, but this time, Calum didn't stop off in the lounge area, nor did he lead her to the basement that housed his living quarters. Instead, he headed straight for the stairs. On the top floor, he turned left. He removed a key card from his wallet and inserted it into the slot.

"After you," he said, gesturing for her to go in first.

Laurella stepped inside… and gasped. The room was the epitome of contemporary luxury. Thick wall-to-wall carpeting covered the living space, upon which sat three deep couches arranged in a U shape, with myriad scattered cushions. Fresh flowers had been placed on the coffee table, and an enormous television set dominated one wall. What caught Laurella's eye, though, was what lay beyond the glass floor-to-ceiling doors.

She kicked off her shoes and curled her toes, relishing the softness of the fibers against her feet, which were sore from standing in heels for hours. She walked across the vast space and flung open the doors. The outside patio was enormous. Around the edge was a glass screen topped with oak wood. Subtle lighting provided a muted glow, but it was the large Jacuzzi sitting proudly on a raised platform that Laurella wanted to sample. And the man standing off to the side, watching her reaction, was the person she wanted to sample it with.

With her eyes on his, she slipped the spaghetti straps off her shoulders and let her dress slide to the floor. Underneath, the red lingerie she'd chosen had the desired effect on Calum. His lips parted, and his tongue swept out to dampen them. He maintained eye contact and the physical distance, but the glint deep within his emerald irises told her he was only just holding it together.

She sauntered outside, hips swaying, and climbed up the steps to the bubbling water. Reaching around her back, she unclasped her bra and dropped it beside her. She didn't need to turn around to know he'd be watching. She could almost feel his burning stare scorching her back.

She hooked her fingers into her panties and slowly, oh so

slowly, slid them down her legs. Once fully naked, she dipped her toe into the deliciously warm water. Sinking all the way down, she turned on her front and rested her chin on her folded arms. Calum hadn't moved.

"Aren't you coming?" she called out.

His steps toward her were leisurely and deliberate. He unfastened his bow tie and let it dangle on either side of his collar. Her belly somersaulted. *Christ.* He looked stunning standing there, like her own personal James Bond.

He undid the top button on his shirt. "Oh, I'm coming," he said, sitting on the side of the Jacuzzi. "I'm coming hard inside you."

She reached a finger inside the waistband of his pants and tugged. "Then get in, lover boy."

His smile, when it came, was slow and sexy. He captured her chin and tilted her head back. His lips brushed hers, but when she raised herself out of the water to deepen the kiss, he pulled back.

"I'll get the drinks." He wandered back inside.

Screw the drinks she wanted to yell. Calum loved stretching the anticipation, and so did she. It was still frustrating, though.

He returned five minutes later, holding a silver bucket with a bottle of champagne sticking out the top in one hand and two crystal flutes in the other. Setting the glasses on the rim of the Jacuzzi, he expertly popped the cork then poured the sparkling liquid into the glasses.

"To us," he said, passing one to her.

"To you getting out of those clothes and joining me in here."

He chuckled. "So impatient, my Laurella."

"I won't be yours for much longer if you don't put out the flames you started earlier tonight."

He rose to his feet, grinning. With painstaking languidness, he unfastened each button on his shirt to reveal the flat, hard muscles beneath. It slipped from his shoulders, and he let it fall to the floor. She growled in frustration, but all that did was make him go more slowly. When he finally dropped his dress trousers, his erection sprang free.

Laurella knelt up and gripped his length. "Get in here this second, or I'm ripping this off."

Calum cocked an eyebrow. "Such violence from one who professes to adore me."

"I may change my mind about that if you don't stop teasing."

He stepped into the Jacuzzi. Once seated, he tugged her astride his lap with her thighs straddling his. "Here's what's going to happen tonight," he said, his voice low and sultry, his teeth nibbling her earlobe. "I'm fucking you in here, then I'm fucking you on the enormous bed that's waiting for us in the bedroom. And providing you haven't passed out on me, I'm fucking you from behind, with the view of the city around us."

Her stomach flipped, and she automatically flexed her thighs.

He tilted his head back and smirked. "From the way you're clenching those delicious legs around me, I take it you approve?"

"Stop talking." She put her mouth on him and felt his lips curving into a smile against hers. He lifted her—such an easy task with the hot, bubbling water acting as a buoyancy aid—and slid her down over his erection. Thank God they'd both been checked out and could ditch the condoms. The all-new sensation of being submerged in water brought an added intensity. Once he'd filled her to the hilt, she went to move, but he gripped her hips, stilling her.

"Let me feel you," he said. "Because the minute you move, I'm going to come, and I don't want to yet."

She smiled. "Whatever you want."

"Oh, sweetheart, I love it when you obey me."

Laurella snorted. "Careful. I've got the upper hand here."

Calum raised an eyebrow. "Oh yeah? How?"

Laurella clenched her inner muscles and gently rocked her

hips. Once. Calum groaned, and his hands tightened around her waist. His cock jerked inside her.

"Have I answered your question?" she asked sweetly.

"Yes," he hissed.

"Am I in charge?"

"Beautiful, you own me."

"Can I have that recorded?"

Calum threw back his head and laughed. "Move, woman. I need to come."

Laurella gripped his broad shoulders, raising and lowering herself. The water sloshed over the sides of the Jacuzzi, and as she went faster, the waves grew in size. At the rate they were going, there wouldn't be any water left. His hand dipped between their bodies, and he pinched her clit hard. It was all she needed to tumble over into orgasm. She threw her head back, incoherent mumblings falling from her lips. Calum's panting grew in volume as he took control of the speed and angle. Then he groaned loudly.

"God, I love you," he murmured against her neck, his arms tightening around her as though he was scared she'd disappear.

Her chest constricted, and her throat grew thick. He'd actually said the words. And his bravery freed her to be brave, too.

"I love you, too. So very much."

CHAPTER 20

Laurella tapped on Zane's office door, a stack of papers beneath her arm. When he called out, she entered and gave him a bright smile.

"Ready to take a final look through the plans?" she asked, referring to their upcoming meeting with the senior leadership of Sorensen's. Since her and Calum's initial pitch and their first delivery, which had gone extremely well, they'd made great strides in building the relationship. If today went according to plan, they had a good chance of Sorensen's signing a large contract. It was a huge deal for Necron, one that would grow the company by at least twenty-five percent, not to mention that Sorensen's had a lot of influence in other markets that Necron was targeting.

"I certainly am." He pointed to the seat opposite. "You could save a tree and bring your iPad, Laurella."

"I like old-fashioned paper."

Zane smiled. "Fair enough. Did Calum make those adjustments to the pricing model?"

"Yes. It's all in here." She handed the papers to Zane and took a seat, smoothing her skirt beneath her.

"And is Eric on board?" Zane asked, referring to their chief financial officer.

She nodded. "I'd go so far as to say he's rather excited about the potential this deal will bring to the bottom line."

"Money is the only thing I've found that Eric does get excited about. But that's what makes him a great CFO."

Zane flicked through the presentation. He made the odd note in the margin and gave an occasional "Mmm."

Laurella waited patiently.

"It looks great," he finally said. "They'd be crazy to turn their noses up at that deal."

"They would, although from what I can glean, it's our supply chain they're concerned with. The fact we made the first delivery complete and on time will have done us a huge amount of good, though. Now we just need you to convince them we can scale up."

Zane blew on the ends of his fingers. "Get ready for a master class."

Laurella laughed. She loved working with Zane, and since this lead had come to fruition, she'd had the opportunity to study and learn from him up close. Zane might come across as a bit of a joker, but when it came to Necron, he was deadly serious. The minute the Sorensen's team walked into the boardroom, the joking would end, and he would settle down to business.

She rose to leave. "Okay, well, I'll grab some lunch and see you in the boardroom at three."

"Hang on," Zane said, forcing Laurella to sit again. "You've been with us almost six months now. I'd like your views on how it's going. Do you think you made the right decision coming here?"

Laurella nodded. "I love it, Zane. I miss my family, of course, and Italy, but I wanted a new challenge." She smiled. "Necron has certainly been that. I never wanted to stay in one company my whole career. I want to test myself, to grow in directions other than marketing. To add value and make a difference. I'm achieving all those things here."

"That's good. Because from my perspective, you've been an amazing addition to the team. A bit of a bumpy start," he said, teasing. "But overall, you coming here has been really valuable."

"I'm glad you think so."

"And what about Calum?"

Laurella frowned. "What about him?"

"Things going well between you two?"

Her frown deepened. "I'm not sure how that's relevant."

"Calum's my best friend as well as a valuable member of the team here."

"And…?"

Zane grinned. "I admire your directness while maintaining a professional façade. I don't mean to overstep the mark. It's just that these past couple of months, he's been so happy. I've never seen him like that in all the years we've known each other. I hope it lasts, that's all."

Laurella kept her gaze even, although her insides did a double flip at his comment about Calum's happiness. "My work and my personal life are two separate things. It complicates matters that Calum works here, but from my perspective, I have never let our relationship affect my work."

Zane shook his head. "Shit, I'm sorry. I didn't mean to insinuate that at all." He rubbed a hand over the top of his head. "Clearly I need to work on my management skills. Forget I said anything."

"Can I make a suggestion?" Laurella asked, taking pity on how the turn in conversation had made Zane uncomfortable. He was a person she liked and respected. She didn't want him to feel awkward around her.

"Shoot," he said.

"Calum is *your* best friend. If you want to know how things are going with his girlfriend, I suggest you ask him." She smiled warmly to let him know she hadn't been offended by his clunky questioning.

Zane returned her smile. "Fair point."

She rose from her chair once more. "I'll see you at three."

Laurella sat on Zane's left, her palms sweating from nerves and anxiety. This was the first big deal she'd brought to the table, and it had to go well. If they got Sorensen's on board, she'd be able to use that as leverage in the discussions she was having with other companies.

She fiddled with her notebook, her pen, her hair, her fingernails. Calum cleared his throat. She lifted her chin. He winked, the movement so quick she almost missed it. She flashed him the briefest of smiles. He knew her so well. He must have guessed she was panicking. She'd put so much work into this deal. They all had. To come out the other side with nothing would be devastating.

After the presentations were over, the lead negotiator from Sorensen's—Brad Novak, a hard-nosed but fair guy—asked a few questions which their team were able to answer with ease.

"I think we can do a deal, Zane," Brad said. "I'll get my legal team to draft the documentation and get it over to you as soon as possible so your lawyers can crawl all over it, too."

Laurella suppressed a whoop, crossing her gaze to Calum, who was also having difficulty restraining his excitement. Zane and Brad shook on the deal, and Brad rose to leave.

"Oh, one more thing." Brad turned to Laurella. "I hope you don't mind, Ms. Ricci, but I'd like to put one of my top marketing guys on this full-time to work with you in developing the brand and advertising campaign to go with the launch. I hope that works for you?"

A thrill ran through her. She'd hoped he'd commit some

resource from their side. It would make getting agreement on the direction she wanted to go in much easier.

"I have no issue with that at all. I look forward to working closely with your team."

"Great. I'll be in touch about the finer details." He shook hands with Zane once more. "Let's get this deal done."

And with that, the Sorensen's team left the boardroom. Once they were out of earshot, a broad grin spread across Zane's face. "We've done it."

"Thanks to Laurella," Calum said, his expression one of intense pride.

"It was a team effort," Laurella said. "I'm so pleased."

"Calls for a celebration," Zane said. "Drink?"

"Rain check?" Calum replied.

Zane glanced between him and Laurella. Then he laughed. "I guess three's a crowd. Go on. Get out of here, both of you."

Calum stood and walked around to Laurella's side of the table. He took her hand, a public display of affection he rarely used at work unless they were alone in her office or his. He lifted her hand to his lips and pressed a soft kiss to her palm. "Come on, beautiful. There's a cocktail at our favorite bar with your name on it."

It didn't take long to reach Jax's hotel. Inside, the lounge area was quiet, although at almost six in the evening, that wasn't too unexpected.

"This is a nice surprise," Jax said, placing two napkins on the bar.

"We're celebrating."

"The pitch went well?"

Calum grinned and slipped his arm around Laurella's shoulders. "Thanks to this amazing woman, yes."

"Then drinks are on the house."

"What do you want, beautiful?" Calum asked as he pulled out a bar stool for Laurella.

"Surprise me," she said.

Jax grinned. "Ah, someone who appreciates my creative talents."

"You'll regret that," Calum said. "Jax has been known to mix the most disgusting concoctions when left to his own devices."

"I take offense at that," Jax said.

"Truth hurts," Calum hit back.

Laurella chuckled. "Every time I come here, I'm always reminded of my family. We can bicker with the best of them."

"I'm looking forward to meeting them," Calum said as Jax poured all manner of alcohol into a cocktail mixer.

"Be careful what you wish for," Laurella said. "My family have a fearsome questioning technique with any would-be suitors."

"I think I'd be up to the task."

A sudden urge to have her family meet the man who'd become so important in her life rushed through her. She tilted her head to the side. "Okay, lover boy. How about we fly to Italy in late August? The Sorensen's deal should be well underway by then, and as long as we're contactable, Zane shouldn't have too much of a problem with us both taking a vacation at the same time."

Calum slipped a hand around the back of her neck, his thumb brushing the soft skin there. "Sounds like a plan."

Jax placed a tall fluted glass in front of her. "Try that. And if you like it, I'm putting it on the menu. I'll name it after you."

"Really?" She took a sip. "That's strong but delicious."

"Just like you," Calum said.

"Smooth talker," she responded with a laugh.

Jax set down Calum's drink and discreetly moved away, giving them privacy.

"Are you really okay with Sorensen's teaming you up with someone on their side?" Calum said.

She nodded. "Of course. Why wouldn't I be?"

Calum shrugged. "What if they're a pain in the ass?"

"I have some experience in dealing with men like that."

He laughed. "Seriously, though. What if they're difficult to work with, or you can't agree on the right direction to go in?"

"Again," Laurella said, "I've got some experience in that area."

Calum narrowed his eyes. "Carry on teasing me, Ricci, and you won't get laid tonight."

She snorted. "As if. One glimpse of my garter belt, and you'll be putty in my hands."

He ran a finger up the outside of her thigh, gently pushing her skirt upward. "You're wearing a garter belt?"

She slapped his hand away. "I might be."

He picked up both their drinks, stood, and began to walk away. "See you later, Jax."

Laurella scrambled off the chair and went after him. "Where are you going?"

"*We're* going downstairs. And *I'm* going to slowly undress you and then peel that garter belt off with my teeth."

CHAPTER 21

"All set?" Calum asked, opening the door to the boardroom. They were about to meet the representative Brad Novak had arranged to be their opposing number within Sorensen's.

"I think so." Laurella set her notebook and pen in front of her. Nervous tension bit at her insides, although she couldn't understand why. The worst was over. They'd secured the deal.

"Relax." Calum reached across the table to still her hands.

She took a deep, cleansing breath, blowing out as Ellie walked in, juggling a tray of coffees.

"Laurella, Calum—Mr. Novak and his colleague are here. Is it okay to show them in?"

"Please, Ellie," she said, gratefully taking one of the coffees.

Calum took another.

Ellie disappeared, returning a few seconds later with Brad Novak in tow. Laurella gave him a warm, welcoming smile— and then her attention fell on his companion, who was a step behind.

Bile rose from her stomach, burning a passage to her throat. A piercing internal scream vibrated in her ears, and sweat drenched her skin even as an icy chill swept over her. *Oh God, no.* It couldn't be.

She couldn't speak, couldn't move. Her heart thumped against her ribcage. *Thud. Thud. Thud.* The heartbeats escalated in speed and intensity.

"Laurella, Calum, it's good to see you again." Brad shook hands with Calum, but when Laurella held hers tight to her sides—because she was frozen in place—a frown drifted across his face.

"Glad to have you here, Brad," Calum said, clearly oblivious to Laurella's terror.

"This is Alberto Vorino," Brad said.

"*Ciao.*" The bastard dared to touch Calum's hand. She curled her fingers into fists, digging her nails into her palms. "Good to meet you."

Vorino's focus cut to Laurella. "*Ciao, bella.* It's wonderful to see you again, Laurella."

Calum narrowed his eyes, and then he smiled. *He smiled!*

"Oh, of course," Calum said, sending a teasing grin in her direction. "You two used to work together."

"Indeed," Vorino said. "Laurella was a wonderful member of my team, although we didn't work together long. I always knew she had so much potential. I'm delighted to see that potential fulfilled."

Still, she sat there, mute. The words refused to come. Fear was a strange thing. She felt as if she'd been put in shackles that made it impossible to move, even though every fiber of her being was screaming for her to run—and never come back.

"Laurella?" Calum's voice broke through her paralysis, a puzzled expression on his face. Her neck felt stiff, and she struggled to lift her chin and meet his gaze.

"Yes?"

"Are you all right? You look awfully pale." The concern was prevalent in his voice, in his posture, in the way his eyes bored into hers.

Stai calmo. *Stay calm. Breathe.*

She pasted on a smile, but it felt all wrong. It didn't belong there. "I'm fine." She forced herself to face Vorino. "What kind words. Thank you." Her tongue felt too thick in her mouth, and her voice sounded strange to her ears.

Vorino smirked, the sides of his mouth curving upward. The bastard. He knew *exactly* what he'd done, yet there he was, pretending everything was okay.

"I know we didn't have the most auspicious of goodbyes, but I can forget it—if you can."

Forget it? She'd never forget what he'd done to her. If she lived to be a hundred, it would remain with her. Calum had soothed her ravaged soul. He'd shown her tenderness and love. He'd made her believe in fairy tales. But sitting there, facing the man who'd brutally attacked her and unable to utter a word, she felt the hole Calum had filled in her heart tear open with such force that she struggled for breath.

"It was a long time ago. I'm sure we can be professional." That wasn't her speaking. It couldn't be. Who was this imposter, this woman who managed to calmly sit there without launching across the table and scratching Vorino's eyes out until he bled? *Like he made me bleed.*

"Oh, that's right." Calum laughed. "She took your job at Spirito. No wonder the atmosphere has turned a touch cool in here."

Brad looked over at Laurella. "Are we going to have a problem, Ms. Ricci?"

From the corner of her eye, she saw Calum staring at her, an expression of concern on his face. Dredging up every ounce of strength she still had within her, she shook her head. "Not at all. Alberto has always been a very talented marketer. I'm sure we'll make a very good team."

Over my dead body. Or preferably over yours, you utter bastard.

"Excellent," Brad said. "Then let's get to work, shall we?"

While the three men discussed the best way to manage the account, Laurella's mind whirred, desperately searching for a way out of this untenable situation. She came to only one conclusion: if Vorino stayed on this account, she couldn't.

But how would she explain it to Calum and Zane? She couldn't tell them the truth. It was too painful. Too *personal*. She might be in love with Calum, but only Papa and the CEO of Spirito knew the details of that terrible time. If she told Calum, it would taint their relationship. He'd say it was okay, of course. That he felt the same about her as he ever had. That he still loved her. But they were just words, because once he knew, every time he touched her, every time they made love, he'd see Vorino and the part of Laurella he'd stolen that she would never get back.

No, however she solved this situation, the truth wasn't possible. She'd have to figure out some other reason why she and Vorino couldn't work together. But no matter how hard she searched her mind, she couldn't come up with a plausible excuse.

Laurella struggled through the next hour in a daze. Every time Vorino opened his mouth, she found herself digging her fingernails into her palms so hard she drew blood. She barely paid attention, the words spoken by the men around the table reaching her through a kind of fog. Calum shot the odd confused glance her way, but when she remained like a statue, he led the meeting, saving her—and the deal with Sorensen's.

She came to when Brad Novak got to his feet, only because the chair he was sitting on scraped loudly against the wooden floor. Relief rushed through her. Soon, *he'd* be gone, and she could think again. *Breathe again.* She could strategize and plan her escape from this account. It seemed impossible—*was* impossible. But regardless, she needed to find a way to make it happen.

"I'm looking forward to working with you again, Laurella." Vorino's voice was like a dagger to her heart.

The man had broken her once. He wasn't going to break her

again. She kicked up her chin, steeled her mind and, somehow, managed to form her lips into the semblance of a smile.

"Likewise," she murmured, glaring at the man with barely veiled hatred.

The bastard knew how difficult this was for her. It was right there in his eyes. They held not a trace of regret. It was the same expression he'd worn after he'd destroyed her life. He had refused to believe he'd done anything wrong.

"We'll be in touch," Brad said, shaking Calum's hand. He nodded curtly to Laurella.

"I'll see you out," Calum said.

Laurella began to gather her things when Calum said, "Wait here for me, Laurella. I won't be long."

Dread crept over her like an icy chill, further numbing her brain. *And so it begins.* Calum would want to know what had happened to the excited, driven woman who'd been at the forefront of this deal and why she had turned into this fool—this quiet, uninvolved nonparticipant—in front of their most important new client.

She drifted over to the window and stared down at the busy street below. New York was an enormous city with millions of people living in Manhattan, but there wasn't room for her and Vorino. Why had he come back now? Maybe he'd seen her achieving her dreams and decided to destroy everything she'd worked so hard for—his way of sticking it to her in a final hateful act because he blamed her for the fact that he'd lost his job at Spirito.

Calum burst back into the boardroom, slamming the door behind him. "What the fuck is going on?"

Laurella jumped but remained with her back to him. She couldn't look him in the eye in case he read the truth within hers.

"Not my best day," she said, hoping to inject a bit of humor even as she wanted to throw herself into his arms and blurt out the whole sorry mess. In her dreams, he'd stroke her hair, kiss her temple, and tell her he'd make everything okay. Except this wasn't a dream. It was the worst kind of nightmare. And Calum couldn't help her. No one could.

"A fucking understatement, Laurella. Jesus, Brad just questioned whether you're the right person to work on this account."

Her pulse jolted. Would it be that easy? "Maybe I'm not," she said.

"What the hell does that mean?"

She didn't reply.

Calum made a frustrated noise. "Look at me," he demanded.

She shook her head, tears pricking at her eyes. She blinked furiously until they receded.

Calum appeared at her side. He gripped her arms, turning her until they were standing toe-to-toe. She kept her head bent. He gently tilted up her chin. "Talk to me, please. You were fine until Vorino appeared. Is this because you're embarrassed that you tried to seduce him and then took his job at Spirito?"

He finished with a grin—and she took a knife to the heart. The room began to spin. Did he think so little of her? Did he believe she'd attempt to sleep with Vorino just to get on the next rung of the ladder? *Oh my God.* The man she thought she loved didn't know her at all.

She pushed hard against his chest. "Get your hands off me!"

His smile fell. "Laurella…"

"You think I tried to seduce that disgusting excuse for a human being? Oh, of course that's what you'd believe. Vorino is a master manipulator. A man whose lies trip off his tongue so easily, so convincingly. But you? I thought better of you. Turns out I was wrong."

She clamped a hand over her mouth as fear ripped through her. She'd said too much. No, no, no. She needed to get out of there.

She made a run for the door. Calum got there first. He stood with his back against it, barring her way.

"Wait. Just wait. Talk to me."

She shook her head. "Let me go, Calum."

"Not until you talk to me."

"Let me go!" She shoved him.

Calum was a big man, and he could easily have held his ground, but he must have read the desperation and fear in her tone because he moved to the side. She wrenched open the door.

Calum clasped her arm. "You're scaring me. I'll let you go for now. But we are having this conversation, whether you want to or not."

She averted her eyes, and when his hand fell to his side, she left the room. On wobbly legs, she managed to make it down the hallway. The moment she closed her office door behind her, she broke down. Her legs gave way beneath her, and she sank to the floor. Silent tears flowed. She wanted to bawl loudly but couldn't risk attracting attention. Everything was falling apart. She couldn't think straight, her mind a fog of fear and terror.

Eventually, she staggered to her feet, dried her face as best she could with some wipes, and grabbed her purse. She tentatively opened her office door. Apart from a couple of employees heading toward the kitchen to grab a cup of coffee, the hallway was quiet. She slipped outside and headed for the elevators, the whole time expecting to hear Calum's concerned voice behind her, but she made it to the street without interruption.

She needed to come up with a plan. And fast.

CHAPTER 22

L aurella let herself into her apartment and closed the door. After making sure the deadbolt and chain were securely fastened, she dragged a chair over and stuck it in front of the door—a habit she'd abandoned since coming to New York, but now that *he* was back, the superstition was back, too. At least with the chair there, if anyone broke in, the clatter would alert her, giving her vital seconds that could make all the difference to her safety.

Her legs were still trembling as she made her way over to the kitchen. She opened the cabinet where she kept a small amount of alcohol. Spotting a bottle of whiskey that Calum had brought over a couple of weeks earlier because he often liked a tipple before bedtime, she grabbed it and poured three fingers into a glass.

Her heart ached when her thoughts turned to Calum. Nothing would ever be the same now. While her secret had always existed, it had been buried deep enough for her to pretend it had never happened. But that terrible period from her past had burst into her present, bringing chaos and turmoil and misery along with it.

She collapsed onto the couch and sipped at her drink. What

should she do? The same question was on a loop inside her mind, but each time it came around, she found no answers. One thing was certain, though—Calum wouldn't let this lie. He might not have stopped her leaving the boardroom, but his intention had been there in the flashing of his eyes and the firm set of his jaw. He'd want to know everything. She couldn't lie, yet she couldn't tell him the truth either.

Tears threatened to fall once more. She closed her eyes and took a deep breath, trying desperately to calm the storm brewing inside. Her earlier questions came back to haunt her. Why now? Vorino must have known she was working at Necron. Was that why he'd turned up at Sorensen's? She should have asked how long he'd been working for Brad, but she'd been so shell-shocked at his arrival that she'd barely been able to summon the ability to breathe, let alone address her tormentor.

Her cell rang, but she didn't answer. It was probably Calum, and she wasn't ready to answer his questions. The ring tone stopped, only to start up again. And then it happened a third time.

Laurella pushed herself to her feet. Her legs felt stiff, and her back ached, not to mention the oncoming migraine stabbing behind her eyes, all brought on by stress, no doubt. She snatched up her cell, readying herself for Calum's onslaught.

Except it wasn't Calum calling. It was Caterina.

"Ella," her sister said. "You have to come. Papa's had a heart attack."

Laurella ran into the departures hall at JFK. She headed straight for the Air France desk to pick up her ticket. She'd had to pay a small fortune for a business-class fare, but none of the other airlines had seats until the following day.

There was a short line in front of her. She checked her

watch. The flight left in an hour. She'd be cutting it close, considering the heavy security she'd need to navigate.

"Excuse me," she said to the lady at the front of the line. "My flight leaves in an hour. I only need to pick up my ticket. I wonder if I might go first."

"Shouldn't have left it so late," came the reply as the woman turned her back and began talking to the ticketing agent once more.

Tears welled up behind her eyes, and a sob caught in her throat. "My father had a heart attack." She pushed her ID and reference number across the desk. "Please. Get me my ticket."

The woman had the grace to blush. "Sorry. Of course you can cut in."

Clutching her ticket tightly between her fingers, she ran toward security. By the time she reached her boarding gate, the area was empty. She thrust her ticket and passport at the gate agent, who tutted but at least let her board the flight.

She collapsed into her seat, waving away the offer of a glass of champagne before takeoff. And then it occurred to her that she hadn't told Calum or Zane where she was going. *Shit.* She'd been so panicked after Caterina's call that she'd thrown some things into a bag and jumped straight into a cab.

Taking the coward's way out, she switched off her cell and dropped it into her purse. As soon as she landed, she'd text Zane and let him break the news to Calum, because she simply couldn't bear to. At least the distance would give her some time to work out how on earth she should deal with Alberto Vorino.

CHAPTER 23

Calum exited the elevator on Laurella's floor. He strode down the hallway and knocked on her door. He'd done as she'd asked—given her space. But after three hours had passed without her contacting him, and when he hadn't been able to find her at work, he figured she'd gone home.

He knocked again. No answer.

"Laurella," he called out. "Open the door. We need to talk."

Silence.

"Laurella," he said again, his voice rising in volume, partly through annoyance and partly in case she was in another part of the apartment and couldn't hear him.

Still no answer.

He pounded hard with his fists. "Open the fucking door!"

When she still didn't answer, he removed a multi-tool device from his pocket. She'd given him no choice. Picking locks was something he'd been expert at in his younger years. He'd given it up a long time ago, and although he was seriously overstepping the mark—not to mention breaking the law—something was niggling at the back of his mind. He'd apologize later, and if she wanted to press charges for breaking and entering, he'd take whatever punishment came his way.

It didn't take long before the lock clicked. Pushing open the door, he called her name again. He slipped inside and quickly scanned around, poking his head inside her bedroom. The apartment was definitely empty.

Where the hell are you?

He was about to leave when a piece of paper lying on an occasional table caught his eye. He picked it up. Written in Laurella's neat handwriting was what appeared to be a flight number, followed by a time. He grabbed his cell and punched the letters and numbers into Google. The results returned immediately. *Fuck!* He checked his watch. *Goddamn it, Laurella.* The flight had already left for Italy. She'd run. She'd panicked over whatever the hell had gone on between her and Alberto Vorino and shot back home. Away from him. Without saying a fucking word.

He would *not* allow her to run away from this issue or from him. She was going to tell him what was going on in that beautiful mind of hers whether she damn well wanted to or not.

He closed up, making a mental note to talk to Cole about getting her some decent locks, because he'd broken in far too easily.

Calum didn't even knock on Zane's door, just launched straight inside. Fortunately, Zane was alone.

"Come in, why don't you?" he said with a sarcastic grin.

"I need Laurella's address."

Zane snorted. "Have you had a lobotomy? You spend every spare minute at her place."

"Her address in Italy."

Zane frowned. "Why would you need that? What's going on?"

"We had the meeting with Brad. He brought along the

colleague he wants Laurella to work with, a guy named Alberto Vorino."

Zane nodded. "I know. Vorino's got a fantastic reputation as a branding expert. It'll be a good partnership between the two of them."

"You're not aware of their history?"

"What history?"

Calum updated him on what he'd heard, how the word on the street was that Laurella had basically stolen Vorino's job and then had him removed from the company. He ended by briefing Zane on how the meeting had gone and how weird Laurella had been the entire time.

"Fucking marvelous," Zane said. "This could ruin the whole deal."

"There's more to this, though," Calum said. "My radar is firing like crazy. Something's off. And I'm even more convinced after what I found at Laurella's apartment." He pushed the piece of paper across Zane's desk.

Zane read it, his frown deepening. "This looks like a flight number."

"It is. I'm guessing that Laurella is already on that flight to Italy."

"Fuck!" Zane slammed his fist on his desk. "What the hell is wrong with her?"

"That's what I'm going to find out. Hence, I need her address in Italy."

"You're going to follow her?"

"Damn right I am. The woman I'm in love with has just run out on me over an ex-coworker and didn't even have the courtesy to tell me why. She owes me answers, and I'm going to get them."

He didn't share how much she'd scared him when they'd argued. He believed he'd fucked up in a major way, even if he didn't understand how. The look on her face when he'd accused her—albeit jokingly—of trying to seduce Vorino would haunt him to his grave.

Zane's frown smoothed. "You're in love with her?"

Calum grimaced. "Can you focus please and get me her address?"

"You realize I'd be breaking several data-protection laws."

"I don't care."

With a sigh, Zane walked across to a tall filing cabinet in the corner of his office. After rifling through several folders, he found what he was looking for.

"Her résumé." He passed Calum two sheets of paper. "Her address is at the top."

Calum clapped his friend on the arm. "I owe you."

"Call me when you get there."

Laurella strode through the arrivals hall at Malpensa Airport in Milan. She secured her place in the long line of travelers waiting for taxis then put in a call to Caterina. Her sister answered immediately, and despite her best efforts, Laurella could hear the strain in Caterina's voice.

"Are you here, Ella?"

"Yes. I'm waiting for a taxi. I'll come straight to the hospital. How is he?"

"Stable. Mama won't leave his side, though, so I'm hoping you'll have some luck persuading her to take a break."

"I'll do my best."

Being the eldest of the Ricci children, Laurella had always been the one her siblings looked up to—the sister who would fix things when they went wrong, the one they all confided in. Yet when she'd needed someone to confide in, she hadn't felt able to turn to them, because she hadn't wanted them to realize she was fallible. No, Papa had been the one she'd reached out to. Her wonderful father who, right at that moment, was fighting for his life.

Tears threatened, but she quickly blinked them away. She needed to remain strong for her family. "Are the boys all there?" she asked, referring to her brothers who, at twenty-six, twenty-four, and twenty-two were hardly boys, but she still thought of them as her little brothers. "And Alessia?"

"We're all here. I can't wait to see you, *bella*."

Laurella's heart squeezed. "Me, too. I've missed you, Caterina."

"Just hurry. We all need you."

By the time she hung up with her sister, she found herself at the front of the line. She slipped into the back of the lead taxi and gave the address of the hospital. She'd landed at rush hour, so the travel time into Milan took much longer than usual. Bumper-to-bumper traffic reminded her of New York. A twinge of anxiety as she thought about what Calum would do when he discovered she'd gone pricked at her insides. She missed him already, but she needed to get used to being without him because he couldn't be hers anymore. Vorino had ruined that possibility. She'd thought long and hard on the flight over about how she could remain in her post at Necron but had come to the conclusion that it wouldn't be possible. And that was why, as soon as she'd landed, she'd dropped a text to Zane, tendering her resignation. She had no other option than to leave New York and return to Italy. At least she'd have her family to support her, although she'd also need to come up with a good reason to tell them why she was giving up on her dreams. Severe homesickness should work, although Papa would see right through her lies.

If Papa survived…

She pressed her knuckles against her sternum as pain shot through her at the idea of losing her father. He'd been the mainstay of her whole life, the man she'd always looked up to, whose shoulder she'd cried on when boys at school had tugged on her braids. He was the man who'd laughed with her at silly come-dies on TV—the man whose arms she'd run into when she'd scraped her knee. She loved her mama with all her heart, but she'd always been a daddy's girl.

By the time the taxi pulled up outside the entrance to the hospital, Laurella was gripped by a combination of fear and apprehension. The thought of seeing her strong, capable father committed to a hospital bed with wires and tubes monitoring his heart was something she wanted to run from. Except she couldn't. Her whole family was relying on her to be the one to keep it together.

As she approached the reception desk, her hands started shaking. Delayed shock, no doubt. She hadn't had time to think about things after Caterina's call. Instead, she'd switched into practical mode. Only when she was mere minutes away from the reality of the situation did it really start to hit her. She must have appeared pale beneath her olive skin, because the recep-tionist gave her a concerned once-over.

"Are you all right?" she asked.

The familiarity of hearing her mother tongue filled Laurel-la's eyes with tears. "I'm here to see Matteo Ricci. He was brought in yesterday with a heart attack."

After a few clicks of her mouse, the receptionist nodded. "Here we are." She gave Laurella directions to the *high-depen-dency unit*—three little words that sent fear coursing through her heart.

She arrived at the unit, and something about the quiet effi-ciency with which the nurses bustled around settled her anxiety. This was the right place for Papa to be. She caught the attention of a nurse, who showed her to her father's room.

Laurella hesitated, resting her palm against the door. She needed a moment to collect herself. After a few seconds, she breathed in deeply and went inside.

Six pairs of eyes swiveled toward the door. A strangled noise came from her mama as she scrambled to her feet. Laurella found herself crushed in her mother's arms, and moments later, her siblings all crowded around, each one hugging and kissing her. But the reunion was a hushed one. Everyone spoke in undertones, conscious of Papa lying prostrate in his hospital bed.

"I'm so glad you're here," Mama said, her eyes glistening. She squared her jaw, trying to hold it together for the sake of her children, but the tears fell anyway.

Laurella kissed her mother's cheek, tasting the saltiness of Mama's tears on her lips. "How is he?"

"They've sedated him to give his heart a chance to rest. They're hopeful he'll make a full recovery."

"Thank God," Laurella said.

Her mother captured her hand and led her to the bed. Laurella choked back a sob as she bent over her father. His eyes were tightly closed, and although he looked peaceful, the heart attack had clearly taken its toll. His normally healthy complexion was pale and wan, and his skin seemed thinner.

"Hi, Papa." She kissed him, too, and gently squeezed his arm. The eldest of her brothers, Franco, brought over a chair and, with his hand on her shoulder, eased her into it. She gave him a grateful smile and covered his hand with hers.

"Good to see you, Ella," Franco said. "We've missed you."

Emotion swelled within her. Soon, she'd be back in the bosom of her family permanently, but the thought didn't bring her joy. Instead, an intense sadness rushed through her. She didn't want to leave New York, and more importantly, she didn't want to leave Calum. But that bastard, Vorino, had given her no choice. He might be chasing her out of her adopted home, but she wouldn't let him win. She'd leave with her head held high, even if inside, she was crying rivers of tears.

"Would you all mind if I had a moment alone with Papa?" she said, making eye contact with each member of her family.

They all nodded in understanding. Even Mama. They knew

the special relationship Laurella had always had with their father, and none of them resented her for it.

Her mama and siblings shuffled from the room, leaving Laurella alone with her father. She caught his hand and pressed his palm to her cheek. He didn't even stir. The medication must have been keeping him deeply sedated. Good. She didn't want him awake to hear what she had to say. She wanted to spill her confession without seeing fear and worry cloud his expression and darken his eyes.

"Oh, Papa. He's back. Alberto Vorino has turned up in New York. He's working for a company that Necron is partnering with, and worse, I'm supposed to work alongside him. Except I can't, Papa. I've tried to be strong. I've really tried, but I can't see a way out other than to come home to Italy." A sob caught in her throat. "I've failed you, Papa. I'm so sorry. So very sorry."

Until that point, she'd kept it together, but telling her father opened the dam of emotion. She clamped a hand over her mouth as a scream threatened. The unfairness of it all was too hard to take. She'd put that terrible time behind her long ago. She'd worked hard, gained promotions, honed her skills, and absorbed every piece of knowledge she could get her hands on. Yet in one moment, the walls she'd built had come crashing down. It had all been for nothing.

CHAPTER 24

C alum walked into the arrivals hall and scanned around, looking for the exit. This was a new airport to him, so it took a few seconds to locate it. Spotting the sign, he headed outside and easily found the line for taxis. He joined the back and switched on his cell. He'd had no word from Laurella, despite him basically spamming her inbox with voicemails and text messages. Anger grew within him slowly, like the burning embers of a fire before the raging flames took hold. After everything they'd been through, she had chosen to run rather than talk to him about what was really going on. He didn't want to contemplate what that said about their relationship.

He reached the front of the line and gave the taxi driver the address he had for Laurella. As the car pulled into the crazy traffic to the beeping of horns—followed by what Calum assumed was a rude gesture made by his driver out of the window—he called Laurella once more. This time, the automated message told him her inbox was full and no more messages could be left. *Goddammit.*

He opened the text app. *I'm here, on my way to your parents' house. You can ignore my calls and messages, but you'll find it harder to ignore me. We are talking this through whether you like it or not.*

He didn't expect a response. She hadn't responded to any of his other messages. Still, he hoped. He glared at the screen almost as if he could make a reply appear through sheer force of will.

He texted Zane, letting him know he'd arrived and asking whether Zane had heard from Laurella. The answer came back almost immediately.

Yes. She's resigned.

Calum slammed his fist against the leather seat. "Fuck!"

The cab driver gestured and muttered something in Italian. Calum held up his hand in apology and leaned his head back. He closed his eyes. They were stinging from a lack of sleep and the six-hour time difference. He hated traveling west to east. It was the worst direction to acclimatize to.

An hour later, the taxi stopped outside a large apartment block about fifteen stories high. Calum glimpsed the bright blue of a swimming pool set among communal gardens filled with summer flowers. He paid the fare and climbed out. The driver popped the trunk, and Calum lifted his suitcase onto the roadside. The cabbie drove off, leaving him alone.

Three steps led up to the entranceway. Towing his suitcase behind him, he walked inside. The lobby area resembled that of a nice hotel. In the center was a large round table, on top of which sat an enormous white vase filled with flowers and green foliage. To the left was a bank of elevators, and two women were sitting behind a desk.

"Hi," Calum said, hoping like hell they spoke English because his Italian consisted of three words: *ciao, arrivederci,* and *stronzo.* "I'm here to see the Ricci family." He glanced down at the piece of paper upon which he'd scrawled Laurella's address. "Apartment nine twenty-two."

"Of course, sir," the receptionist replied in accented English —thank God. "If you'll sign in here."

Calum signed his name where she indicated. He rode the elevator up to the ninth floor, anxiety swirling in his stomach.

Not only was he unsure what Laurella's reaction was going to be, but he also didn't know whether she'd mentioned him to her parents, or whether she was even staying with them. *Oh Christ.* What if she hadn't told her parents she'd come home and was currently licking her wounds in a nearby hotel while she plucked up the courage to break the news to them? And he was about to turn up with his size thirteen's and put his foot right in it.

Too late now.

He found the apartment and knocked before he lost his nerve. When a few seconds passed without answer, he knocked again. Still nothing. They had to all be out. Disappointed, he headed back down to the lobby. He'd seen a bench outside. He'd wait for her there—however long it took.

He plugged his headphones into the jack on his cell and stuck on some music to waste time until Laurella turned up.

"Mama, please go home and get some proper rest," Laurella pleaded. "You look so tired. I'm here now. I can take some of the strain."

Her mother shook her head vehemently. "I'm not leaving the hospital. Not until he's fully conscious and I'm sure he's going to be all right."

Laurella met Caterina's eyes over the top of her mother's head. Caterina shrugged, a silent message of acceptance.

"Okay, but if Caterina and I fetch you some clean clothes, will you at least take fifteen minutes to freshen up?"

"If it makes you feel better," she said in a defeatist tone.

"It does," Laurella insisted, raising a brief smile from her mother.

Laurella gave Papa a kiss before she and Caterina left.

"Do you mind if we take a quick detour to Luisa's so I can check on the children?" Caterina asked. Luisa was her mother-in-law.

"Of course not," Laurella replied. "I'm desperate to see them, too. I just wish it was under happier circumstances."

Caterina squeezed her hand. "Papa will be fine. He's strong as an ox. Plus, do you think he has the guts to leave Mama?"

"Fair point," Laurella said, and the two girls laughed together.

Mama and Papa had the most wonderful marriage. They'd certainly set the bar very high for their children.

They both lapsed into silence, and Laurella's thoughts turned to Calum once more. It had only been forty-odd hours since that fateful meeting with Vorino, yet it felt more like forty years had passed. She still hadn't plucked up the courage to switch on her cell. She couldn't bear to hear the confusion in his voice. No doubt, he'd have gone to her apartment by now and found her missing. Would he be worried or just angry? Either way, she needed more time before facing him.

Laurella's nieces barreled out of the house. Their squeals of excitement at seeing their aunt after a six-month absence momentarily soothed her agony. She swept them up into her arms, hugging them tightly.

"Let me look at you," she said after they broke apart. "Oh my, how you've grown."

"How long are you staying?" Callie, her eldest niece, who was five years old, asked.

"I'm not sure yet. But I'll make sure I have plenty of time put aside to spend with you."

"Now," demanded Isabella, who had just turned three.

Laurella laughed. "Not now, but soon."

Isabella pouted. The beginnings of a wail were diverted by Luisa, who swept her granddaughter into her arms before dangling her upside down by her ankles. Isabella's crying soon turned into peals of laughter.

They spent a few minutes with the children, then Luisa distracted them with some cookies and milk so Laurella and Caterina could escape without fuss. After another fifteen minutes in the taxi, they arrived at their parents' apartment block. The familiarity of home brought tears to Laurella's eyes.

Her sister didn't even need to ask what Laurella was feeling. "We had a wonderful childhood growing up here, didn't we, Ella?"

Unable to speak, Laurella simply nodded. The two girls were walking up the steps when a familiar voice called out her name.

Laurella's breath caught in her throat. She shouldn't have been surprised, but interestingly, she was. Slowly, she faced him.

"Hello, Calum."

CHAPTER 25

It had only been two days, yet he drank her in like a man stumbling across an oasis after being lost in the desert. Dark circles gave her eyes a bruised appearance, and she was clinging to the woman next to her—clearly a relative, given the family resemblance.

"Laurella," he said, his voice clipped and cold, even to his own ears. "We need to talk."

She shook her head. "Now isn't a good time."

She went to walk inside. He sped across the short distance and gripped her elbow. "I'd say now is a perfect time."

The woman next to her narrowed her eyes. "I'd thank you to take your hands off my sister." Her English was not as clear as Laurella's, but the fire in her eyes made up for any loss in translation.

"It's okay, Caterina," Laurella said. "Go inside and get Mama's things. I'll be straight up."

"Are you sure?"

Laurella nodded. "Go on, now. Give me two minutes."

Caterina reluctantly left, glancing over her shoulder several times as she went inside. Calum waited until Laurella's sister had disappeared from view, and then his anger and hurt spewed out.

"Are you going to tell me what's going on?" he snapped. "You refuse to give any details of what the problem with you and Vorino is. You disappear from the office without a word and run away to Italy with your tail between your legs. You don't return any of my calls or texts. Zane is worried sick that the deal with Sorensen's is about to go down the pan because, apparently, you've *tendered your fucking resignation*. I fly all the way to Italy to talk to you, and you tell me 'Now isn't a good time.' What the fuck, Laurella? Just so I'm clear, when *would* be a fucking good time?"

She squared her shoulders, and her eyes sparked in defiance. Her hands came to her hips, and she glared at him. "When my father isn't lying in the hospital having suffered a heart attack."

She might as well have shot him with a Taser. He actually staggered backward a couple of steps and blinked rapidly. He opened his mouth in horror. *Jesus Christ.* He was a fucking idiot. He hadn't even given her time to explain, just launched into a tirade that she didn't deserve. He, on the other hand, deserved everything coming to him, and by the look in her eyes, he was about to get it.

"Shit, I'm sorry—"

Her hand flew in the air. "I don't have time to spar with you today, Calum. My sister and I have come to pick up some of Mama's things, and then we're going back to the hospital."

"How is your father?"

"What do you care?" she said, her tone full of bitterness.

He grimaced. "I deserved that. But I do care. If you just shared what's in that head of yours, I wouldn't be left wondering."

She threw her hands up. "Oh, so it's *my* fault you jumped to the wrong conclusions."

"Stop twisting my words," he said, irritated.

"Whatever," she said.

His lips twitched. He always found it amusing when Laurella came out with an unusual—for her—English phrase.

"Do you think this is funny?" she asked. "Actually, forget it. I have to go."

She turned away and stomped off. Calum ran after her, reaching her before she could burst through the doors to the lobby. He wrapped his arms around her waist and pulled her against him, her back to his front.

"I'm coming with you whether you like it or not," he murmured, his lips right next to her ear.

She wriggled. "Let me go, Calum."

"Not until you calm down."

"Go home."

"Not without you."

He sensed what she was about to do, but he didn't move out of the way quickly enough. Her elbow crashed into his ribs. He grunted, but despite the pain, he managed to hang on to her.

"God, you are one frustrating female. Stop fighting me. Where else would I be but beside the woman I love when she's falling apart?"

His words must have stripped all the fight from her, because she sagged in his arms. He eased her around to face him, but her gaze was firmly fixed on the floor, her chin trembling.

"Look at me," he said.

Slowly, her head came up. Her eyes glistened with unshed tears. She'd never looked more beautiful.

"I can't talk about what happened back in New York. Not yet. I need to put all my energy into my father and my family."

He nodded. "When you're ready, I'll be here."

CHAPTER 26

Over the next few days, Papa made a slow and steady recovery. Having Calum by her side gave Laurella strength so she could, in turn, give support to her family. Calum had shown his charming side and won each and every one of them over, including Caterina who, after a couple of frosty exchanges, had come around in the end.

He'd kept to his word and hadn't asked her anything further about her meltdown during the Sorensen's meeting, but the conversation couldn't be avoided forever. And she was dreading it. So many years had passed, during which time she'd buried that event so deep that she sometimes went weeks without thinking about it. Yet now, the painful images were at the forefront of her mind, and she *hated* it.

On the day her father was being released from the hospital, Laurella found herself alone with him. He waved away her offer of help as he padded about his hospital room, collecting his things.

Once he'd placed them all on the bed, ready for packing, he stiffly sat on a chair and patted the one next to him. "Come sit with your papa, girl. Time to share what's bothering you."

Laurella feigned surprise, even though she was anything but.

Papa always had been able to read her, and much as she'd tried, hiding things from him always ended in failure.

"Everything's fine, Papa. Especially now that you're well enough to go home."

He gave her that face that said *Don't lie to me* and shook his head. "Will you never learn, girl? I've known you for thirty years. Ever since that day I held you in my arms, my firstborn, and you opened your eyes and looked at me, I knew we had a special connection. And still, you think you can keep secrets from me."

Laurella's knees trembled. She risked a glance at the door, hoping someone would enter and save her. It remained stubbornly closed.

"No one is coming, and if they do, they'll be told to leave," Papa said. Sometimes she was sure he shared the inside of her head with her. He patted the seat once more. "Sit."

With nowhere to turn and no one to save her, she trudged across the room and reluctantly did as he'd asked. He captured one of her hands, tucking it between both of his. Silent, he waited for her to speak.

A swell of emotion rushed through her. "Vorino is in New York."

Her father heaved a breath and increased the pressure on her hand. "Tell me every detail, Laurella. And don't you leave out a single thing."

Laurella briefed her father on what had happened during the last few weeks in New York. He listened without interruption, though his keen mind would record every detail. When she finished, his arms came around her.

"You have to tell Calum," he said. "You cannot carry this burden alone. I might be ill and old, but even if I were blind and senile, I'd still be able to tell the strength of that man's love for you."

Laurella's vision blurred. She lifted her head and stared into

Papa's eyes. "What if he doesn't look at me the same way afterward?"

"Pah," her father said, his hand slashing through the air. Despite the heavy subject matter, the familiarity of that action brought a smile to Laurella's lips. "Then he's not the man for you. Except I think he is, and I'm never wrong. He might not be Italian, but I'll try not to hold that against him."

Laurella's smile widened. "I love you, Papa."

"Love you, too, girl. Now, let me finish this packing so I can get out of this godforsaken place and go home."

Laurella helped her mother clear away the dishes after dinner. As usual, Mama had made far too much. Laurella had grown up with tables groaning under the sheer weight of food. She scraped leftovers into the waste as excited chatter floated in from the dining room. Calum had been accepted into the bosom of her family. He'd even survived the severe grilling from each of her brothers. Having brothers of his own no doubt helped.

"I suppose you'll be going back to the States now that your father is on the mend?"

Her mother's question came completely out of the blue, and Laurella was unprepared to answer it. Whether or not she returned to America was completely dependent on how her conversation with Calum went. If, as she feared, he rejected her once he knew the truth, she wouldn't be going anywhere. And even if he remained by her side, she still didn't know how she could go back with Vorino there. Certainly, her career at Necron was over. If she did return to New York, she'd have to find another company to take her on, and that wouldn't be easy in the current economic climate. Plus, it would be difficult to explain why she'd decided to leave Necron after only six months working there.

"I expect so," Laurella murmured noncommittally. "I'd like to stay a little longer if that's all right."

"What's with you, girl?" Her mother flicked a dish towel at her backside, a method of teasing she'd used since they were all young children. As Laurella dodged out of the way, chuckling, her mother said, "You can stay as long as you like. If it was up to me, you'd never have left in the first place."

"If it was up to you, we'd all still be living in this apartment, driving each other crazy."

Her mother's wistful smile tugged at Laurella's heartstrings. "I miss those days."

"You might now, looking back," Laurella said. "But then, I seem to remember you begging for us all to *go away and leave you in peace*."

Mama shrugged. "Be careful what you wish for, I guess."

At the nostalgic tinge to Mama's voice, Laurella folded her inside her arms, hugging her tightly. "We're all still here, Mama. Whenever you need us, we're here."

Mama clung on. The hug only lasted a second, but it gave Laurella an insight into how much she'd had been missing them all. Alessia was the last of the siblings, and she would be leaving for college at the end of the summer.

And then the moment was over. Her mother bustled to the fridge and removed an enormous tiramisu, enough to feed the whole apartment block, let alone her family. "Okay," she said, forcing a huge smile. "Dessert."

"Honestly, Mrs. Ricci," Calum said, rubbing his stomach as a second helping of tiramisu was placed in front of him. "I couldn't eat another thing." He sent a helpless glance Laurella's way.

She laughed. "Mama, take pity on him. He's not used to the size of Italian meals."

"He needs feeding. There's barely an ounce of fat on him."

"Leave the man alone, Hayley," Papa said. "Besides, Laurella told me before she wants to show him around our beautiful city at night."

"I did?" Laurella said.

Her father widened his eyes in a silent message.

"Yes, I did," she said, understanding his escape plan a few seconds too late. Fortunately, her mother didn't notice the slipup.

"You must take him to see the Santa Maria delle Grazie," Mama said. "And the Duomo. Oh, and not let's not forget the Leonardo da Vinci statue."

"Mama, stop," Laurella said. "We'll probably go for a wander around the streets and see what we come across rather than do a fully organized tour. Honestly, I think you missed your calling. You should get a job with the tourist board."

"Sorry, Calum." Mama grinned apologetically. "Milan is such a beautiful city. That's why I never left."

Papa cleared his throat. "What my beautiful wife means to say is that she never left because Milan is *my* home, so she made it hers because she loved me that much."

The similarity of her mother's life with her own touched Laurella deeply. She nudged Calum's arm, anxious to leave before she was overcome with emotion. "Let's go. I think you've seen enough of Italian family dynamics for one night."

Laurella suppressed a giggle at the speed with which Calum got to his feet. "Thank you for having me." He took hold of Laurella's hand.

The two of them almost ran for the front door.

Outside the apartment, they started to laugh. "You survived the Ricci grilling," Laurella said.

Calum snagged her around the waist. "A warning would have been nice."

"That would have been boring."

"Yeah." He touched his nose to hers. "For you."

She tilted her head. "They like you."

"Jesus. I'd hate to see what happened to someone they didn't like."

"Oh, those people are buried in the walls," she said with a straight face, but then she laughed once more. All the stress of her mad dash from New York a week before, followed by the hospital vigil and Papa's recovery, had made her a little crazy.

"It's good to see you laugh again," Calum said, dropping a quick kiss on her lips. "And as much as I want that to continue, we need to talk."

He might not have wanted her to stop smiling, but knowing how difficult the upcoming conversation was going to be wiped the grin right from her face.

She breathed out a heavy sigh. "I know we do. There's a nice quiet bar not far from here."

They wandered into town, and after about fifteen minutes, Laurella turned down a narrow alley and stepped into a cozy bar, an old favorite of Papa's. She hoped that telling Calum her dirty little secret while being there would make it easier somehow. Or at least, it might give her more strength.

They found a table toward the back where it was less crowded. After ordering their drinks, Laurella took off her jacket and hung it on the back of her chair.

"Nice place," Calum said, glancing around. "This is my first trip to Italy. I'd definitely like to see more."

"More than the inside of a hospital or my parents' apartment, you mean."

He grinned. "Something like that."

They quieted as the server wandered over with their drinks. Laurella sipped her coffee. She would have preferred a stiff drink, but keeping her wits about her was probably a better option. Her leg bounced up and down, and she only realized she was nibbling on her nails when Calum tugged her hand away from her mouth.

"Go at your own pace," he said gently, as if talking to a frightened child. "There's no rush."

She nodded and swallowed. *Oh God.* This was awful. She'd thought all this was behind her. She'd told this story twice, and each time had been like slicing through her guts with a rusty knife. Telling Calum would be worse. She knew it.

Taking a deep breath, she began. "I started working at Spirito as an intern. Fresh out of college, I had a lot to learn. But I was hardworking and ambitious, and it wasn't very long before I began to move up the career ladder. When I was twenty-six, I found myself temporarily transferred to Alberto Vorino's department."

She took another breath and, with trembling hands, drank a little more coffee.

"Actually, do you mind ordering me a whiskey?" she said, changing her mind. "I don't think I'm going to get through this on caffeine alone."

Calum's mouth twisted with worry, but he simply squeezed her hand and called the server across. After her whiskey had been delivered, she drank a healthy mouthful. It burned on the way down but warmed her insides in preparation for the oncoming chill.

"Alberto was riding high at the top of his career. He'd cata-pulted Spirito into the big leagues with his brand definition and tight, targeted marketing campaigns." She laughed bitterly. "There's no doubting the man's talent at least."

She picked at a stray bit of fluff from her skirt. She needed to avert her eyes. Looking at Calum's worried expression was making this so much more difficult.

"After about three months, he started to notice me. I found myself invited to senior-management meetings, asked to under-take projects that were way above my level of experience, but I've never shied away from a challenge, and when I successfully implemented them, more were forthcoming.

"Then one day, I received a meeting invite. It was for six

that evening. Late, but not unusually so. We often worked into the night when deadlines had to be met. I assumed another large project was coming my way even though I already had a full calendar."

She picked up her whiskey and studied the amber liquid swirling inside then drank another larger-than-recommended mouthful.

"I expected there to be other people, but when I arrived at Vorino's office, he was alone. On his desk was a bottle of prosecco, a couple of glasses, and a few snacks." She squeezed her eyes closed and breathed deeply through her nose. "I asked him what was going on, and he said it was a celebration, a thank-you of sorts, for all the hard work I'd been doing. He said I deserved a treat."

From the way Calum's face hardened, he'd already guessed where this was going, but maybe not the extent of it. He deserved the full, unedited truth, however disgusting and hideous it was.

"I felt uneasy. I should have listened to my instincts and left, but he was my boss, a very senior figure in the organization and the man who could make or break my career. So I stayed." She shrugged. "At first, everything seemed fine. We had a drink and chatted about the latest project I was working on. He told me how impressed both he and his entire team were with me. How glad he was that I'd been temporarily moved to his department. He even joked that I'd soon be pushing him out of his job. I began to relax. I remember he topped up my glass, so I must have finished the previous one, although I can't say for sure."

She paused as their server came by to ask if they needed anything. Calum waved her away with an irritated flick of his wrist and a curt, "No."

Laurella touched his arm. "She didn't know it was bad timing."

"Then she should learn to read body language." His face softened. "Sorry. Go on. I mean... only if you want to."

After a further sip of Dutch courage, she continued. "It was getting quite late. I was conscious that the floor beyond Vorino's office had quietened, and outside, it had gone dark. I rose to leave. He asked me to stay a while longer, but I said that my parents were expecting me home for dinner, even though they weren't. I headed for the door, and I almost got there when he lunged at me. He slammed me, face-first, up against the wall. His arm came around my neck, and I remember I couldn't breathe properly. I panicked." Hot tears burned behind her eyes, and she blinked to clear her vision. "He was like a man possessed. He told me I owed him for all the chances he'd given me to further my career—and that night was his turn to collect."

She swallowed and closed her eyes, only opening them again when Calum's warm hand covered hers.

"You don't have to say any more." His voice might have been calm, but his eyes burned like coal.

"No, I'd like to finish." She grimaced. "I always thought I'd be the sort of girl who'd fight in a situation like that. But when it came to it, I froze. I can still smell his foul breath as he panted in my ear. I can feel his hands, roughly tearing at my underwear. I remember how painful it was, even though I wasn't a virgin." Tears leaked from the corners of her eyes and trailed down her cheeks, but she didn't brush them away. She straightened her spine. "After he'd… finished, he told me that if I breathed a word to anyone, he'd tell them I offered him sex to further my career—that I was so ambitious I'd do anything to climb the ladder. I was desperate to get out of there, so I agreed I wouldn't tell anyone.

"When I closed the door to his office, and he remained on the other side, I can't begin to describe the relief I felt. I didn't even wait for the elevator. I ran into the stairwell and out onto the street. My parents' apartment was only about a twenty-minute walk from Spirito, and a stroll I'd often taken, but I ran the whole way home. I was so scared he'd come after me. I'd have taken a cab, but I left my purse in the office."

A nerve ticked in Calum's cheek, and his hands were curled into fists, showing his fury. "And did you tell anyone?"

"Not right away, no. But the following morning, I broke down and told Papa. I'm sure you've seen over the past week how close I am to my father, but even so, telling him was one of the most horrific things I've ever had to do. To tell a man who adores the very bones of you how another man had violated you, done terrible things to you, and then see something change behind his eyes, something you know will never go back to the way it was… that's what broke me."

"Jesus, Laurella," he muttered, pressing her hand between both of his. "I'm guessing you didn't go to the police, because that fucker is still walking around."

"I couldn't." She shook her head violently. "I couldn't do it. Papa plays golf with the CEO of Spirito, and so, with my agreement, Papa told him. The CEO removed Vorino from his post that very day. I don't know what was said or agreed, and I didn't want to know. All I cared about was that he was gone from my life, and I could go on working for the company I'd grown to love."

Calum's face darkened, and then a look of absolute disgust distorted his features. "Fuck. I accused you of trying to seduce him. Oh God, baby, I'm so sorry. So, so sorry. No wonder you ran. How can you ever forgive me?"

She squeezed his fingers. "You didn't know."

"That doesn't excuse my behavior. I should have read the signs. I was so flippant with you back in New York."

She chuckled, and it felt good. "Calum, you're you. You don't read signs."

Her teasing didn't bring on a smile. "I don't deserve you."

"I won't lie. It hurt that you thought me capable of such a thing, but none of that matters now. You know everything, and it feels good not to have to hide it from you anymore. I love you.

211

And loving someone means you forgive them. I could have told you everything then and there, in New York, but I didn't. It's not all your fault, Calum."

"And you never heard from Vorino again?"

"Not until he walked into the boardroom last week."

Calum covered his face with his hands and rubbed hard. When they fell back into his lap, a faint tinge of red stained his cheeks, and a muscle flickered in his jaw. "You sat there, with that… that… *animal* for an hour. *An hour*. Jesus Christ."

She shook her head. "I was determined not to let what happened ruin my life, and by going on, by being successful, I win. I'm not a victim. I'm a survivor."

"You're amazing."

She smiled. "My trip to Italy wasn't running away, Calum, but it did give me time to think. I can't work with Vorino. I'm sorry."

His eyes widened. "Fucking hell. Of course you can't work with him."

"But don't you see? This means that I'll have to leave Necron. Which means I'll also have to leave New York. Without a job, I'll lose my work visa."

Calum leaned forward and gripped her hands. "You're not going anywhere. I will not have that man chase you from your job, your home. From me. I will sort this out with Zane."

"No!" She yanked her hands away as panic swelled within her. "You can't tell him. I don't want people judging me, looking at me differently. Feeling sorry for me."

"Take it easy," he said, his voice steady and mild. "I won't tell him anything, but you have to let me talk to him." He reached for her hands once more. "You're the woman I love. You belong with me. Zane trusts me. Can you?"

A fluttering set off in her abdomen. "So you still want me, after… now that you know?"

His nostrils flared, and he stiffened his spine. "Did you really think I wouldn't? That what *he* did to you would change one thing about how I feel about you?"

She nibbled at her bottom lip. "I wasn't sure what you'd think."

"Oh, Laurella." He rose from his chair and tossed some money on the table. "Come back to the hotel with me. Nothing has to happen, I just want to hold you. I don't want you out of my sight. Not tonight. Not ever."

Relief rushed through her. She took his outstretched hand. She hadn't lost him. He still wanted her. "I'll come back with you—on one condition."

He frowned, worry lacing his handsome features. "What?"

"That *something* happens."

CHAPTER 27

Calum and Laurella fell through the door of Calum's hotel room. Her lipstick had smeared where he'd put his mouth on her during the elevator ride, and his shirt had come loose from his jeans where she'd snaked her hands up his bare back and scored his skin with her nails.

She tore open his shirt before he'd even kicked the door. Buttons bounced off the nearby wall then hit the floor. He kicked off his sneakers when her fingers went to his zipper. She dragged his jeans down his legs, turning them inside out in her haste to get them off.

"Slow down." He grabbed her hands, stopping her. "We've got all night."

"No. We haven't. I need this. I need you, and I need it fast, Calum. Please."

There was a kind of wild desperation in her eyes, almost as though she was testing him and waiting for him to fail but praying like hell he didn't. Despite his verbal assurances, it was the physical evidence she needed to fully believe he still loved and craved her the way he always had.

"All right, beautiful. Your way. This time," he added with a grin.

She crossed her arms over her body and tugged her T-shirt over her head. Her skirt followed, as did her lingerie. Then she appeared to lose her nerve, or wonder what her next move should be, because she stood there, slightly trembling, nibbling on her fingernail.

Calum lifted her, hooking her legs over his hips. He pressed her up against the door he'd slammed shut less than two minutes before. He crashed his mouth down on hers, hard, and thrust his tongue inside.

She moaned, her hands digging into his hair. She tugged hard until he feared she'd pull it out by the roots. It didn't matter, though. However she needed to do this was the way it would go down.

She twisted her head to the side. "Now," she gasped.

He pushed inside her, one quick movement. She cried out. He paused in case he'd hurt her.

"Don't stop," she muttered.

He thrust into her again and again. Her thighs clenched around him, clinging on so she didn't fall. Not that he'd ever let her fall.

"More," she said. "Harder, please. Faster."

He dug his fingers into her ass and gave her what she demanded. What she *needed*.

And then a tremor racked her. He couldn't take his eyes off her, even though she wasn't looking at him. Her legs trembled, her orgasm taking her to a place he wanted her to never leave—because wherever that was brought her ecstasy.

She buried her face in his shoulder, her teeth lightly grazing his skin. "I love you," she whispered in his ear.

Her declaration was all he needed. He came, the urgency and speed of his own climax surprising him with its intensity. He pressed his mouth to her neck, tasting the perspiration on her skin while he waited for his cock to stop jerking.

Slowly, he lowered her legs to the floor. She lifted her chin, meeting his gaze.

215

"Thank you," she said.

"For what?"

"For letting me be me."

His heart squeezed. *Christ*, he loved her. Bending his head, he gently kissed her soft lips. "Let's go to bed, beautiful."

Calum waited until he was certain Laurella was fast asleep. Then he eased her head from beneath his arm. She stirred but didn't wake. He carefully tucked the covers around her and padded out of the room, closing the door behind him.

The minute he had space to himself, anger bubbled within him, leaving a burning trail so fierce only retribution would put out the flames. Vorino had to pay for what he'd done to Laurella. Every time Calum thought about what had happened to his woman—*his fucking woman*—sickness churned in his stomach, and murderous thoughts consumed his mind.

He wouldn't be able to get Vorino removed from the Sorensen's account without sharing what Laurella had told him, but he'd made a promise to her, and he wouldn't break it. No, there was only one way to get Vorino off that account. The man himself had to resign and agree to leave New York.

And to get him to do that, Calum needed help. Which meant he had to share Laurella's story with one other person. Someone he trusted with his life, who would be discreet and understanding, who would never let him or Laurella down.

Cole.

He checked the time. If Cole was pulling a day shift, he'd be finishing right about now. He dialed his brother's cell. It rang out once, twice, a third time. Calum was about to hang up and redial when Cole answered.

"Hey, bro. How's Italy? Great news about Laurella's dad being on the mend."

"Yeah. They released him from the hospital today," Calum said, speaking in hushed tones in case Laurella woke up.

"That's really great. When are you coming home?"

"I'm not sure yet. There's a bit of a complication."

Calum recounted how Vorino had attacked Laurella. He kept it brief and shared relatively few details, but even so, bile burned his throat, and he kept having to take deep breaths to stop himself from throwing up. He thought of her suffering, of how much pain that bastard had caused, of his cocky fucking expression as he'd sat across the board table from her, knowing what he'd done. *Fuck.* Calum wanted to maim, to kill, to destroy the bastard. Vorino had taken a piece of the woman Calum loved. Well, fuck him. Calum might never be able to help her get that piece back, but he'd be damned if Vorino was getting away unscathed. That fucker had to suffer.

Cole didn't interrupt once. Only when Calum fell silent did he speak. "What do you need?"

"I want him gone. Out of New York. Once that's happened, I'll think of a way to make him pay, because he's not getting away scot-free. But my first priority is making Laurella feel safe, and the only way to do that is to get him as far away from her as possible."

"Okay, I hear you. Let's catch up when you get back, and we'll come up with a plan."

"Thanks," Calum said. "I knew I could rely on you."

"In the meantime, I'll talk to Draven." When Calum began to interrupt, Cole continued. "Don't worry. I won't share any details. Plus, Draven's perfect for this type of job. I swear he only joined the police force so he could legally shoot people."

Calum laughed, the heavy weight that had been riding him hard since Laurella's horrific revelation momentarily lifting.

"Okay. Let me talk to Laurella. I'll be in touch."

"Morning, beautiful." Calum brushed Laurella's hair off her face and bent to kiss her.

She stretched and made a wonderful contented sound. "Morning. How long have you been awake?"

"Long enough. You hungry?"

"A little." She leaned up on one elbow, her other hand curving around his neck as she stole a second kiss.

"I'll order room service, then I want to talk to you."

The lightness disappeared from her face, and her expression grew shuttered. He caressed her cheek with the back of his hand. "Trust me?"

She blinked and nodded. "Okay. Coffee and a croissant for me."

He dialed room service and returned to the bedroom. Laurella had the covers pulled up to her chin and was gazing at him warily.

"I want you to come back to New York with me."

Her face paled. "I don't think I can."

"I'm not leaving you here, and I'm not letting you give up your career because of a piece of shit like Vorino. Look, don't be mad, but I spoke to Cole."

Her face crumpled. "Calum…"

He raised a hand in the air. "I shared the bare minimum. He's very discreet, I promise. Cole has a rather interesting partner at work, and the two of them are going to help deal with Vorino."

Her eyes darkened with worry. "What are they going to do?"

"We'll come up with a proper plan when we get back to New York. It won't cross too many lines. I'd guess one look at Draven, and Vorino is going to shit his pants."

Worry was replaced with curiosity. "Why?"

Calum laughed. "Come back to New York with me, and I'll introduce you."

CHAPTER 28

Laurella cried when she said goodbye to her parents, partly because going back to the States meant leaving them behind, and partly because of what was waiting for her back in New York. Despite Calum's promises to ensure her safety and his insistence she would not have to have anything to do with Vorino, the walls she'd constructed to protect herself were crumbling.

Curled into Calum's side on the trip back to New York, she tried to forget the potential horrors awaiting her on the other side of the Atlantic. She trusted Calum, couldn't bear to live without him, but she couldn't lie to herself—the thought of being back in the same city as Vorino almost sent her into a meltdown.

In New York, they got into the back of a taxi, and Calum gave the address of Jax's hotel. She knew why, of course. He'd arranged for Cole and his mysterious partner to be waiting. The thought of facing them, even though Calum assured her Cole would be discreet, gave her the chills. But worse than facing them was allowing Vorino to win.

Calum's arm around her waist warmed and comforted her. They walked up the steps and into the hotel. He didn't pause outside the lounge area to greet Jax. Instead, he ushered her straight toward the door that led to their living quarters.

Laurella stepped into the family room. So much happened since she was last there—a lifetime could have passed. Her overwhelming feeling, though, was one of safety. She'd originally wanted to go directly home, but Calum had been right to bring her here.

"You okay, beautiful?" He pressed a kiss to her temple. "Want to have a nap before Cole and Draven arrive?"

She shook her head. "A coffee would be nice."

"Coming right up." He pointed at the couch. "Sit down, and I'll get it."

She gratefully took a seat, grabbed a throw off the back of the couch, and wrapped it around her legs. She wasn't cold—far from it—but she craved the comfort the soft fabric provided.

"Draven's a very strange name."

Calum looked up from pouring milk into two cups. "He's a very strange man." Then he grinned. "Actually, that's not fair. He's different, that's all."

"Different how?"

"You'll see."

She pulled a face. "You could give me a little hint."

Calum grinned. "He's the complete opposite to any of us."

"In what way?"

Calum pointed his chin at the doorway at the sound of heavy footfalls on the stairs. "You're about to find out."

Laurella twisted her head as Cole stepped inside. He smiled warmly. "Welcome home, you guys."

"It's good to be—"

She trailed off as a man who surely had to be Draven followed Cole into the room. Her mouth fell open. He was a giant. He had to be at least six feet, eight inches tall, and darn it if those biceps weren't larger than Calum's thighs. He was covered in tattoos and wore a full beard. Around his waist was a thick leather duty belt with a gun in plain sight.

He scared the shit out of her, and supposedly, he was on her side. Calum was right. Faced with this tank of a man, Vorino would surely return to whatever rock he'd been hiding under for the last four years.

"This is my partner, Draven."

"Hey," Draven said, his low voice rumbling through his chest.

"Um, hi," Laurella said, casting a worried glance at Calum.

"Good to see you," Calum said, striding across the room. He shook Draven's hand and went on to briefly hug his brother. "Coffee?"

"Sounds good," Cole said, sinking onto the couch beside Laurella.

She suppressed showing relief when Draven took the chair. Having Cole on one side and Draven on the other would have made her feel as if she'd been bookended without an escape route.

Cole briefly touched her arm. "How you doing?"

Her answering smile was tight. "I'm good."

He nodded, immediately catching that she didn't want to discuss it any further. "So," he said as Calum passed coffees around, "are we going to talk about the elephant in the room? And by that, I don't mean Draven."

A guffaw burst out of Draven. She looked over at him. Their eyes met, and he winked. An instant sense of safety rushed through her. He was like a shield, and if she stood behind him, no harm would come to her.

Calum passed a piece of paper to Cole before sitting beside Laurella. He captured her hand in his. "Here's where he's staying. He hasn't been here long enough yet to figure out a permanent place to live, so you'll have to contend with hotel security."

Laurella frowned. When had he found out Vorino's address? He shrugged one shoulder, a faint smile playing around his lips.

Cole gave the paper a cursory glance and stuffed it into his pants pocket. "Any no-go areas?"

Laurella frowned. It was like they were talking in code.

"I'd like to say no," Calum said, his laugh harsh. "Do enough that he gets the message loud and clear. I don't want either of you getting in trouble over this."

Draven laughed. "Trouble's only going one way: his."

"Please," Laurella said. "Calum's right. I don't want you getting into trouble on account of me."

Cole gently patted her shoulder. "You're family, Laurella. No one messes with my family and gets away with it. You leave the worrying to us." He climbed to his feet and cocked his head at Draven. "Might as well pay an early visit to our friend. I quite like the idea of starting the weekend off scaring the shit out of the fucking coward."

Draven heaved his huge body to his feet. "Amen to that, brother."

"Get some sleep," Cole said to Laurella. "We'll be back when we're done."

"There." Cole pointed at a space on the street not far from the hotel where Vorino was holed up.

Draven parked behind a yellow Hummer and set the brake. He twisted in his seat. "How do you want to handle it?"

Cole grinned. "Remember that drug pusher who beat his girlfriend to a pulp and then tried to wriggle out of it by saying she deserved it because she'd given him a bad hit of heroin?"

Draven nodded, a gleam in his eye. "Hell, yeah."

"Kinda like that."

"Aren't you bothered he's already met Calum, so he'll know exactly who you are?" Draven asked.

Cole hitched a shoulder. "Do I look like I care?"

Draven opened his car door, glancing back with an evil grin. "Then let's go have some fun."

They walked inside, being careful not to draw attention to

themselves—well, as much as they could hope with a man as colossal as Draven. Fortunately, the one receptionist on duty had a line of people waiting to be dealt with, so she didn't even look their way as they crossed the lobby over to the bank of elevators.

The two of them rode up to the fifth floor in silence. They didn't need to speak because they worked together as successfully as a well-oiled machine, in perfect harmony.

They padded along the hallway until they reached Vorino's room. Cole rapped once with his knuckles.

"Yes," came an accented reply.

"Room service," Cole said.

"Wrong room."

"I have this room, sir."

"Wrong room," came the voice again, more irritated the second time around.

"Sir, please. If I return this food to the kitchen, I'll be fired. Can you at least sign my ticket to prove that I came up here and tried to deliver it?"

Vorino grumbled, and a rustling noise sounded on the other side of the door. It opened.

Draven launched forward. He grabbed Vorino around the throat and shoved him backward. Cole closed the door and followed his partner inside. Vorino was clawing at Draven's large hand as he applied just enough pressure to instill panic. Vorino's eyes bulged when Draven lifted him a few inches from the floor.

"Put him down," Cole said.

Draven glanced over his shoulder. "Spoiling my fun already?"

"No, but I want him conscious when he shits himself, if only for my own amusement."

"Fine." Draven dropped Vorino, who gasped for air. He bent over, hands on his knees, trying to catch his breath. He eventually managed to stand upright, and his eyes wildly darted around the room, looking for an escape route that didn't exist.

"It's you?" he rasped, his eyes firmly on Cole. "Wha-what are you doing here?"

Cole grinned at Draven. "He thinks I'm Calum. Tell him who I really am."

Draven stepped in close. "Your worst fucking nightmare, dickface."

Cole touched Draven's arm, moving him to one side. He stood toe-to-toe with Vorino.

"Settling in well in New York?" Cole asked.

A frown drifted across Vorino's face. "I-I don't know what you mean."

"It's a simple enough question. Are. You. Settling. In. Well?"

Vorino spluttered a response but made no sense.

"Fuck this," Draven said, pulling out his Glock and shoving the butt under Vorino's chin.

"No!" Vorino's face turned ashen, and a distinct odor of panic drifted over to Cole. "God, please. Don't hurt me. I haven't done anything."

Cole laughed, the sound short and bitter. "Yes, you have."

"You've got the wrong man. Please, you have to believe me."

Cole took a menacing step forward. "I don't have to believe a fucking word that comes out of your mouth. I know what you did. And I'm going to make you regret it."

At the terror in Vorino's eyes, a sense of satisfaction crept over Cole. He'd bet the slimy bastard hadn't given a second thought to Laurella's fear when he'd violated her.

"Please, tell me what I'm supposed to have done so we can sort out this mess." His gaze sliced to Draven who still had the gun pressed tight against Vorino's chin.

"Drop the gun," Cole said.

Draven did as Cole had asked. He knew the drill.

"Thank you," Vorino said, his hands pressed together in prayer. "Thank you so much."

Cole's fist smashed against Vorino's jaw. He fell backward, hitting his head on the wall. He cried out, which turned into a muffled scream when Draven clamped his large hand over Vorino's mouth. Draven dragged him to his feet, holding him upright, which allowed Cole to punch Vorino hard in the stomach. He grunted as the air was pushed from his lungs, and when Draven released his hold, Vorino crumpled to the floor, his body curled into the fetal position. He sucked in air at a rapid rate as if his lungs were begging for oxygen.

"There's something about a chickenshit excuse for a man that makes me want to puke," Draven said, poking his toe into Vorino's ribs. He barely touched the man, but that didn't stop Vorino from letting out a squeal. Draven dropped onto his haunches, his face up close. "Make one more fucking sound, and I will end you."

Vorino whimpered and tried to get to his feet. Draven put his large boot on the piece of shit's stomach, holding him to the floor.

"I don't know about you, partner, but I'm getting bored. And you know what happens when I get bored."

"Yeah." Cole laughed. "I do."

A dark stain spread out from Vorino's groin area, the smell of urine filling the air. Draven screwed up his face. "Fuck me. Chickenshit *and* pisses his pants. Can I end this guy?"

"No!" Vorino cried out. "Please. God help me."

Cole crouched. "He won't help you. There's only one thing that can help you now."

"What? I'll do anything."

"Anything?" Cole asked.

"Yes. Just tell me what you want me to do, and I'll do it."

Cole nodded at Draven. "Get him up."

Draven stuck his hands underneath Vorino's armpits and pulled him upright. Cole got in his face, nice and close. "Here's what you're going to do. You're going to call your boss and tell him you've decided New York isn't for you. And then you're going to leave Manhattan. No, strike that. You're going to leave the United States and never set foot on these shores again. We have enough rapists of our own. We don't need imported ones."

Vorino's eyes widened as he finally caught up. And then he blinked rapidly.

"Is that a yes?" Cole asked.

Vorino nodded vigorously.

"Good. You have two days. I will come checking. And if you're still here…" He cocked his head in Draven's direction. "I'm going to give him free rein to do whatever he wants. He's very thorough, and he likes to take his time. It won't be quick. It *will* be painful."

Vorino's eyes darted to the side, where Draven was barely managing to hold back a smile.

"I'll go," he said. "I'll do whatever you want."

Cole's lips curved upward. "That was never in question." He nudged Draven. "Let's go."

Draven put his face up close to Vorino's, whose whole body shook. "You and me, sweetheart. Make one wrong move, and it's just you and me."

They left him standing there with a bloody nose and bruised ribs, stinking of the evidence of his cowardly status. Outside, they high-fived.

"Easy money," Draven said, his booming laugh echoing down the hallway.

CHAPTER 29

Laurella clung to Calum's hand because if she didn't, she might run screaming down the street instead of stepping through the double doors that led into Necron's office building. Although Calum assured her no one there knew what had happened, she couldn't help wondering if every nod in her direction or every furtive glance was because the office gossip train was in full flow. *That's her, the victim*, she imagined them saying.

Well, she wasn't a victim. Not then. Not now. Not ever.

"You're trembling," he said, squeezing her hand. "Where's my tenacious, headstrong woman?"

She gave him a tight smile. "In Italy."

Calum brushed a kiss to her temple. "To everyone here, you went home because your father was sick. It also happens to be the truth."

"But what about Zane? What did he say about my resignation? What will he say about Vorino?"

Calum shook his head. "Stop worrying. I told Zane it was a reaction because you were in shock about your father. He understands. And Cole assured me Vorino's out of here. When Zane shares that piece of news, just act surprised."

She gnawed at her bottom lip, only stopping when the metallic taste of blood flooded her tongue. "Okay," she said, her voice so small she barely recognized it.

Calum strode down the corridor toward Zane's office, nodding curtly at a couple of staff members who walked past. Laurella almost had to jog to keep up with him. He paused outside Zane's office and raised his hand to knock.

"Ready?"

"Not in the least," she replied, drawing a wide smile from him.

He rapped once on the door and entered.

"Hey, you're back," Zane said, getting to his feet and walking around his desk. He shook Calum's hand, followed by Laurella's. "How's your father?"

She smiled. "He's doing well, thank you. He'll need to rest and do as his doctor tells him, but as long as he's sensible, they think he'll make a full recovery."

"That's great. I'm so glad you decided to come back." Zane waved at the chairs in front of his desk. "You're just in time, actually. Brad Novak is on his way over. He should be here any minute."

A bolt of fear rushed through Laurella, and her face heated, but Zane didn't seem to notice anything out of the ordinary.

"Why?" Calum asked casually.

"He's taking me to lunch. And you know me. Never one to pass up a free meal."

Calum pulled a face. "How did he sound?"

Zane frowned. "Fine. Same old Brad. Why wouldn't he be?"

Before Calum could respond, there was a brief knock at the door. Ellie poked her head inside. "Brad Novak's here, Zane. Do you want me to show him in?"

"Please," he said, rising from his chair once more.

Laurella clenched her hands into tight fists when Brad came into the room. She risked a glance at his face. Impassive, businesslike. Normal.

"Brad, please come in. Would you like coffee?"

Brad shook his head. "Not for me. Laurella, Calum, good to see you. I hear your father hasn't been well, Laurella. I hope he's on the mend now?"

"He is, thank you. Sorry I had to leave so suddenly. I hope everything is still on track." She cast a fishing line and hoped Brad Novak would bite.

"Yes, we're all good, although I have had to make a slight change in personnel. Alberto has left the company."

Laurella held her breath. She glanced between Calum and Zane.

"That's a shame," Zane said, saving Laurella or Calum from having to say anything. "He seemed like a good guy. Nothing serious, I hope?"

"He didn't share the details, only that he had to return to Italy for personal reasons." Brad shrugged. "It happens. I'm recruiting for a replacement, but until then, Laurella, you'll deal directly with me."

"Of course," she murmured.

"I'll give you a call tomorrow. We'll set up some time in the calendar. Shall we go, Zane? I've made reservations at a great little Japanese place."

After Zane and Brad left for lunch, Laurella's breath left her lungs with a whoosh.

She turned her head to look at Calum. "It's over," she said, relief coursing through her veins.

He lifted her hand to his lips and kissed it. "Yes. It's all over."

CHAPTER 30

Laurella stepped into her apartment and closed the door behind her. She locked it and put on the chain. She sighed tiredly and dropped her bag on a nearby chair then glanced at her watch. Forty-five minutes until Calum was due. Plenty of time to grab a shower and get changed. He was taking her to the theater that evening to celebrate being home.

Home… yes, that was how she now thought of New York. Being back in Italy for those few days had taught her that she wanted more. To go back there permanently would have been the wrong thing to do, although if Cole and Draven hadn't managed to scare off Vorino, she wouldn't have had a choice.

Cole hadn't spilled all the details of what happened when he and Draven had gone round to Vorino's hotel, but what he had shared had been enough. Vorino was a coward at heart, like most bullies, and he wouldn't risk going up against the likes of Cole and Draven. She was glad Calum had stayed out of it. The last thing she wanted was him getting into trouble for her, although she knew how difficult he'd found it to hand off the task of dealing with Vorino to his twin brother. Calum was such a *manly* man that he couldn't have liked standing back. But he'd done it for her, his willingness to follow her wishes offering yet more ironclad evidence of his love.

She padded into the bedroom and quickly undressed. Stepping into the shower, she bent her head and let the hot water cascade over her, washing away the stress of the last few hours. The day had gone much better than she'd imagined. Everyone had been so welcoming, so glad to have her back. She was starting to understand what Calum had said to her all those months before: small companies were like family.

After a few minutes, she got out and wrapped herself in a large towel. She dried off and went into the bedroom then removed the blue lingerie Calum had referred to in Chicago. Chuckling to herself, she slipped on the panties and fastened the bra. She knew what his response would be when he undressed her later that evening.

With gentle strokes, she brushed her hair, easing out the knots. She really did need a haircut. She liked to wear it long, but the extra inches made it difficult to manage. That place down on Sixth and Forty-Third had a decent hairdresser. She'd call in the morning and see if they could fit her in over the weekend.

She plugged in her hairdryer, but as she went to switch it on, she paused, wrinkling her nose. What was that smell? It was vaguely familiar. Where had she smelled it before? She didn't get a chance to investigate because a strong arm came around her neck, and she was yanked backward.

Her knee hit the edge of the dresser, and pain ballooned outward. She screamed, arms and legs flailing as she tried to get her assailant off her. She caught him with an elbow to the ribs, and he grunted and leaned back, which gave her enough room to twist out of his hold.

She sprinted for the kitchen, but he was on her before she got there. His arm came around her throat again, and this time he applied so much pressure she struggled to breathe. *Oh God, what's happening?* Panic and fear froze her brain. He was much stronger than she was—too strong for her to do anything.

Her gaze fell on a kitchen knife lying three feet away on the counter. Using every ounce of strength, she lunged.

And missed.

Her attacker slammed her face-first against the wall. Pain exploded in her cheek, knocking her sick. He grabbed her arms and pinned them above her head. He smelled of garlic, booze, and stale sweat.

"You'll remember this position from last time."

She heaved violently. Every inch of her body crawled with revulsion and disgust as she realized who had her. That was the smell—his cologne, buried underneath the other more prevalent scents.

Her mind screamed out in agony. *No! Not again.* She would *not* let him do this to her again.

She tried to breathe through the panic, but like a snowball, it built from deep within her. Sweat drenched her skin, and her heart pummeled against her ribcage. He managed to trap both her wrists in one of his large hands, and he slowly rubbed the other up and down her spine.

"Have you missed me, Laurella? Missed how hard I made you come last time? You like it rough, don't you, *cara mia?* Well, don't worry, because that's what you're going to get."

He licked the back of her neck, forcing a repulsive shudder from her. She tasted vomit at the back of her mouth.

"I think about our night together often. But then you had to ruin everything by *lying*! You destroyed my life, but I'm a patient man. I bided my time, and when my opportunity came around, I took it." He was panting. Her stomach lurched from the stench of his breath. "I was hoping to toy with you for a bit longer, but then you sent those *thugs* after me."

Stay calm. Keep your wits about you. You're no match for him physically, but you're smart. Think your way out.

"What thugs?" she said, playing the innocent. "Alberto, please?"

"Please what? Please don't hurt me? I've waited four years for my revenge. Your pretty-boy American won't be interested in my little Italian whore by the time I've finished."

How long had she been home? Twenty minutes? Calum wouldn't get there in time. Acid burned her throat, but she forced her body to relax, to stop fighting him—to make him think she'd yield and give him what he thought he was owed.

"Please let me go so we can do this properly. I can make you feel good, Alberto, but not like this."

He hesitated, his grip loosening from around her wrists. "Don't play games, Laurella."

"I'm not. I didn't realize how much I'd missed you until we met again. You're right. Calum is no match for you." The words scored her heart. *Please forgive me for what I'm about to do, il mio amore.*

"Then why did you just lunge for that weapon? Why send those thugs to scare me off?"

"I didn't know it was you," she said, thinking on her feet, praying she'd be able to go through with what she needed to do. "I thought I was being attacked and reacted like any woman alone would do. And I don't know anything about any thugs. Maybe it was Calum. He's crazy jealous of our history." She wriggled against him, hating herself, *hating him* for what he was forcing her to do. His erection pressed against the crease of her bottom, and her stomach reacted violently. She gagged, but fortunately, he didn't seem to notice.

She sucked in a deep breath through her nose to calm the oncoming nausea. "I'm glad you're back, Alberto. I was a stupid girl back then. But I'm a woman now. A woman who knows what she wants. And she wants you."

He trembled with what she assumed was pleasure then dropped her arms and spun her around. His mouth crashed down on hers, his stubble tearing at her tender flesh, his tongue almost choking her as he thrust it inside her mouth. She urged her body to comply and her mind to switch off.

She pressed lightly a hand to his chest and pushed. When he drew back, she forced a smile. "Slow down. There's no rush." She caressed a hand down his cheek. "Let's go into my bedroom where we'll be more comfortable." She added a coy smile followed by a girlish giggle. "I might even let you tie me up."

His lecherous gaze raked over her, and he licked his lips. He took one step back. It was all the room she needed. She lunged for the knife. Her fingers closed around the hilt. She spun around, holding the blade out front, her hands trembling, even though she tried so hard to still them.

"Don't come near me," she said, tears dripping down her cheeks and blurring her vision.

Vorino recoiled in shock, but he recovered quickly. He sneered. "You're not going to hurt me."

"I will if you ever touch me again," she cried, "I'll do it."

His eyes narrowed, and then he lurched forward. He grabbed her wrist, shaking the limb hard, trying to get her to drop the blade. But she held on. With everything she had, she clutched the hilt, her only chance at survival, because if Vorino violated her for a second time, it would kill her.

She formed a fist and swung her other arm backward then hit him in the face with as much force as she could muster. Pain shot through her hand. She screamed, hoping one of her neighbors might hear and come running.

He closed in on her. There was a struggle. Laurella fell backward. Vorino tumbled on top of her. She hit her head on the floor and felt herself go woozy. *Don't pass out. Don't pass out.*

They wrestled. As the last vestiges of strength left her, a sharp pain sliced through her side, and then a warm wetness spread across her abdomen. He was heavy. So heavy. She couldn't get him off. He gurgled deep in his throat. Laurella reached a hand between them. When she brought her fingers up, they were covered in blood. She didn't know whether it was hers… or his.

She heaved at his chest. He rolled to the side. And then she saw it. The kitchen knife sticking out of his abdomen. His eyes lolled back in his head, and a rattling noise came from his chest.

Laurella stared, frozen in shock. There was so much blood. It pooled beneath his body. Thick, dark, gloopy. He was dying. She knew it, but instead of rushing to help, to try to stem the loss of blood, she watched as the life drained out of her tormentor.

She'd killed a man. And she would pay.

CHAPTER 31

C alum exited the elevators, excited at the thought of the evening ahead. Laurella had mentioned going to see the play *Miss Saigon* several times before she'd rushed to her father's aid. She'd been under so much stress for so long, and he wanted tonight to be special, so he'd bought the best seats in the house.

The elevator doors had barely closed when a scream reached him. He set off sprinting. That scream had come from Laurella's place. He rattled the door handle of her apartment, but it didn't open. Scuffles and thudding came from inside.

"Laurella!" he yelled, slamming his shoulder into the door— once, twice, a third time. The wood creaked and splintered, and the door sprang open.

The scene that greeted him was like something out of a slasher movie. Laurella was propped up against the wall nearest the kitchen. She was in her underwear, the lower half of her body covered in blood as well as smears of red on her arms and chest. To her left was a man with a knife sticking out of his abdomen.

"Jesus, baby, what happened? Are you hurt?"

The man's face was staring vacantly at the ceiling. *Vorino*. A swell of anger built up inside him. He fell to his knees beside

Laurella. She had an empty stare that scared the shit out of him. He checked her over. She seemed to be unhurt, which meant the blood was Vorino's.

He gripped her arms and shook her slightly. "Laurella, look at me," he demanded.

She didn't respond, her eyes firmly fixed on blood splatter that had painted the wall.

"Laurella!" He shook her again.

She turned her head. "He's dead," she said flatly. "I killed him."

Calum's heart squeezed. If that bastard had hurt her, he'd kill him all over again. "What happened, beautiful? Talk to me." Her vacant stare scared the shit out of him.

"I don't know how he got in. I locked up. I know I did."

Riddled with guilt, he cursed. He'd meant to mention her crappy locks to Cole and get him to send one of the experts over from work to fix them, but it had slipped his mind. *Fuck.* It was all his fault.

"Did he hurt you?" he asked, terrified of the answer.

She shook her head.

Thank God.

"I'm going to call Cole."

"No!" She gripped his arm. "I don't want to go to prison."

He recognized the signs of shock. Her pale, clammy skin, rapid breathing, and enlarged pupils were all giveaways. He pulled her against him and kissed her hair. "You're not going to prison. This is America, sweetheart. He broke in. All you did was defend yourself. Cole will sort everything out, I promise. But I have to call him."

He eased his cell out of his pocket and dialed his brother. When he answered, Calum gave him a very brief rundown.

"I'm on my way," Cole said. "Sit tight, and don't touch anything."

Calum hung up. He got to his feet.

"Where are you going?" Laurella asked, her tone panicked.

237

"To get you a robe."

He went into the bedroom, returning with a bathrobe. He wanted to bathe her but didn't dare in case forensics needed to take swabs. He wrapped her in the robe. Her whole body shuddered and trembled, but with some encouragement, she leaned into him.

Cole arrived fifteen minutes later, Draven in tow. The two of them took one look at the scene and then over at Calum.

"We have to call it in," Cole said.

Within minutes, Laurella's apartment was swarming with officials. Detectives questioned her, and forensics took their swabs. Laurella answered quietly but fully. Cole promised to take her down to the station the next day to make an official statement. The police bagged her clothes in an evidence bag, including the robe Calum had dressed her in when he'd found her, and then they were told to leave.

Calum found another robe which he swaddled her in. He packed her an overnight case, and then took her back to his place. She hadn't said a word on the journey home in the back of Cole's squad car.

Calum left her sitting on his bed while he turned on the shower. He glanced at his watch. Two in the morning. She must be exhausted, but he couldn't let her sleep with that filth's blood all over her.

He walked back into the bedroom and gently eased her to her feet. "Let's get you cleaned up."

He slipped off her robe and quickly took off his own clothes, then climbed into the shower with her. She stood with her head down as he washed every trace of blood, every trace of *him* from her body.

Once clean, he dressed her in one of his T-shirts. He combed the knots from her hair and then he dried it. Throughout the whole process, Laurella didn't speak. She looked like a lost little girl. His heart clenched with sorrow for her, while his anger burned.

He drew back the covers and helped her into bed then climbed in beside her. He rested her head on his chest and curved his arm around her shoulders. It took an age, but eventually, her breathing evened out, and as exhaustion took over, she fell asleep.

Calum, though, lay awake, his mind racing as he went over the last few hours. She'd said Vorino hadn't hurt her, both to him and the police, but the fact remained that he'd found her almost naked. What had gone on in those minutes she'd been alone in the apartment with that bastard that she had chosen not to share? He had to know. He couldn't bear the thought of Vorino's hands on her.

Eventually, he fell into a fitful sleep. When he awoke, he was lying in an empty bed. Fear shot through him, and his body shook.

"Laurella?" he called out, scrambling out of bed. He'd half tugged on his jeans when she appeared in the doorway to the bathroom, a toothbrush in her mouth. She held up a finger then disappeared back inside. He sank onto the bed as his legs gave way.

She was back a moment later. "Sorry. I didn't mean to worry you."

"Are you okay?"

She shrugged. "I've had better nights."

He held out his arms and was relieved when she virtually threw herself at him, a very different response from the previous night. "I'm so sorry, Calum."

"For what?"

"For zoning out on you."

He grinned. "Zoning out?"

She returned his smile. "Looks like I'm becoming more American by the day."

"I knew we'd wear you down."

She laughed then. It was brief, but he'd take it.

He cradled her jaw. "Baby, I know what you said to the

239

police, but I'm more worried about what you didn't say. Please talk to me."

Her face fell. "He was going to assault me again. So I played along."

He frowned. "What do you mean?"

She covered his hand with her own. "I couldn't beat him physically, so I made him think I wanted him." Her head dropped, her gaze fixed on the floor. "I kissed him. It disgusted me, but I did what I had to do to survive." She hitched one shoulder. "I'm so sorry if you think I've betrayed you."

If that bastard wasn't already dead, I'd fucking kill him.

He gently nudged up her chin. "I couldn't love you more."

CHAPTER 32

After a long day spent at the police station where, as Calum had promised, she hadn't faced any charges, they headed over to Calum's place. Laurella opened the door that led down to his living quarters, but Calum put out a hand to stop her.

"What's the matter?" she asked, frowning.

He pressed a soft kiss to the top of her head. "I'm so goddamn proud of how you dealt with what's happened. You're my hero. I'm in awe of your strength, your courage, your guts. I'm so lucky you chose to be with me." She opened her mouth to interrupt, so he placed a finger over her lips. "I know I can be an ass sometimes, but I'm working on it. I'm in this for the long haul. Nothing you could do would make me not want to be with you. But I need you to promise me one thing."

She held back on a bite of anxiety that twisted her gut. "What?"

"You will always trust me enough to share what's going on in that beautiful mind of yours. I know you find it hard to share sometimes, but you need never be that way with me."

Her vision blurred, and she nodded. "I promise."

He curved his hands around her face. "I love you. So fucking much."

Her heart almost burst with adoration for this complicated man who, over the last few months, had tested every single one of her limits. Despite the painful and tempestuous start, their future held only happiness.

With her hand firmly in his, Laurella headed down the familiar stairs at Jax's hotel. At the bottom, she found the whole Brook family waiting. Well, except for Nate. The youngest Brook brother hadn't been seen since that one night she'd met him.

Indie shot across the room and hugged her. "I'm so glad you're okay," she said, her eyes shining with sincerity. "I'm here if you ever want to talk. Woman to woman."

"Thank you," Laurella said, a little taken aback by the exuberant response, although it was lovely all the same.

Jax squeezed her shoulder, and then she found herself wrapped in Cole's warm embrace. "You did so well today, Laurella. I know it wasn't easy."

"I'm just glad they believed me."

"Of course they believed you," Calum said. "That fucker broke into *your* apartment, and you defended yourself."

"Well, it's behind us now. I just want to forget it."

"And on that note, let's eat," Indie said.

Laurella flashed her a grateful smile. She and Indie didn't know each other very well, but the other woman had correctly guessed that Laurella wanted the conversation to move on. Maybe Indie would become a friend, someone she could go shopping or to the movies with or who'd be a sounding board when she wanted to moan about Calum. She missed her sisters and her girlfriends back in Italy, and as wonderful as Calum was, a girl needed her friends.

After dinner, Indie and Jax disappeared upstairs to take over the bar, and Cole muttered something about meeting his buddies for a drink. Laurella found herself alone with Calum. His eyes smoldered with an intensity that had her toes curling.

He placed his hands on her hips and moved her closer to

him. "I knew, from the moment I first saw you sitting in *my* chair in the boardroom, that you'd be trouble."

Laurella smiled. "*Il mio amore*, you wouldn't have me any other way."

EPILOGUE

C ole strolled with Draven across Times Square, the bright lights of the city he loved making night feel like day. Their shift was almost over, and Draven was trying to persuade him to head out on the town. It was Saturday night, after all. But after a week of pulling twelve-hour shifts, he craved sleep.

"How's Laurella doing?" Draven asked.

"She's one tough girl," Cole said. "She's bounced straight back, and even though Calum wanted her to take some time off work, she insists that she's going back Monday."

Draven laughed. "I bet he loved that."

Cole grinned. "He doesn't have a choice. She's got him under the thumb."

Draven laughed again. "I never thought I'd hear those words in relation to Calum."

"Neither did he."

A scuffle broke out at a bar across the street, and they broke into a jog. When the troublemakers got a look at Draven, they sobered up fast. He had that effect on most people, although the odd dick took it as a sign that Draven was up for a fight. Those idiots soon learned the hard way.

They headed back to the station, but as they passed by a

coffee shop, something made Cole glance inside. He stopped dead in his tracks.

What. The. Hell. Millie Frayser.

Shock rolled through him. What was *she* doing back in New York? He stared harder, making sure he wasn't mistaken. Ten years had passed since she'd fucked off with Tanner, the captain of their high school football team. Yet it might as well have happened yesterday, because the passage of time hadn't dimmed the devastating blow of rejection clawing at his gut. Nor had it taken away the nasty taste of being passed over not once, but twice. Although, could it be called rejection when he'd kept his true feelings buried deep inside?

"What the fuck are you gawking at?" Draven asked from several feet ahead as he realized Cole hadn't kept up.

Cole turned his head in Draven's direction, then back toward the coffee shop.

"Cole!" Draven said.

"It's her," Cole said obtusely.

Draven frowned. "Who?"

He came to his senses as a rush of excitement was followed by resurgent feelings of anger and resentment bubbling to the surface.

"The woman who should have been mine."

THE END

Ready for Cole? Grab your copy here
and read on for a sneak peak of Chapter 1

HIS TO PROTECT - CHAPTER 1

Fire scorched Cole Brook's lungs, and his jaw hung open in an imbecilic fashion, but as much as he must look like a total idiot to anyone bothering to pay attention, the damned thing wouldn't close. He couldn't stop staring through the greasy, fingerprint-smeared window at *her*. Millie Frayser. The girl—now woman—who'd been one of his closest friends at school, and who'd rejected him not once, but twice.

Except that wasn't fair. Millie hadn't been aware of his secret obsession with her. Instead, she'd been mesmerized by his brother's charisma. When it came to thrills and excitement, Calum's domineering personality was impossible to resist. To Millie, Cole had simply been her buddy. The *nice one*. The invisible man who'd been relegated to live in the shadow of his utterly captivating sibling whose brooding yet charming temperament had demanded the spotlight.

Calum had drawn Millie in, like a moth to the proverbial flame, then tossed her aside with astonishing speed.

Cole had given her a comforting shoulder to cry on like the good buddy he was. She'd blurted it all out, and he'd bitten his tongue and listened to her sobs and her questioning of where it had all gone wrong.

Cole's stomach twisted at the memory. He adored Calum, idolized him even, but there were times when he hated his guts. The day he'd so harshly broken off his fledgling relationship with Millie, refusing to offer any explanation, had been one of those occasions.

Millie had rebounded, hard. Except instead of rebounding into *his* arms, Tanner Bailey—captain of the football team, arrogant jock, and total dick—had seized his chance and picked her off so easily. Within a week of their high-school graduation —which also happened to be the day she'd turned eighteen— Tanner had put a ring on her finger. They'd moved to Chicago, and Cole hadn't seen her since.

And now, here she was. Back in New York. So many years had passed since he'd last laid eyes on her—and yet, as he stood there gaping, time folded in on itself. It felt like only yesterday when he'd watched her get married. She'd unwittingly stolen a piece of his soul that day, leaving behind a wound other women hadn't been able to heal.

Sure, he'd had girlfriends. He hadn't exactly lived like a monk this past decade. But none of them had touched him in that hidden place reserved for *The One*—the place Millie owned.

Cole jerked out of the past as long-buried childhood resentments threatened to hurtle to the surface. Sweat dampened his palms. He peered through the window once more. She'd barely changed from all those years ago, save for the crinkles around her eyes. Shoulder-length, coffee-colored hair, oval face, a dimple on her left cheek. Hypnotic mocha eyes, although he couldn't see them right then because she was staring into her coffee. Cole had spent a good proportion of his youth craving for her to turn those eyes on him with the same hunger she had with Calum.

A pang in his chest he'd long since forgotten returned. She was even more beautiful now, the innocence of youth replaced with an intoxicating maturity. No one else came close to making him feel such a profound ache as the woman on the other side of the glass. Her light had shone so brightly she'd dazzled him.

She could have been his. *Should* have been his. Why hadn't he told her how he felt? Why hadn't he fought for her, staked his claim? Given her a chance to notice *him*—the real man behind the façade he showed the world, rather than simply Calum's shadow?

Because you're a dick who'll do anything to avoid conflict.

Bullshit. Not true. He wasn't afraid of conflict, although he preferred to seek solutions, mediate, search for common ground.

It was no surprise he became a cop. Resolving hostilities, displaying tact and diplomacy? He had all those attributes in abundance. Protecting those he loved? Fucking Zen master.

Fighting for something *he* wanted more than life itself? Yeah, he sucked ass.

Draven, his partner in the NYPD, an all-round bearded, tattooed badass, appeared at his shoulder.

"Feet glued to the sidewalk, dickhead?"

Cole looked at Draven. "It's her," he said, nodding toward Millie who still hadn't noticed the two cops gawking at her through the window. She was too fixated on her coffee cup, as if it had the answers to every question she'd ever asked. "The one I let get away. I haven't seen her since high school."

Draven glanced between Cole and Millie, and then his gaze settled on Cole, a deep frown drawing his brows low.

"Are you high?"

Cole grinned. "When it comes to her, I've been stoned my entire life."

Draven pointed his chin toward Millie. "So go talk to her. I'll sign you out."

Cole hesitated. Did he really want to tear open a wound that had never quite healed? He could walk away right this second, try to make himself forget he'd seen her, carry on with his life.

Except apart from his work, he didn't have a life. He had an existence.

"I should come back with you," he muttered.

Draven rolled his eyes. "Your shift's over. Go get some, before your cock shrivels up and dies."

"Fuck you," Cole said to Draven's retreating back, and then he laughed to cover up the nerves swarming through his body. His legs shook, his mouth dry as a cracker. What would he find to say to her after all this time?

He heaved in a breath and then lightly tapped on the window. Except it was more of a thump than a tap. *For fuck's sake!* Her unexpected appearance had thrown him so much, he couldn't even knock on a fucking window right.

Millie jumped, her eyes darting in his direction. She paled and knocked over her coffee. Grabbing a handful of napkins, she mopped up the spillage with short, jerky movements. Her gaze returned to him, and she openly stared, her lashes brushing her cheeks as she rapidly blinked.

Oh shit. She probably didn't recognize him. No wonder she'd spilled her drink with a burly cop banging like hell on the window. He took a step back, half turning away before he made even more of a dick of himself.

When a flicker of recognition crossed her face, he made a decision—too late to back out now. He pushed open the door to the coffee shop, simultaneously dreading a put-down while relishing the chance to spend time with her, to bathe in the warmth of her gaze.

A couple of diners glanced over at the tall, broad-shouldered cop filling the doorway, then returned to their food. He removed his peaked cap and stuck it under his arm. Scuffing a hand over the top of his head, he made his way over to Millie's table and smiled.

"Millie, hey. It's me. Cole Brook. We, um, we went to high school together."

He inwardly groaned. He sounded like a complete jerk.

Millie scooched to the end of the bench, stumbling when

she got to her feet. He put out his arm to steady her, but she'd already righted herself.

"Cole, of course I remember."

They hugged awkwardly, and he breathed her in. She smelled amazing. Even after all these years, the scent of her shampoo—vanilla—triggered a memory bubbling beneath the surface, only to burst free, bringing with it joy mingled with resentment that she'd never been his. But Christ she was thin. She'd been on the petite side in high school, but he could actually feel her bones sticking through her sweater.

"You haven't changed a bit," she said.

Still the invisible man, huh?

He brushed aside the uncharitable thought and smiled. "Sorry to scare you by thumping on the window like that. What are you doing in New York?"

She averted her gaze, slid back into her seat, and then began to fiddle with her watch strap. "Let me get you a coffee. Do you have the time?" She glanced around looking for the server, made a haphazard attempt to attract her attention by waving her hand in the air, then let her arm fall back to her side when the waitress served another customer. "Mustn't have seen me," she muttered, more to herself than to him.

"Coffee would be good." Cole slipped onto the bench opposite. He caught the server's eye and gestured. "Can I get two coffees over here?"

She acknowledged his request and went to fetch the pot.

"You must have the Midas touch," Millie said with a glimmer of a smile. And then her head dropped, and she picked at a tiny scratch in the table.

The hairs on the back of Cole's neck stood on end. Something didn't sit right. The Millie he remembered had been confident, energetic, life and soul of the party. The woman sitting opposite was gauche, awkward, almost timid.

She lifted her chin in his direction. "You always did want to join the NYPD."

A brief thrill rushed through him that she'd remembered his childhood dream. "Yeah. Almost ten years and counting now."

"Do you like it?"

He nodded. "Best job in the world."

"No ambitions to be Chief of Police?"

He chuckled. "Not one. Being on the street is where it's at. That's where you can make a real difference in this job. I'd go crazy sitting behind a desk all day having to manage budgets and crawl up the asses of politicians."

"Well, you certainly cut a dashing figure in that uniform," she said, following up with a shrill laugh.

He schooled his expression to hide his surprise at the compliment, not to mention her choice of words. *Dashing?* Nope. The Millie he knew wouldn't have used such flowery language. What the fuck was going on? He thought about probing, but just as quickly, he dismissed the thought. She was acting so out of character, all nervous and jittery. Being grilled by a cop—albeit one she'd gone to high school with—might send her into meltdown. Or have her scrambling from her seat and vanishing into the Manhattan crowds.

The waitress saved him from responding by arriving with their coffees. Cole added cream and one sugar. He stirred and then set the spoon on the table. Picking up his cup, he blew across the top of the drink, and then took a sip.

"Are you back for good or just visiting?" he asked.

"For good, I think."

A grin inched across his face. And then he remembered she wasn't free to chase, and the grin faded. "How's Tanner?"

She blanched, her eyes downcast. Her fingers closed around her coffee cup, and she tapped her nails against the side. Her hair fell in a veil, covering the right-hand side of her face. With a jerky hand, she tucked it behind her ear. "I don't know," she said with a shrug, adding, "We split up a few days ago."

"Oh?" Yeah, he was fishing, but something about her anxious expression when she spoke about Tanner had Cole worried. He arranged his face into one of sympathy, but not pity. In his experience, most people didn't react well to pity.

She lifted her eyes to his, two deep pools of warm chocolate that had him leaning forward in his seat like she was gravity pulling him in. Yet behind the eyes that had invaded his dreams since he was a young man lay pain and suffering. Whatever had transpired in her life, the last ten years had changed her from the girl he knew to the troubled woman now before him.

"I've left him," she stated, accompanying her words with a glance out the window.

"I'm sorry," Cole said. A blatant lie. He hated that she'd married Tanner. He'd never been the right man for her—and nor had Cole's twin—because, dammit, *Cole* was the right man.

"I'm not." Her face took on a faraway expression. Then the shutters came down, making her hard to read.

"Is he still in Chicago?"

She nodded. "At least I hope so." She chewed on her lip, and her eyes briefly closed. "He doesn't know I'm here, and I'd prefer to keep it that way for as long as possible."

Cole studied her, his earlier disquiet raging inside his head. Something was very wrong.

"He won't hear it from me. We weren't even friends. I haven't seen him since he left New York with you on his arm right after you turned eighteen."

A look of surprise crossed her face. "You remembered?"

I remember everything.

He gave her a faint smile. "I guess."

"What about you? Married? Kids?"

The abrupt change of subject was telling. Deflect attention, block others from digging too deeply, turn the conversation around to them. Most people loved to talk about themselves and would barely notice they'd been manipulated. Not him. He recognized the signs because he used the same tactics. He'd cede control to her—for now. Give her space, because the vibes pouring out of her said she needed it, badly.

"Neither."

"Oh." She tucked her hair behind her right ear and then immediately freed it, a habit she'd always had—and he'd always adored. "I thought some lucky girl would have snapped you up by now."

She already did. Except she doesn't know it.

"Married to the job, I think."

"Yeah, I hear that about cops. They're supposed to make terrible husbands."

Her answering smile was tight. What he wouldn't give for a full-on beaming grin, or one of her throaty laughs he remembered so fondly.

"Oh, I don't know, some make it work. I guess it depends on finding the right woman who understands the demands of being married to a police officer."

She nodded in agreement. "So, how's Calum? Still breaking hearts?"

Did her voice lift at the mention of his twin? His chest burned with jealousy. Still, *still* Calum was on her mind. Ten fucking years, and his brother featured center stage, whereas he got banal conversation. Fuck if he'd let his annoyance show, despite the painful lump in his stomach.

"He's off the market," Cole said, watching her response carefully. "Her name's Laurella, and she's awesome. Exactly the kind of girl he needs. Very good at putting him in his place."

She blinked rapidly, her eyes widening in surprise at his curt response. "Sorry, I didn't mean to pry."

Fuck. Way to go, dickhead. Say something to make her feel comfortable and do it quick.

He lightened his tone. "Jax runs a hotel now, right here in Manhattan. He opened it last New Year. It's doing great. You should stop by for a drink sometime."

"A hotel? Wow, that's terrific."

"Yeah." He flashed her a grin to take away the sting of his earlier words. When her face softened, he breathed a sigh of relief. "We're all shareholders, but he and his girlfriend, Indie, do most of the work, along with the staff, of course."

"And Nate? What's he up to these days? He was always such a sweet kid."

Cole rolled his eyes. "And then he grew up. He lives out in California. He's an actor. Doing pretty good, too. We don't get to see very much of him."

Her lips pulled to the side. "That's a shame. Then again, he always struck me as very different to the rest of you. A real independent kid. I'm not surprised he's flown the nest."

Cole nodded. "Me either. Nate's his own man. Jax is gutted, though. He tried so hard to keep us all together when Mom and Dad died. It still hurts Jax that Nate got as far away from New York as he could without leaving the country."

A brief frown drew her eyebrows low. "Yes, I remember that about Jax. Family first."

Cole nodded. "Always."

An awkward silence fell between them. Millie removed some money from her purse. She dropped it on the table. "It's been lovely to catch up with you, Cole, and I'd love to stay and chat, but I have an appointment to view an apartment early tomorrow morning, so I need to get some sleep. I just hope it works out. My savings won't last long if I have to stay in a hotel much longer, especially without a job."

Cole pushed the ten-dollar bill back across the table and replaced it with a bill of his own. "This one's on me."

"You don't have to do that," she said, although she did give him an oddly grateful look. "But thank you."

She shuffled along the bench and stood. A surge of panic hit him. He couldn't allow her to simply walk out of there without convincing her to meet with him again.

He hastily got to his feet. "How about dinner tomorrow night? Again, on me."

She gnawed on her bottom lip, frowning. "I'm not sure…"

"It's only dinner. I've lost touch with most people from high school. It'd be fun to reminisce about old times."

She plucked a stray hair from the corner of her mouth. "I'd love to, but I need to channel all my energies into finding a job. I appreciate the offer, though."

Dejected, he half turned away, and then an idea came to him. It might cause problems with Calum—big-ass problems—but he'd find a way to calm the situation. He always did, right? All he was doing was helping a friend in need.

Keep lying to yourself, dickhead.

"I might be able to help you with the job situation."

A dash of hope lit up her face. "Really?"

"Yeah. I can tell you all about it over dinner. You have to eat, so you may as well eat with me."

She nibbled on her fingernail. "I get the feeling you're not going to take no for an answer."

He winked. "You know it."

She faltered, then gave him a shy smile. "Okay. Dinner it is."

Buzzed with energy at winning her over, he beamed. "Great. Seven okay? I'll pick you up."

She nodded, reached for a napkin, and scribbled down an address. She handed it to him. "That's where I'm staying."

Glancing down, Cole repressed a wince. The place was an absolute shithole—frequented by hookers, pimps, and petty criminals looking to hide out until the heat died down. God only knew what the apartment she was viewing would be like if this was her temporary accommodation. He made up his mind there and then. She didn't need to search for a job, because he'd found her one—as The Miller-Brook's new front desk clerk.

Realizing he hadn't spoken, he looked up. "I'll be there. Good luck with the apartment."

If I have my way, you won't be there too long.

With a tentative smile and jerky nod in his direction, she picked up her purse, slung it over her shoulder, and left. She passed the window of the coffee shop and waved, then disappeared into the crowds.

Cole stared down at her neat, precise handwriting. He opened his wallet and tucked the napkin inside.

Millie had been hesitant, but at least she'd agreed to dinner. He was determined it would be the first of many. He stuck the money underneath the salt shaker and, with a lightness in his chest, set off for home.

FROM MY HEART

Thank you so much for reading Against All Odds.

Writing Calum and Laurella's story was one of the most joyous times I've had as an author. I completed a first draft during NaNoWriMo in November 2017 where this book just poured out of me. Sometimes when an author is writing a character, for some strange reason, they resonate more deeply than others. Calum Brook is that character for me. Yes he's blunt and uncompromising, and at times, downright irritating, but as I was writing his story, he stole a little piece of my heart that will always belong to him.

I'd love to hear what you thought of Calum and Laurella's journey to their HEA. Please feel free to get in touch via email, Facebook, Twitter or by signing up to my reader group

Next up is Cole and Millie. I can't wait to introduce you to the quiet Brook Brother—or is he? Looks can be deceiving, and Cole Brook has hidden depths.

His To Protect will be released on January 3rd 2019.

To be kept up to date, and to share in exclusive excerpts and cover reveals be sure to sign up to my reader group (if you like email) or my facebook group, Aces and Hot Reads (if you don't!)

Would you consider helping other readers decide if this is the right book for them by leaving a short rating on Amazon? They really help readers discover new books.

BOOKS BY TRACIE DELANEY

The Winning Ace Series

Cash - A Winning Ace Short Story

Winning Ace

Losing Game

Grand Slam

Winning Ace Boxset

Mismatch

Break Point - A Winning Ace Novella

Stand-alone

My Gift To You

The Brook Brothers Series

The Blame Game

Against All Odds

His To Protect

Web of Lies

ACKNOWLEDGMENTS

Yet again, I have so many people to thank. If I miss anyone out… I'm so so sorry. Please know that I appreciate every single one of my team.

To my wonderful hubs for not complaining when I disappear for hours at a time, locked in my study while I bash away at my keyboard, and for the endless supply of coffee. You still make the best coffee I've ever tasted.

To my editors, Sarah and Emmy. Really, ladies, you've made my words sing. I can't thank you enough for your insight.

To my critique partner, Incy—thank you, thank you, thank you, from the bottom of my heart. I remember sending you a first draft of Against All Odds with a tinge of fear because I adored Calum so much, and I wanted you to adore him too. Thankfully you did, although you still shared a few amazing nuggets that strengthened the story no end.

To Louise. My Rock. You've been there since the very beginning and I appreciate you more than you'll ever know. Thank you for everything you do, and the constant giggles on Messenger. Don't ever change. You're perfect.

To my alpha reader, Allison. You are THE BOMB, lady. I am so, so thrilled to know you and to work with you. I'm so glad you loved Calum as much as I did—even if you did think he was a gigantic ass at times (LOL).

To Lexi for believing in me and this book. Not long until Nate... who is yours (swapping for B seems like a good deal to me!)

To Del. Thank you for being so selfless with your time. Your feedback really is appreciated. Calum would like me to point out that he is so much more than sheer entertainment value!

To my ARC readers. You guys are amazing! You're my final eyes and ears before my baby is released into the world and I appreciate each and every one of you for giving up your time to read —and point out the odd errors that slip through the net!

And last but most certainly not least, to you, the readers. Thank you for being on this journey with me. It still humbles me to think that my words are being read all over the world.

If you have a couple of minutes, would you consider leaving a short review on Amazon? Reviews really help readers discover new books, and they're particularly important for up and coming authors. You'd be helping more than you know

ABOUT THE AUTHOR

Tracie Delaney realized she was destined to write when, at aged five, she crafted little notes to her parents, each one finished with "The End."

Tracie loves to write steamy contemporary romance books that center around hot men, strong women, and then watch with glee as they battle through real life problems. Of course, there's always a perfect Happy Ever After ending (eventually).

When she isn't writing or sitting around with her head stuck in a book, she can often be found watching The Walking Dead, Game of Thrones or any tennis match involving Roger Federer. Coffee is a regular savior.

You can find Tracie on Facebook, Twitter and Instagram, or, for the latest news, exclusive excerpts and competitions, why not join her reader group.

Tracie currently resides in the North West of England with her amazingly supportive husband and her two crazy Westie puppies, Cooper and Murphy.

Tracie loves to hear from readers. She can be contacted through her website at
www.traciedelaneyauthor.com

41517916R00160

Printed in Poland
by Amazon Fulfillment
Poland Sp. z o.o., Wrocław